Moon City
Slaughter Man Series

A Limbus, Inc. Novel

By
Benjamin Kane Ethridge

JournalStone

JOURNALSTONE
YOUR LINK TO ARTISTIC TALENT

JournalStone books may be ordered through booksellers or by contacting:

JournalStone
www.journalstone.com

ISBN: 978-1-942712-65-7   (sc)
ISBN: 978-1-942712-66-4   (ebook)

Library of Congress Control Number: 2016949886

Printed in the United States of America
JournalStone rev. date: September 16, 2016

Cover Design: Eddie Fazekas
Face: istockphoto.com #5778102, Standard License, by Dphotographer
Moon: Adobe Stock, #69786163, Standard License, by Dmitrijs Mihejevs

Edited by: Amy Huntley

Moon City
Slaughter Man Series

A Limbus, Inc. Novel

Chapter 1
The Killer in Moon City

My hand stretched forth with the candy wrapped in reflective red foil.

"You'll take this. You'll take this because there's no other choice. It's what you need. All creatures go after what they need. Even children," I told it.

A Deitii child with pale skin and black mirror eyes stared back at me. It wore a simple gray tunic and was shorter than most five-year-old humans, but the being held an intelligence in its eyes that made it more than just a simple lifeform. Its mouth was a flat line and all of its expression was communicated through its eyes. My hand clenched the candy and the foil crackled with my impatience.

"I don't need this. I can give this gift to anyone... But I'm choosing you," I said.

The Deitii only blinked, but made no other movement. Slowly, it reached out to take the candy.

Dark red bamboo structures framed the area in the darkness. It was nearly impossible to see, but the crinkling of paper indicated the alien was opening the candy. My eyes clarified on its shape. It pushed the candy, a helix-shaped pink thing, past fish-belly white lips. Perfectly square amber teeth descended into the candy. The lips closed and the jaws grinded.

"We can work together. We can be friends. There is nothing to be scared of. I just wanted to gain your trust. There is so much we can do in this city," I went on.

The chewing stopped and the lips smoothed into a straight line again.

"I know your kind isn't talkative. I guess that makes sense, since you're the same species as God, the one who invented everything and yet says nothing to anybody, but I still would like to ask your help to find others like you. I need—"

A strange squeal erupted from the creature's mouth. It grasped its throat. From its mirrored eyes ran sapphire tears.

"I need you to go to sleep. Because this city needs your help."

The Deitii collapsed to its knees. Its eyes rolled back from mirrors to foggy white. The creature passed out and rolled onto the ground on its side. I could see my reflection in the murkiness, but I didn't want to linger on it.

Never much cared for my looks. I always knew it was what was inside that made the universe need me. Not that abnormally tall, I was a well-built human man in the clothes of a manual laborer: washed-out gray pants, a loose-fitting black denim tunic with deep pockets and leather tie-strings.

I found myself accidently looking back at the mirror surface of the creature's eyes. Again my eyes fell away from my reflection. I didn't want anything to do with it. I'd rather stare at the creases of my dusty work boots. My features were not distinct, not handsome nor ugly, just mediocre most often. The only times I'd seen my true face come out was through anger or after intercourse, but perhaps the latter was one in the same for me. I could look up to a bedroom mirror beyond my burnt-blonde hair, grown out to my shoulders in sweat-clumped prison bars, and see that thing that needed to get free.

I imagined that what happened next, what happened to me after I finished with the Deitii would do the same, and although it would be a release, a revelation, and a resourcing of all the power in the universe that rightfully belonged to me, there would still be anger. A trail of anger that could be measured in light years. This anger, I had wasted my life on, until discovering my true purpose.

I knelt near the body and withdrew the bonesaw from my left tunic pocket. It was a compact device, but just as brutal looking as a four-hundred-pound battle-axe.

Flickering shadows danced on a nearby red bamboo wall, rhythmic with my gruesome fruitage. A nauseating sound of bone splintering away filled the dark with its maniacal music.

Using my tunic sleeve, I wiped sweat away from the stubble across my upper lip. A rich, cherry-colored blood came off on the sleeve. Not sweat after all. Yet, still the sign of hard work. Honest work. Not evil. Not good for that matter either.

I felt an explanation was needed for any lingering spirit. "It is true I am no murderer of Deitii children. I'm liberating you from this sick place, so this is no death." I considered the inert form for a moment, unsatisfied with my solemn declaration. "And judging by your height and weight, you are four hundred years old, and so I deem you no child, despite your species' length of age."

I closed my eyes a moment and took a deep breath. There can be no room for deception, I decided. From myself. From the universe. I had to call these things out as true or lose myself in despair.

"Not murder, but I am robbing you of something precious. There can be no mistake about that. It is for the best, however. It is for the best of everything."

I examined the shallow puddle in my hand in the flickering torch light. The dappling of cerebral spinal fluid danced with orange, red, and purple colors that swirled and combined and contracted. I'd seen it many times before and still regarded it with awe, licking my lips, salivating, before viciously sucking all the fluid through my stinging teeth like a starving savage.

A short, yet ringing crash came from a distant alley, stopping my feast. I gently wiped at my messy lips and narrowed my eyes down the alley.

A tabby cat bolted down the alley. It passed me and I watched it with a newfound coldness washing over me.

"What spooked you, little friend?" I asked, returning to my search down the alley again. "What indeed..."

My body began to tremble. My eyes got that fire and ice sensation. I recalled staring at my own eyes once while standing in my kitchen and looking through the window, like two bright silver suns spread from the back of my eyes to the front. They were mirrors, just like the Deitiis', and with that change I became more like them; I became closer to the power that forged the universe. Just as it was now. Through the darkness of the alley, everything brightened and I saw everything with such clarity there might as well have been a supernova hanging overhead in this immense cavern, a volatile, deadly power that belonged only to me. And my work.

Near a dumpster not far away, I saw what had frightened the cat. I saw his hunkered form and the black camouflage akin to planetary raiders and mercenaries. He was, not surprisingly, holding a high-powered rifle. After my first sips of the Deitii's spinal fluid, my senses enhanced immediately. The clarity afforded to me allowed my eyes to scroll across the serial number at the edge of the stalk of the mercenary's weapon and the tiny flicks of perspiration fallen nearby from his hair.

I flared my nose for a moment, took a step back, making a silent retreat. Then I ripped my Thalulus Repeater off my hip and fired at him. Dodging the yellow explosions with greater intensity each foot traveled, the mercenary sprinted for a side alley and I swiftly pursued.

The alley broke away into the Bleeding Cave Market District. Uncountable red-bamboo structures lined the modern-looking street. Stalactites dripped down from the dark heavens and stalagmites rose from the ground, a large one splitting two lanes in the main thoroughfare. There was no traffic, however. It was late, indicated by empty streets and unlit markets.

I fired my weapon once more as the mercenary rounded the large stalagmite. The man put his head down and charged for a straw-and-board fence. He scaled it with expert grace. I snorted, a vengeful bull, and leapt into the air so agilely it felt dreamlike, a wish fulfilled. One of my boots touched down on top of the fence, momentarily giving me the extra step I needed before springing forward and—catching a garbage can lid straight in the face.

I maintained balance but staggered forward, howling in rage and blindly pulling my weapon up to fire again. As my vision reestablished, the mercenary was nowhere to be seen. The stretch between these shops was less developed and more cavern-like. Water dripped slowly into staggered puddles. There weren't many places for anyone to run or hide; the cavern wall ahead made a discernible dead end.

I moved slowly, eyes and gun covering the area.

The hissing sound of air released to my upper left. The mercenary ascended the roof of a small warehouse via grappling hook. I caught a glimpse of his neck as he climbed through a patch of nearby torchlight. In dull blue-green ink was the tattoo of a stomach on fire with a devilish smiley face in its center. The tattoo of the Princess of Ganymede. It had been altered by the smiley face, but the flaming stomach, the insignia of everlasting hunger, could not be mistaken. She no longer had people in this region though. For all I knew, she no longer had anyone doing anything. She'd been incapacitated for some time.

Nevertheless, I would find out. With three measured steps, I bounded up the walls of the alley to the warehouse roof after the mercenary. The impact on my ankles gave me pause, however. I hadn't drunk enough of the Deitii this evening, and though I became stronger with every feeding, I was pulling the source of its power heavily with this chase. And the power was waning. I had to kill this problem and return to the corpse before the reg police found it in the alley.

The roof had several dozen yurts constructed of imported gray palm fronds and joining structures resembling thin, charred bones. With my gun extended, I walked through the silent shanty town, glancing from silent yurt to silent yurt.

"You are a veteran of the Ganymede wars then," I said loudly so the hiding assassin could hear me. "The Princess's coat of arms. You fought for her... And yet, now, you are after me and the Princess's mighty stomach has been sour for years, unable to function as it once did." I stopped and listened for anything that might give away the mercenary's position, but heard only the soft rustling of wind through the cavern, gently upsetting the fronds on the yurts. "She doesn't need mercenaries anymore, my dear, murderous friend. So you belong to another group. Come out and talk to me, tell me everything, so I might kill you and the rest of your ilk."

A smallish whine came from behind me. I whipped my head around to a girl standing next to a yurt with a sharpened stick in her hand. She looked about six years of age.

I pointed my gun at her. "You need to go night-night."

The child held up her stick and her bottom lip quivered in

terrified defiance.

I licked my lips and took aim.

The child took off and I lowered my weapon a little for a better range of sight. As I predicted, the mercenary scrambled out of the shadows, running for the same yurt as the child. *I hope the heroism is worth it.* I fired at the mercenary, riddling the nearby yurts with blossoming holes of fire and escaping smoke serpents.

The chick ducked into the yurt I'd almost completely destroyed. The mercenary followed shortly after inside and I emptied the rest of my cartridge into the yurt's remaining leafy fabric in a frenzy. The façade slowly caught fire, which crept from the base up the left side. The fire extinguished by the time I stepped in front of the yurt. The countless holes ran with thin, pale smoke crawling up the frond walls. The digital read-out on my Repeater counted down to twenty as it cooled, and the two microfans in the weapon spun fiercely. I watched as the timer reached zero and the cartridge readout changed to read, AMMO, and then READY.

I leveled my gun at the yurt again and fired five more shots. Afterward, I watched for a moment and then scratched my leg with the warm weapon. With little ceremony, I lifted the entry flap aside.

I walked through the three-chamber yurt. In the first chamber, two parents grasped each other tightly, wide-eyed in terror. In the second chamber, the child lay prone on the ground, appearing to have been killed. Unfortunate that the mercenary would get her killed.

A disturbing thought entered my mind, a memory, a distant, timeless recollection of when God created mankind. It had not started with the male form, but the female form—the memories settled in my mind as though they were my own, as though I had been the Creator all along. I fondly remembered my experimentations on how the growth of every cell would be, how the tissues would work together, how the organs would form strongholds and unify like my other creations, but would power a brain far superior to the primates before that. I recalled watching these cellular acrobatics and the progression of the female human form. This memory sparked in my mind because this little girl reminded me of the *first* such child in that progression of growth. Very similar in facial structure and skin tone. It was a pleasant memory filled with much nostalgia, for this was long before I created other species with three, then ten, then hundreds of different genders and possibilities of DNA varietizing.

These were not my memories, I understood, but those impressions the Deitii shared with their one greatest offspring, the Lord God, or whatever. I was certain It, whatever It had been, was dead now though, and that role in the universe could only be filled by one person willing to see through the suffering and the torment of limitless power.

As this sweet concept ran through my mind, the child stirred and rolled over, revealing a large bruise on her ribcage, which she rubbed at, grimacing. *Live to fight another day.*

Leaving the girl, I continued to the next chamber and found a rip through the bottom of the wall where the mercenary likely escaped. Losing my composure, I tore through the wall of fronds and rushed forward to encounter a rooftop door. I pulled at the cold, damp wooden handle and flung the door open.

I charged down the stairs. A firearm discharged rapidly and I fell on my back and slid down the stairs, as bullet holes peppered the old mortar in dusty gray pirouettes. Three bullets missed my head by an uncomfortable proximity, one even connected and scratched a line of blood at my right temple.

The sting fed my anger and I thrashed to my feet, firing my Repeater blindly down the stairwell. After a moment, I ceased firing and glanced down the stairwell and estimated the drop—about three floors—and I pitched myself over the side without another thought. On the bottom floor, I landed with less ease than my earlier jaunts, my ankles and leg bones buckling instead of absorbing the impact. It was shadow silent though and the pain was transient still, the ancient taste of the Deitii still on my tongue. I poised my weapon at the stairwell and waited for the mercenary to come running into my trap.

A door slammed just a floor up. The mercenary had somehow sensed my descent, even though it had been quick and soundless. I bolted out the exit door, trying to not let my frustration guide my actions. I needed to know who this man was before I killed him. I couldn't let my eagerness for blood overrule something so valuable. One dead mercenary wouldn't be the end to my problem. Two more heads would grow on this monster if I didn't seek out its heart.

The exit led to a field of pitchweeds. Over the dense, knee-high, coiling black plants, I spotted the mercenary making his way through. He was far ahead, but not uncatchable. The field sloped severely downward. I grinned as the mercenary stumbled and fell down the hill. My grin vanished as my own feet outpaced themselves and I tripped forward and rolled after him. I regained myself, spitting out the spicy mustard-like taste of a pitchweed leaf that had rubbed across my gums. The field thinned out toward the outskirts of the Devil's Gullet, a ghetto I'd not visited since my aimless childhood wanderings.

I took another shot, this one finally connecting. It struck the mercenary in the shoulder and a plume of shredded black fabric erupted from the wound in his body armor. The force of impact only made him stagger forward onto the main street. I followed him, waiting to get in a better incapacitating shot.

The area was a series of small cave apartments I wasn't acquainted with. Litter and homeless people filled the streets. Abstract graffiti covered the walls in various shades of red, giving the entire area the look of innards. I gained on the mercenary through this surreal setting. He looked behind his torn shoulder armor and realized he was about to be taken. No fool, this one. He took out something from a hidden pocket, flicked his thumb at it and dropped it into the street.

Grenade.

Shit.

I broke sideways on my heels, skidding through the dirt road. I tried to fall back, out of the grenade's range. A startled homeless man nearly bowled me over. I caught him by the neck and held on for a shield. I heard the detonation. A resounding pop and rushing sound. Rocky debris and dust blew out amidst screams.

As the smoke cleared, my human shield let out a ragged sigh. His rotten face was covered with small micro-cuts, but he wasn't otherwise harmed; we were well enough away from the explosion. The street, however, had a series of spidering cracks running through it. I glanced around, trying to wager where the mercenary ventured off to this time.

The filthy old bum struggled under my grip. "Hey," he said, breath like vapors from an outhouse. "Can you let me—?"

I pushed him forward, disgusted and frustrated to seeing red.

The bum stumbled out and the road beneath him collapsed inward in ragged pieces. He fell through with a short, vanishing scream.

I watched in shocked silence. Two steps forward and that would have been me—though it would take a lot to kill me after all the Deitii I'd consumed over the last month.

I lifted my eyes, feeling slightly dizzy. The mercenary had encountered something similar up the road and stood very still before a giant rift in the street. I couldn't help the smile forming on my lips. I lifted my Repeater and took aim.

A cracking noise followed by an unsettling rumble came from beneath me. I wasn't on stable ground either. I took a step forward to what looked like solid ground. It held my weight, but I wasn't certain how long that would remain true. I navigated a few more steps forward, noting the mercenary's slow progress. I lifted my gun again, aimed, and just as I fired, I pitched sideways as the ground fell out from under my boots. I sprung forward to a shaking piece of cavern floor and decided I needed to run for it.

Large pieces of the brittle rock floor fell out behind me. In my disorienting sprint, I wagered the mercenary had taken the same tact and ran full force as well, leaving a network of gaping holes in his wake. I bounded over the holes, several fracturing larger as I landed on their other side.

The ground firmed, thankfully, as my pursuit led to the new desalination plant. The mercenary had gained more ground than I'd wanted; he was already outside the plant and deploying his grappling hook up a slender metallic chute in the cavern wall. Water steadily coursed down the chute and obscured the mercenary as he quickly ascended.

I would have preferred taking him in the open. The plant would have operators and more hiding places and opportunities for escape. I couldn't give up though. The chase would end with answers and this man's death. I lunged forward, scrambling up the chute, into the cascading water. This place would be the mercenary's tomb. I would end his life here. Laughing in morbid delight, I moved with the ferocity of a supernatural beast, clawing up to its first bloody birthday.

Chapter 2

Miles away from the desalination plant, in a cold transport station, Dean Fulsome was arriving at Moon City for his first time. His vision did not come into focus so much as it seemed to unpeel layer upon layer of fibrous images, some looking real enough to touch and others resembling a graphic on a computer monitor. All of them were indescribable things, mechanical devices without meaning, biological organisms without life. He wondered, as he often did when going through an interstellar membrane transport, if the images were actual things hidden from the rest of the universe, or just the untangled bits of his imagination.

He was getting closer to Moon City. For him, he'd just left Earth minutes ago, but the trip had taken the better part of a month. That idea soured his stomach. There were better, fancier transport protocols capable of taking him to his destination in Earth time, but he hadn't been with Limbus, Inc. long enough, he supposed, to get the nifty travel accommodations.

A disintegrating orb of color washed down his field of sight, and through a black fog, he began to make out the giant form of the Moon City transport tunnel. Movement back and forth slowly revealed the long, blue membranes hanging there like a futuristic car wash. They pulsed as his body formed and reformed through them, converting him from light particles into cellular matter again. He never understood why the membranes flapped. There were never any wind currents in the transport stations; the alien technology just moved independently, doing their job with the passionate relentlessness of a robot.

Dean spotted a transport technician furiously typing at his console. Sweat beaded across his brow and he spoke urgently into his headset. The tone of his voice indicated the call was to a personal friend. Still, something looked wrong.

Just as he thought that, one of the membranes slipped past him and left something cold and sharp in his side.

That had never happened before. And he'd gone through his fair share of membrane transports by now.

The technician kept typing away. "Dean Fulsome, director of Solar System Operations, engaged with a one-way pass." He waited a moment and nodded. "Yes. Yes. No. Just him. No, he—no, I know he's a director, but they haven't given him Golden clearance. Of course my baby can convert on the gold level. These membranes are from last year. Yep. Pretty much brand new. Talon Corp, sure. X5000 series." He waited another second, wagging his head side to side impatiently. "I know who Fulsome is. Not a complete dumbass over here.

"Yeah, I know what he did, but obviously that doesn't grant him privileges with the more expensive, energy consuming transports... Right? Well, because Limbus can be cheap bastards at times. Wait! Hold on! I knew something wasn't coming through right. He's passed the fifth series. Wait, wait, that doesn't make sense. How did he skip over so soon? Oh this isn't right. Shit! Something is wrong. No clue. Look, baby, I'll need to call you back. This guy's going to come through sooner than he thought. I'll give you a call later. Want your body too. Yeah. Oh hell yeah. Bye."

In the next second, Dean saw only blinding, hot, white light. He felt his body staggering forward into the light and supple hands catching him around the shoulders. As the light receded, he could see the technician more clearly. His mouth was moving but no sound came forth. In his hand, he held what looked like a sky blue cloud. The cloud's intense color and form shrunk and Dean could now see it was a robe. He ran a hand over his face to make sure it was still there. His beard stubble scratched his palms and made him feel like a real person again. Bringing his hands over his head, through his hair,

Dean felt the slight bald spot he'd been cultivating in the back for a few years now. *It's just a cowlick.* His ribs hurt on both sides, as they always did after transport. He touched the tender surface and winced. Definitely a real person, he concluded. It was then he realized he could hear again too.

"How are you feeling, Mr. Fulsome?"

"What... happened?" Dean's voice sounded foreign to him for a moment. It was always this way at first though. "The trip was faster than I thought." He smacked his lips. "Feel like I'm going to toss my cookies."

"You skipped some membranes," said the tech. "I can only imagine there was interference with the transfer somewhere. This was a locked mission though... So unless it was from Limbus itself, I have no clue who could have known your transfer path."

Dean snorted. "Someone who didn't want me to make it here."

A look of dread passed over the young tech's face. The band of the headset through his blond crewcut made him look slightly ridiculous with the wide-eyed expression. "They don't pay me enough to know all that."

"Me neither. You got your records in order? They'll blame you, you know."

"Shit," muttered the tech. "Yeah, I always document everything."

"Keep it all handy when they come asking—"

Dean fell sideways without warning, and the tech grabbed him by the arm. "Shit, mister, your lips are turning blue."

"Feel raw," said Dean. "Something ain't right. Came through those membranes too fast. One of them didn't pass me through correctly. Do you know how to decode a Quantum Flu?"

"Say what? Hey, man, I just got my Membrane Trans cert. Only been at this for three Earth months."

"Shit... They spare only the best people for me."

Something tickled Dean's cheek. He touched it and brought away a tear of blood. "Oh nice."

The tech froze. "Holy shit. You're—"

"I know, I know," Dean replied. "Look, where is the operative who was supposed to meet me here?"

"Shouldn't we call medical?"

"They can't fix this. It's light particle anatomy and membrane programming. Where's the operative?"

The tech stiffened. "I have a private letter for you."

"Open it. Read it to me."

"I'm not supposed to."

Dean wiped away another blood tear and glared at the tech. The younger man swallowed and nodded. "Right away." He pulled out the postcard-sized envelope and tore away the top. With some difficulty, he pulled out the slip of paper and narrowed his eyes as he read it. "*Have the mark. Will rendezvous with you at the mayor's representative's office.*"

"Bullshit," Dean spat. "Do you have interagency email?"

The tech nodded.

"Send him word to meet me here. It's contractor77@limbus.gal.net."

The tech began to return to his console and stopped. "Are you sure we shouldn't get you a medical unit?"

"They can't do anything for me. Neither can the mayor's rep. The contractor will know how to recode this Flu though. I know his skills. He isn't just a mercenary. I need him here, to fix this... and keep it quiet."

The tech went to the console and began typing. "I haven't heard from him in over four hours though. What if he doesn't show?"

Dean collapsed to the ground with a grunt. "That'll certainly be discouraging."

The tech finished the email. "Okay, sent. Now, what should I do next?"

Dean took a deep breath. It tasted like copper and charcoal. "Try to get in touch with Tasha Willing. She'll know where to find... the operative, if he can be found. Hope that's soon because otherwise I'm not going to last long for this adventure."

"I don't have access to Ms. Willing... I'm sorry."

Dean tried to keep his annoyance at bay. "Call the Solar System office and tell them Dean Fulsome is requesting Tasha. She'll come through. Hurry your ass up, kid. Really. My insides are turning... soft."

Returning to the keyboard, the tech made the call and waited. Into his headset he spoke with a quivering voice that didn't instill

Dean with much confidence. "Yes, I'm at the Moon City membrane transport station. I have a Dean Fulsome here and he urgently requests Tasha Willing. He has acquired Quantum Flu from an interrupted membrane transportation event— but— but— he's— yes, but you don't understand. He's getting really sick."

Almost on cue, blood poured from Dean's nostrils and steam lifted from his feverish blue skin. The tech looked over and saw this, beginning to visibly shake. "She's outside com boundaries. Well how do we get her? We need help! He needs help!"

Dean shook his head as though to tell the tech to forget it. He waved him to come over instead. "Don't waste the effort. If Tasha's outside of com range, there's nothing to do now but wait for the Op to show."

The tech slowly approached him. "How can this be happening? You're the Slaughter Man. Aren't you?"

"Sure, that's me, if you like the name. I don't really, but go ahead and have at it."

"You killed the Princess of Ganymede?"

"No I didn't."

"But you stopped her. You're a hero. People like you don't get the Quantum Flu."

"As you can see, that ain't true, and I'm not a hero. Don't deserve any of the credit. People just like stories."

"The Princess caused the extinction of three prime intelligent species, all by herself, right? Just from her appetites?"

Dean grimaced at all the talking. "Dunno the stats. She isn't a good thing, person, creature... whatever. Good Christ my stomach is twisting."

"I'm so scared," the tech told him.

"Oh yeah," Dean moaned, "and that would be why?"

"I'm going to lose my job if I let the Slaughter Man die."

Dean smiled, despite himself, and closed his eyes.

It all seemed so clear in his recollection, so close to his heart, so near to his timeline. But it wasn't. When he thought about that conversation he had with Sandra, it was more than two months ago now. He was sitting on his plaid sofa, an awkward-looking thing with lacquered wooden sticks for a frame and cushions as uncomfortable as they were unsightly. Nobody could say the sofa didn't match the overall country-cabin type décor however.

Sandra, he could see her clearly in his memory, was sitting on the plaid recliner across from him. The wall behind her was a series of stacked logs like an old school cabin, but the huge window cut within them showcased the giant futuristic office lobby peopled with hundreds of Limbus, Incorporated employees walking around purposefully. Dean still wasn't used to it completely, and he could tell neither was Sandra.

She drank the rest of her Fanglion Lager from her pilsner glass. She reached for the remainder of the bottle's contents. Dean stared absently at the golden star on the label: *Home star system brewed! Neptune Lagered!* The bottle had made a condensation ring on his rustic coffee table, but he'd never been one to bother over coasters. Sandra, he knew, would take care of it later. Those types of things did bother her, but she could be patient in taking care of them. Patient, for a time.

She took careful time to pour the strong beer into the pilsner. She stopped at halfway, considered this, and then decided to polish off the bottle. That she drank beer instead of wine coolers had always impressed Dean. She didn't mind drinking something harsher to discover what it could offer. He supposed, as a man, he was very much a complex tasting beer, definitely not a liqueur.

She drank half the glass and Dean snorted. When she looked at him critically, he studied his hands in awkward silence.

"I know it's a lot to take in," he told her carefully. "So whatever you think is best, I have to go with."

Taking another sip, Sandra narrowed her keen, brown eyebrows over the glass. When she lowered the glass, he knew she was pissed. Thoroughly. "That's big of you, Dean. You're giving me permission to call you an asshole."

Dean grimaced and rubbed the back of his neck, wishing something would explode outside or someone would call for help, just to take him out of this moment. "Sandy, that's not exactly—"

Her hazel eyes flared. "No. That *is* what you're saying. You are suggesting I go into Hyper Sleep—"

"No, I said *stasis*. Hyper Sleep cannot be legally interrupted by anyone. Stasis can be broken by friends or family."

"I'm not a moron, Dean. I know that."

"You're making it sound like you'd be trapped though. They can pull you out whenever they need to, and I will *pay* for the duration. Whatever it is. Whatever you choose."

"I know what stasis and Hyper Sleep are—"

"I didn't say—"

"I don't care which is more expensive or what the civil rules of which are. I just know I'll be putting my life on hold for a very long time. For twelve years—"

"I only obligated myself to one Moon week. That'll make the return trip eleven and a half years. It's not twelve."

She gave him a look then that could not be clearer: *don't push me any further than you are right now. Don't.*

"Sorry. Look, the Radiance Pathway is in position, so the transport to Moon City will only take a month. We can talk when I get there. It's not like you'll need to wait ten years to hear from me again. Take your time and decide what you want to do. You can even wait until I'm done with my assignment, that way it's perfectly timed. I wish I could take the same membrane pathway on the way back, but in that system, there are limited options for return. And they haven't granted me Golden Transport."

"I'm sure you fought them very hard on that too."

"I did try," Dean replied softly. "That's outside their budget. Look, I insisted I go right away, so I could hop on the Radiance Pathway. If I went when they were asking it, on a different pathway, it would be three times longer."

"I love how you talk about this like you're being so accommodating."

"I'm *trying* my best."

"Why do you have to do this?" she asked. She shook her head slowly, disgust palpable on her pretty face. "Moon City is not even in the Solar System. You are not the director there. Why are you going way the hell out there? Is there not plenty of bullshit for you handle here?"

He took a deep breath. "The Deitii are being murdered. You and I both know how important they are."

"Given, but they have a contract mercenary out there tailing the Moon City Killer. Let him do the job and you can handle everything remotely. You aren't an assassin. Why the hell do you need to go and risk... *everything?"*

"There are political things that need sorting out," said Dean, "and Limbus needs to establish a firmer hold on Moon City. I told you this already."

"You aren't a politician either, darling. You're a director of operations and they *don't need you there*. That's it. That's all."

"You can have your mother wake you from stasis for all the holidays and birthdays. You don't have to miss anything major you aren't willing to miss."

"I'll miss you, you big, dumb, stupid fucker."

Dean leaned back on the couch and the wood flexed with annoying stridence. "Come on, Sandy."

"Periodic visits with my mother. You haven't even thought this through. This is Limbus Inc. we are talking about. Are you out of your mind? I'd have to get approval for her to know about this organization."

"I worked as a sticker at the slaughterhouse not that very long ago, but I'm not a moron either, okay? I've already got the paperwork in hand to give your mother clearance. I figured she'd be the only one you could trust."

"You're evading the real subject here, but I'll play along for a moment. Say I go with this and say good-bye to you, put my job on hold, and go into stasis. I drag my mother into this and tell her to wake me up every Thanksgiving. The rest of my family, including my step-father and my real father, have no clue where the hell I am for most of the time, *for more than a decade*. You expect my mother to keep that lie for me? I'll disappear off the face of this earth."

"But come back occasionally—"

"Yes. I'll see my nieces and nephews grow up through a string of holidays that'll feel like a few months, when in fact, I'm missing out on LIFE. People might die or get sick or get divorced, or all sorts of things... But I'll be sleeping... Waiting for you. I love you, but seriously, Dean."

As much as he didn't want to say it, he did. "I know it's not worth it. You don't have to do it."

"Would you?"

"Absolutely, but I only have an uncle with advanced Alzheimer's and dementia who I haven't spoken to in seven years. I get why it's harder for you."

"Forget family and friends." Something shadowy and judgmental passed over her face. "Would you wait for me if Limbus told you *not* to?"

Dean stood up, knees crackling slightly, and grabbed a tumbler of whiskey on the rocks situated on the empty fireplace mantle. Even though Sandra liked beer, she was more refined than he, choosing something more expensive and brewed from alien technology. Dean's was Canadian Club whiskey. And it tasted fine. He took a big tug of it and leaned against the mantle. "It's funny," he said, pausing for a moment to choose his words right. "My ex-wife used to give me hell for not being enough. You though? You don't want me to go anywhere, achieve anything."

Sandra almost dropped her pilsner. "You're joking, right? I'm not talking you out of a promotion here. For you, this is different. You go through that membrane transport, go do your politicking on Moon City for a few weeks, and then you're back through the transport station. It'll feel like no time has passed for you, especially if you talk me into stasis. You'll come back here, twelve—eleven and a half years later. I'll be waiting for you and we can pick up right where we leave off. But if I've not been sleeping all that time, I'll have moved on and that scares the hell out of you."

"Sure it does. Of course it would."

"If they need you so bad, why can't they get you the Golden Membrane Transport? At least on the return trip? I don't mind waiting months, but damn it, Dean! Tasha Willings gets to GM transport and she's only a master recruiter. You're a director."

"Tasha is the daughter of an owner and she's worked for the company for over a hundred years. And the Golden protocol sometimes removes years off your life. I'd come back about two years younger. You wouldn't care for being four years older than me. You don't even like being two years older."

"I'd get over that pretty quick if I knew you were back in a couple months rather than a decade. I'd like it much better than having my family think I was abducted, killed, and dumped in a forest somewhere."

"I ain't getting the Golden treatment, Sandy. This conversation doesn't matter. I'm getting the same membrane transport protocol that all the other directors get."

After pressing her pouty lips firmly together for a few seconds, she sighed and calmly asked, "So you won't appeal this?"

"I actually tried. They wanted Hunter on it, but they can't find him."

"Idiots. He'd have been a much better choice."

"Thanks."

Sandra finished her beer and closed her eyes for a moment. "I love you."

"You know I do too."

"I've never felt this way before about anyone. I know you loved your wife—"

"But she didn't love me, and so that makes this better. This is real. We are real. Please think about what I'm asking. We *are* worth this, Sandy."

She began to tear up. He knew better than to console her. She didn't like crying, and if he brought attention to it, her emotions would transform into coldness or anger. He let her be. He gave her the moment.

"I'm just not so sure I can wait it out, asleep or not asleep," she admitted, dragging a knuckle across the large tear forming in her left eye. After this she regained herself and nodded. "It's just *really* hard, Dean."

This was his cue. He put down his whiskey and walked over. For a few seconds, he thought over what he could say, what he could do here. In the end, he awkwardly put his hand on her shoulder. She sniffed and shook her head.

"Get down here and hold me, you dufus."

He knelt next to the recliner and wrapped his arms around her, then rested his head on her shoulder. Her perfume was like sandalwood and cinnamon and sex, and it always drew him closer to her, like the homing beacon he needed to land in the fog.

"I'm sorry for this," he said.

"You're a good man, Dean. I just wish you'd stick up for yourself more."

"I do. I appealed this. I did."

She ignored him and went on. "Sometimes—and don't take this the wrong way—but sometimes I'm sorry I fell in love with someone like you. It isn't what I needed when I came to work here. Things are strange and chaotic and I didn't *need* anything like this. But I don't want anyone else."

"Me neither."

"I will wait… for a year before I decide on the stasis. If a year goes by and I still can't bear to be without you, that's when I'll do it."

He looked up at her and nodded. It wasn't the answer he hoped for, but it was better than an outright *no*. "Thank you, Sandy. Even a chance is better than knowing I'm going to lose you over this."

"No matter what, I'm going to change the décor in this place when you're gone. I've wanted to do it since I moved in."

He chuckled at this, feeling better when the conversation headed elsewhere. "It's comfy though, right? Warm feeling, like camp?"

"I never went to camp and now I'm kind of glad."

Dean tried on his best fake frown. "You don't feel at home here?"

"Maybe, if I were Goldilocks."

He squeezed her midsection, wanting to make love to her then, but also knowing it might be pushing his luck. Instead, he grinned and said, "I don't care what I return to, just as long as you're here when I do."

He remembered the look she had given him then. It was serious, like she wanted to believe him, but wasn't sure. They did make love a few moments later, but they never discussed his trip to Moon City again.

In fact, Dean couldn't recall any other conversations after that night. He remembered nothing more as he concentrated on the tech's blood-covered hands gripping his own. He was gritting his teeth, trying not to overreact to how white the flesh of his arms looked and how his fingers looked undead as they clawed into the transport tech's wrists. Dean's arms had slightly perforated in some places and the blood oozed out, rich and red and tiny shards of light flexing through them from the Quantum Flu.

Ricky Agate, the Crimson Operative, had better get there soon. Otherwise, it didn't matter if Sandra waited for him or not, Dean the Slaughter Man would be over.

He closed his eyes then and hoped his first moments in Moon City weren't going to be his very last.

Chapter 3

My search for the mercenary continued onto the main process floor of the desalination plant. This place must have served all of the Bleeding Caves and possibly other nearby territories. I had this wretched idea just then, like what it might feel like to poison the water supply, just let thousands die because I deemed them unfit for survival. There was power in that, power I deserved. After all, I knew what had made them, so I deserved to unmake them. It went beyond just understanding the stitching of flesh and bone and sinew and biological fluid. I knew how the atom had been created. I knew where electrons came from. I knew where it all originated.

My heart.

My giving, impatient heart.

I gazed across the darkness of the vast processing chamber. Red and amber lights, some of which flashed liked hellish police lights against the hanging stalactites and wrought iron catwalks and plastic water tanks, illuminated the walls. I couldn't find the mercenary, and it was starting to unnerve me. I'd followed him closely enough. It was upsetting he'd slipped away. He was very good for a human. Very good.

You're human too, I reminded myself, but then squashed it.

No I wasn't.

I hadn't been for a long time.

The Deitii spinal cocktail feeding my blood had changed all that, brought awareness.

A trapezoid of white light opening in the darkness brought me out of my musings. A utility worker walked out of a nearby office with a clipboard in hand. It was hard to distinguish the figure, but the hips and roundness of the chest painted her as female. All of her face was indistinct, save for her dark brows knitted in annoyance.

"Take your artwork out to the outer caverns," she said wearily. "You Noggins were told—"

"I'm not a Noggin," I told her.

"I don't care what you are. You have to leave."

"Absolutely. But my friend is in here. He's lost his way. Might you help me find him?"

The utility worker grew more upset by this. "And your friend will be told the same thing as you. Leave at once."

I took my eyes off of scanning the dark corners of the installation and brought them back to her. She took a step back as I approached. I didn't give her another moment. I pounced. She broke her clipboard against my shoulder. It actually *really* hurt. I reacted by punching her in the face and she collapsed, her nose pushed inward in a bloody mess. She dropped on her hip, dead before she hit the floor.

Another door opened from above, a gaping white-hot maw in the dark. A new form emerged, this one taller and broader in the shoulders. It banged heavily down the catwalk stairs. The light from the open door below gave his pensive face some detail. The man was dressed in the same gray and white, striped jumpsuit as the woman I'd just destroyed. He was reading a long, hook-shaped gauge, an expression of distracted interest and bewilderment focused there.

"Cathleen," he called out, "there's another spike in total dissolved solids. Fifth one today—"

Just then, he caught sight of me and froze at the bottom stair. I smiled and lifted my hands, surrendering.

"Hey, I just came to apply for a sampling job. I think I startled her and she collapsed. Call the medical regent."

The man focused now on the slumped-over form at my feet. "Cathleen?"

I bent over and retrieved a part of the splintered clipboard she'd struck me with. "She said you needed this."

The man didn't have a chance to form a word before I winged the jagged blade of wood at him. It sliced through his neck, almost decapitating him. Blood spilled across the catwalk steps and he dropped to his knees. I noted the red letters on his gauge, FATAL ERROR, and I couldn't fight off a smile.

I sensed I was being watched. Perhaps it was my newfound powers, perhaps it was just intuition. The mercenary sent to kill me lay out there in the shadows, watching. Maybe afraid, maybe curious, a mix of both, but whatever the case might have been, his eyes drank me in.

I felt it.

"Who do you work for?" I asked, my last word a booming echo in the chamber. After a moment of silence, I went on. "I am not a sadistic type, believe it or not."

Still no response. I laughed and massaged my neck thoughtfully. "I just thought since I had a captive audience, I'd like to show you what was in store."

The continued silence began to piss me off. My eyes darted around, trying to lock on something meaningful. "What agency do you work for? The Titan Group? Survivors of Ganymede? GalactiaBank? The outer monarchy? Although I doubt you'd worry with me when they're at war with the Fanglions."

The murkiness of my *knowing* shifted; this was how it was with the remainders of the Deitiis' old power. It came in high-rising and low-crashing waves. I knew where the mercenary was then. I couldn't distinguish him visually because my eyes were not heightened but my awareness was. I withdrew my Repeater and took aim for a single support cable high above. I fired and neatly cut the cable apart. The entire upper catwalk crashed down at once. A shadowy figure rolled out of the falling structure and leapt on top of a water processing tank. I took aim and fired again. A round shattered the left side of the mercenary's helmet, revealing his square jaw and bronze skin. A small stream of blood pelted down and his left hand went up in reflex. With another shot, I got him in his left hand. A micro-explosion of blood burst from the wound and the mercenary cried out, the first time I'd ever had the pleasure of hearing the contours of his voice.

I ran for the tank and spotted the mercenary as he opened a heavy iron door in a non-distinct wall in the darkness—he had to have studied this place beforehand. Whoever this man was, he was not easy prey. In fact, I smelled a richness in his blood indicating a greatness that might have terrified me had I not been a walking god. This man wasn't the famous mercenary, Christopher Agate, that I'd read about in the news... but this man was related to the same greatness somehow. This was his relative. A cousin? A brother? With how time-warped space travel could be, it was possible it was his son, father, or grandfather as well.

The door slammed shut as I arrived. It had an airlock wheel, and with one solid slap, I spun at a maddening pace, the force popping the iron door open on its own as the wheel completed its circuit.

I rushed inside. On the second floor above, I saw the mercenary inside an office, beyond a thick pane of glass. He was throwing switches and pushing buttons.

An alarm blared then and a digital readout behind the office window read BRINE DISPOSAL ACTIVE, and there were flexing patterns of lines indicating progress. Blasts of brine water rushed from the countless clay pipes in the walls. The chamber started to fill. And quickly. The level of brine rose over my shoes in a matter of a minute or less.

I turned to the door behind me. I heard a click and a turning of gears. A bar of red light glowed above the door, indicating it being locked, I supposed. Still, I tried to wrench on the door's wheel. It didn't budge, and I didn't have enough strength left in me to make it come undone. I looked back up to the office. A resounding snap and clunking, followed by a red light illuminating over the office door, specified that room was also sealed off to me.

The mercenary now did look down. He smiled, his long, black bangs almost touching his thin, but pleasantly red lips. With a patronizing wave of his hand, he departed to the back of the office. I saw a door open and he disappeared. Despite myself, I smiled. This wasn't it. He couldn't kill me. He was good, but that didn't matter. He was only good for a human. We weren't the same. I smiled wider and chuckled.

I dashed for the ladder to the second-level catwalk. My hands and feet slapped against the rungs mechanically, the vibrating hum of metal underneath them, its energy helping me ascend. I crashed down the catwalk to the office door. I tried to crank the wheel, but the door was just as sealed as the one down below. I glanced over the railing. The level of foamy brine water lifted rapidly. It was well over three feet deep and increasing. I looked around, trying not to be too frantic because it was humiliating. I turned my sight inward and called on whatever form of power I had left. I had plenty left to look *through* the world. My eyes roamed around, colors flickering from black to silver. The cavern walls thinned. I began to see through them. I went and dragged my hand over the wall.

I found a very thin section. I ran my fingers delicately over the rough surface where the rock wall wasn't as deep. I considered it a moment, stepped back, then began kicking it with all I had. Pebbles and clumps of rock fell away, but not significantly. I continued harder, gritting my teeth, giving it my all. I glanced over my shoulder and noted the rising water. It scared me how fast it was coming. I'd drown after a time.

I'd drown.

It made me remember a different time in my life. Something that happened around ten years ago at the mineral pool. There were so many kids and parents roaming around, enjoying themselves, and there I was, at the edge of the cavern pool, staring at my ugly, knobby toes. The thoughts going through my mind rang back clear, recalled completely as though whispered into my inner ear. *You're going to go home, aren't you? She'll call you feeble. She'll wonder why you didn't give her more bedroom time with Jack. She'll say that when she was your age, she'd swim all day, that she was in control of her life even as a child.*

I wiggled my toes and edged closer to the water.

But you aren't her. The last time you almost drowned, her boyfriend, Ryan, was there to rescue you. He was a good man. But she doesn't keep those kind around. Because she's in control of her life—she makes it what she wants. She creates children and lets them go off on their own... And fall. She doesn't care what happens to us. I only stayed when the others left because I was afraid. What if she knew how I'm not going to be afraid ever again? What if she knew I'd rather die than ever be her plaything? I'm in control. Me.

I looked back on that younger man, snarling as he leapt into the pool, and then sank beneath the sapphire water and dropped to the bottom. There, that younger man closed his eyes as though to be transcendent of the crushing water around him. But that didn't last long. His eyes shot open. He began to struggle. Bubbles erupted from his mouth. They covered everything.

I honestly couldn't remember how I survived that day. I couldn't remember saving myself and I couldn't remember anyone coming to assist me. All I remember were the thousands of bubbles around me, just as there were now, surging up to me on the brine water. I'd not let them claim me again. I took a step back and kicked a melon-sized divot out of the wall. I kicked it again, but buckled backward in pain. My knee throbbed and the joint felt wrong, disengaged now. Limping, I ventured over to the office again and put my hand hopelessly against the wheel. The brine water sloshed down over the catwalk, having filled more than half of the chamber.

Time was short.

I returned to the thin place in the cavern wall and kicked with my other leg. Some pebbles crumbled away, but still no progress to boast of.

I double-timed my kicks, water flinging up each time. The water level had become ankle-deep and I found it more difficult to continue at the same pace.

When the water reached my waist, I began punching the wall, leaving bloody fist prints against the cold, gray moon rock. In moments, the water reached my chest. I punched the wall in a feebler attempt, but the water current drifted me back.

Then all those salty bubbles broke at my chin.

Next, my head bobbed underwater. I swam to the surface for a little air. I went back under for a moment, but when I tried to surface for air a second time, there was no space left; my oxygen-hungry lips kissed the rock ceiling and found nothing. I searched frantically, the brine burning my eyes. There was nothing to save me in the murky darkness. I was alone with the pressure of the water squeezing my body and the massive crackling sound of rock above, below, and surrounding me. The cracking turned into a bass moaning, like some mythical death whale coming to see me to an underwater grave. The moaning gave way to a high-pitched whine that ended in a tremendous roar. An unseen force tugged my body down and pulled it through a jagged opening. Rock knives sliced through the right side of my torso, but I paid them little mind as the world went from endless water to unlimited air.

I was poured onto a catwalk outside the chamber. Brine water blasted out and rushed from the hole I'd started and the water pressure finished. The new area of the desalination plant bridged across an abyss. I couldn't hear the waterfall splashing below, so it was indeed a long drop. I rolled away from the torrent, coughing and heaving for air. With considerable effort, I crawled a few feet and reached out for the catwalk railing to haul myself up.

Something caught my eye. I moved a wet shock of hair from my eyes. Below me, on another catwalk, stood the mercenary, a cellular phone to his ear. It was greatly difficult to bring back my incredible new sight, but with concentration I brought him closer into focus and heard the words emerging from his mouth.

"I would have saved the indigenous had I found the subject earlier... I'll get his name, you putz, after I fish his body outta that brine chamber. I don't want Limbus involved in an autopsy. The data should be mine. They wanted the Moon City Killer dead... piss off, you're a hundred galaxies away. Speaking of, I'd like to share the data with you. Only you. I'll finish the autopsy later today and then I have a meeting with some Grettish Friars... well, I live dangerously, what can I say? So let's talk about getting that membrane transport configured so I can get off this moon and to you...

"No, I think Fulsome should be coming into the transport station any moment now. Yes. And they aren't giving me Golden protocol for transport. No shit that sucks, but I'll talk to the Grettish and see if they have a nearby wormship that will secure passage. Well, yeah... after you and I meet, I'd like to get back to Earth before the next thirty years rolls on. I'll just have to pay the Grettish well. I've done it before."

I crept down the catwalk, mindful of my every step. The mercenary's voice boomed in my ears as I drew closer. I stole a glance down the hall and noticed a dark gray conduit running down the ceiling. It had yellow stenciling on the side that read MAG-COIL LINE - BNO4EV. Interesting, I thought. Definitely going to use that.

"Whatever, man," the mercenary continued. "That's your stance, no matter what reality you're in this time. Keep your opinions to yourself... No, I'm not *being* an asshole—you are the asshole. Yeah, I'll be at Mom's birthday party if I get that Grettish airline ticket. Rub it in, you dipshit. Okay. Bye."

The mercenary put away his phone, grimacing, and held his wounded hand. He took a couple careful looks around and started to move down the hall. My excitement got my heart racing along with his.

The mercenary froze and then spun around, gun in hand. I watched him through the wall I hid behind. He'd somehow detected me. He swayed back and forth, uncertain of my whereabouts. "Come out and we can talk."

I laughed. "That's some funny shit right there."

"Fine. It's going to be a fight, so just bring the fight."

"I'm glad you've decided you're in control," I said, "but in this universe of puppets and puppet mastery, you are tangled in your own strings."

The mercenary now had my location and he walked softly toward me, gun raised. "Please show me that pretty forehead of yours so I can split it for you."

"You should try it," I whispered.

"No more talking," the mercenary replied.

"You can hear the heartbeats of an entire planet if you concentrate— an old man fifty miles away having a heart attack feels like a delicious war in your brain."

The mercenary cocked his gun. "I said shut the hell up, freak!"

"Oh, but you know I'm not a freak."

The mercenary looked frightened for the first time. Beads of sweat formed on his forehead and upper lip. His gun shook in his hands.

I calmed myself. "Sorry... But you really should try it."

"Try what?"

"The cerebral spinal fluid from the Deitii."

He edged closer, licking his lips. "I think I'll pass."

"It feels like experiencing your own birth, not just as a child, but as the child and the mother simultaneously. Every important thing that connects the empty stretches of the cosmos suddenly makes sense. It's all stitched together in a way both beautiful and fulfilling. For once, you don't feel at the mercy of the world, the galaxy, the universe, anything."

"Sounds like any powerful drug."

My laugh was a sad one. "I've tried those. It's not. It's the difference between being mortal and immortal, and you should know by now that I'll never get over it. I'll never give it up. It isn't addiction. It's a realization."

"It's murder. And you will die."

I smiled. "No, my mercenary friend. It is you who will die. And every other person who replaces you. I'm not stopping here. I'm going to keep eating. I'm going to keep growing. I'm going to take control. Of your friends, of your family, of everyone and everything, everywhere."

"Not with a bullet in your head. You ain't no god."

"I'm learning as I go," I told him.

I took aim at a black box connected to the conduit line and fired. Immediately, the grappling hook system on the mercenary's back pulled upward, attracted to the exposed magnetic coil. The man was yanked off the ground and pinned to the conduit. His gun fell to the floor.

I drifted into the hall and kicked his gun into a dark corner. The mercenary struggled to free himself, but the straps for his grappling hook system were stuck between his body and the conduit. He couldn't have been more trapped if I'd planned it ahead of time.

"This must be so embarrassing for you," I said. "I will say that it was fun meeting you. And I'll grant you this, you didn't make it easy. You must have seen a thing or two in your day."

"Go to hell!"

"By the way, who do you work for?" I asked. "Tell me and I won't drag this out. I should really get back to that Deitii."

"You do whatever," he said through his clenched teeth.

"Is that so? I've got enough to figure it out already, but if you save me the effort, it'll save you pain."

"You... Do... Whatever."

"Whatever?" I pulled out my serrated bone knife from my interior pocket. It dripped wet with brine, but the rawhide lace-wrapped handle still provided a solid grip. "This knife is made from a composite of crocoshark fangs and devil stone, or I guess it'd be stuck up there right alongside you. Fortunately for me."

I wearily looked him over a moment, knowing he wouldn't break, but I wasn't in the mood for another evisceration.

"Hate for our little chase to come to this. Innards spilling out, always a big yucky. It gives me the willies. But whatever—"

I lifted the point of the knife to his belly.

"Wait!" he cried out.

I smiled. "Oh yes, deary, what is it?"

"So you're no longer interested in who I work for?"

"That'll take care of itself. Once your people come to collect your body, I'll know."

"You don't know my people very well."

"But I know you and your type," I said. "You won't tell me, even when your organs are pouring out the large hole I make in you. I can't decide if I like that type of loyalty or honor. It seems kind of, I don't know, wasted on a bunch of invisible people not standing around to give a shit."

I raised the knife again.

"But I give a shit," said the mercenary and he thumbed something off his belt. It was small and spherical, off a loop.

I watched as the grenade fell to the floor and rolled over to the wall.

"Goddamn it!" I yelled and sprinted down the hall. An explosion of smoke and electricity surged around me. Flames burst forward and caught my coat on fire. I wailed in surprise at the stinging pain and pulled the coat over my head. I lost balance and crashed to the ground, luckily, as a giant wave of fire roared overhead. I twisted around and pulled it off. As flames overtook the coat, arcs of electricity raced through them.

Electrodischarge incendiary... Smart, that one.

I peered down the hall, full of fire and smoke and running fingers of blue electricity. "But he's blown to bits, none the less."

I strolled through the debris. The beams overhead had split and rolled with smoke. After navigating some of the fiery chunks of metal and rock, I spotted something on the ground. Lowering down on my haunches, I took it up and had a gander. It was a business card.

LIMBUS, INC.
ARE YOU LAID OFF, DOWNSIZED, UNDERSIZED?
CALL US. WE EMPLOY.

I smiled. "That's fantastic. Well, Limbus, I am out of work, after all."

A rustling sound came from far down the hallway. I perked up and raised my knife, grinning so hard my teeth hurt. "You still with us after all, my dear mercenary friend?"

I walked down the hall to investigate, but found no other traces of the man. I knew he'd escaped. Otherwise, the smell of his blood would be intense in my nostrils.

I needed to return to my kill though. I guess I'd have to pay him another visit. Him and any other Limbus employees. Wonderful. I looked forward, very much, to that.

Chapter 4

Dean opened his eyes. They stuck together for a moment, causing him some panic; he flinched and rocked around. A distant voice told him to remain calm, but he didn't know if the voice belonged to another person or if his subconscious had decided to lecture him. He lifted his hand, which seemed to weigh fifty pounds, and brought it to his face to scrub away the film and crud that had collected at the side of his eyes. A bitter ball of mucus clung to the back of his throat, tasting of blood but possessing the texture of a raw egg. He tried to clear it but it was holding on back there. *Lovely.*

His presence of mind returned to him and the membrane transport room in the Moon City station took shape once more. At first, he thought perhaps the tech had saved him from the Quantum Flu, but as he tried to move, he realized the grip of the illnesses still held firm. He'd only awoken because he'd gained enough strength to endure the pain again, but passing out once more was definitely in his future.

"How long... was I out?"

"Two hours." The tech checked his screen with dread. "Still not out of the woods, but I'm glad you're awake."

As though to purposely disappoint the kid, Dean passed out again. He wasn't sure how long he was out this second time around, but when his eyes slid open again, the tech hovered over him.

"Thank God," he whispered. "If I let the Slaughter Man die, I think I'd become famous for all the wrong reasons."

Dean's voice was a hoarse croak. "Kid, you're fine. You didn't do anything wrong. Just keep it together. It'll be fine. We just have to wait for that butthead Crimson Op to show."

"Wait no longer. The butthead has arrived."

Widening his eyes, Dean tried to focus on the man walking down the side corridor to the transport room. Well-muscled and tall, the man's clothing was torn and burnt in places and he had several alarming wounds on his right shoulder and mid-torso.

"Good shit, Ricky Agate," said Dean. "You've got to look worse than I do."

The mercenary staggered forward. "Really? I must look incredibly fucked up because I've seen the bottom of outhouses that look better than you."

Dean coughed for a moment and then sniffed some blood back into his sinus. "Still hanging at the bottom of shithouses, huh? I thought people were supposed to leave the anal stage at some point during childhood. Maybe you should look into that in your weekly sessions."

Rick crashed into the transport console and rudely pushed the tech away. "I did consider that once, truth be told, but your mom likes the anal stage."

Dean shut his eyes to rest them. "If I wasn't dying right now, I'd have a comeback for that."

"You ain't dying, Slaughter Man. Shit, I nearly got blown into a million pieces an hour ago by a man high on Deitii spinal fluid. You? You're solid. Quit bitching."

"Yes, master."

"Good, you're catching on."

Dean's stomach rumbled loudly. "Is it possible I'm hungry and still dying?"

"Knock it off." Rick's fingers continued to fly over the keyboard. "I'm not feeling sorry for the likes of you. I'll introduce you to some Moon City cuisine when this is done."

"I feel like I haven't eaten in a very long time. It's even bad for membrane transport. What time of day is it?"

"Thirty-six a.m."

"Oh man," said the tech. "No wonder you're hungry. It's almost time for tri-breakfast."

Dean shook his head. *"Thirty-six* a.m? Not hearing you right."

"No, you are. Orbital period around the gas giant here is eighty-four hours long. Noontime is forty-two o'clock p.m. Welcome to Moon City."

With a wince, Dean tried to sit up. Wasn't happening. "Shit, I should have read the briefing closer."

"Don't worry. We'll get you a bottle of some Constalife pills, and you'll be able to deal with the long days. It'll adjust your circadian rhythm, change your cardiac frequency and increase brain function longevity. It's good shit."

"Doesn't sound as good as tri-breakfast." Dean glanced at the tech, who grinned despite everything else.

"I know what you mean. I skipped bi-breakfast completely today," said the tech.

"And somewhere a hobbit died." Dean tried to laugh but it hurt.

"Shut up, you two," said Rick. "You're making me crazy. I have to concentrate. Half my body feels like it's been in a toaster set on inferno."

Something inside Dean's head broke then and shards of slicing pain jabbed down his spine. He let out a wail as a wetness spilled from his ears and nose. The blood smell was inescapable. He wiped some away and regarded the scarlet rivers threading around his deathly white hand. Sparkles lit through them, stars burning hotter, consuming all…

"Damn it! Hold on, Dean!" shouted Rick, and he pounded on the keyboard furiously. "I almost got connected with your DNA signatures and where they were halted. Who in the hell did this to you? Piece of patchgate crap!"

The tech floated above Dean like a bewildered ghost. "He's not doing so well."

Dean couldn't turn his head to Rick, but he still heard the keyboard going and the mercenary's rough retort, "Thanks for the update, you cockeyed platypus. Like I really need shit from you right now."

The tech looked over in hurt disbelief, and suddenly, Rick let out a triumphant shout. "Holy hot damn! I got through the cross-code. Dean, man, somebody really wanted you dead."

Dean still held his hand out before him. The sparkling pinpoints of light in his blood faded and wisps of steam escaped from under his fingernails and the corners of his eyes. He took a deep, wet breath of air as his muscles tightened from his neck to his midsection to his ankles. A sense of renewed energy coursed through him now that he wasn't under the influence of dimensional arrest. He struggled to rise.

"Don't get up yet," cautioned the tech.

"I'm good," he replied.

Rick walked down the short flight of steps and stood before him. "Oh yeah. Good as muddy holy water."

Dean flipped him off. The gesture tired him more than he expected though, and his hands dropped to his chest.

"Why not go get something to clean him up?" Rick told the tech. "Since you're just sticking around like corn in a turd."

The tech huffed, but made no comment and hurried off. Dean chuckled. "You're pretty hard on the kid."

"Hey, screw that kid." Rick took one knee, a playful grin on his face. It belied his injuries and his general ghastly appearance.

"What's up with that?"

"No reason," Rick replied. "Just feel like being a jerk today."

"One of those days?"

"Happens every time I almost blow myself up with one of my own grenades. I'm trying to work through my issues."

"Well, I wouldn't know anything about that, just got a Quantum Flu."

"Yep. You're a wuss."

Dean pushed up on one arm. "So tell me about the Moon City Killer. He's the one you ran into today I take it."

"All business. Love that about you. My brother and you would be great friends."

"He's a better contract mercenary than you."

Rick made a face like he might laugh or punch Dean in the nose. "If you weren't right, I'd regret disabling that virus on you. Yeah he's a putz, but he's the best. So I gotta be nice."

"But you're the greatest man you've ever had the pleasure to know."

Rick turned even more serious. "It's been going on for almost five Moon months now. The Deitii have lost around twenty of their children. It's never the adults, just the children. And they have a limited number of those, you know, since they don't mature for hundreds of years and most Deitii I've met are thousands of years old. I've been reading like crazy since I got here. Fascinating stuff."

"Sandra and I attended a meeting from Alien affairs a few months ago," said Dean, wincing at her name. "It was a presentation on how the Deitii control their population."

"Makes sense when you live for millennia," Rick replied. "There are only about forty left in Moon City. The young Deitii's blood donations are vital here for the production of Constalife. The older of the species is not as potent. That's what this guy is doing. He's feeding off the cerebral spinal fluid in the brains."

Either hunger or revulsion twisted Dean's stomach. "What?"

"I know. Pretty raw, ain't it?"

The tech walked up with a wad of several paper towels to offer Dean. Rick eyed them carefully. "Those aren't double-ply. They won't soak up a damn thing."

"We don't have those."

"Well figure it out. Go get something to clean this man up, you cocktail boner."

The tech now got visibly upset. "Hey, why are you being so nasty?"

"Because I didn't get to kill today." Rick shooed him off with a dismissive gesture. With a roll of his eyes, the tech left once again.

Dean took a deep breath. He was exhausted still but didn't feel like he sat at the threshold of death anymore. "Why is this guy eating the brains of Deitii children?"

Rick adjusted some hardware on his belt that seemed to bother him. "We know that the Deitii have some amazing chemical properties in their DNA, but when I reported my findings with the company's director out here, I got a file on the Deitii that added up to what I'm thinking is rubbish."

"You think you're being fed something? Wouldn't be the first time Limbus turned against itself internally."

Rick shook his head and squeezed the bridge of his nose. "No, I think this data was legitimate. I even think the director actually *believed* what it said."

"Which was?"

A shadow passed over Rick's face and he stared off into space for a moment. Dean thought he would need to prod him further, but then he spoke. "Do you believe in God?"

"Come again?"

"God? The guy with the long beard and robe."

"Sure," said Dean. "Maybe. I don't know."

"When you think of Him, or It, do you think of a supernatural thing?"

"I'm not religious. I don't think about it at all."

"I hear you," Rick replied. "I didn't either... But this data file, it essentially says that Limbus knows exactly who created the universes."

"And how does this tie into our guy?"

"The Deitii are blood related to the species of the being who created the universe. They are similar to what early primates are to mankind. The Deitii share ninety-nine percent of their DNA with God, according to the data file. That's why their blood has so many unknown applications and seems to have almost magical powers. Personally, I think Limbus needs to find some better scientists. Everything has an explanation and this just sounds like a quick way out."

"Sounds that way. I agree."

The tech brought over several clean, blue shop towels. Dean accepted them and wiped off his hands and face. The tech went back to his station to run diagnostics while they continued to talk in lower voices.

"I think our Moon City serial killer believes the rumors," said Rick. "I think he believes eating Deitii brains will turn him into a god. I'll give the theory some credence here, despite my skepticism... That son of a bitch was strong and moved like no other mark I've ever tailed, and he managed to escape death easier than should've been possible. His diet is definitely making him powerful. Not a god maybe, but powerful."

Dean tossed aside a blood-saturated towel and smacked his lips. "Damn, do I need to get some sleep..."

"No. You need some Constalife pills. You'll be in a world of hurt if you sleep right now. It's the worst jet lag of your life. Trust me."

"Bring it on then," said Dean.

The sounds of a swelling beach tide and seagulls emitted from a cell phone on the control desk. Dean and Rick both glanced over at the sound.

"That's me," said Dean. "Hey, can you grab that for me, kid?"

The tech finished typing and swept the translucent device off the desk and brought it over.

"They transferred all your ring tones to your offworld phone?" Rick asked. When Dean said nothing, he added incredulously, "Upon arrival?"

"Membership has its privileges," Dean muttered, taking the phone and nodding thanks to the tech.

Rick shook his head. "I need to be more forceful with my contract next time. Just wish they gave us Golden Transport."

"Agreed," whispered Dean hoarsely.

He knew the caller. The beach ringtone was his reminder of Sandy. She'd thought it was cute and lovey-dovey, but he'd actually done it unconsciously—just needed a separate tone to know he absolutely needed to answer when she called; she wasn't a woman who would be sidelined for long.

"Hey, sweetheart," he said. The phone stung against the flesh of his ear, his body still not completely recovered from the Quantum Flu.

"You told me you'd call when you got there. I expected to be leaving a message! You've got about twenty of them from me in various emotional states." She chuckled nervously.

"Yeah, I'm very sorry. Ran into a bit of complications outside the membranes."

"Are you okay? Did something happen? Your voice sounds gravelly."

"No, I'm fine," he lied. "Everything went okay. Just wiped out."

Out of the corner of his eye, he saw Rick arch his eyebrow.

Dean cleared his throat. "How was this past month? To me we just talked like a few hours ago."

She said something inaudible and he asked her to repeat herself, which always annoyed her. "Things are okay," Sandra said. "Work has been busy. There have been a few new recruits that have occupied my nights. You know how Limbus goes."

"Yep, I do."

"You don't sound like you want to talk."

"No, I do. Like I said, it hasn't been as long for me as it has for you, and I'm out of sorts. Can I call you back later?"

"Really? Are you for real?"

"Hey, come on, give me a break," he said, growing more embarrassed with the other eyes watching him.

"Yeah, sure, call me whenever," Sandra replied curtly.

"Hey, I love you," he whispered. "Just let me get my head on straight."

"Sure thing. No problem at all."

She hung up before Dean had the chance to say anything else. Rick and the membrane tech shared the same amused smirk.

"Ah, was that your old lady, Slaughter Man?" the tech asked, his grin getting bigger. "I could tell by the tone of your voice!"

Dean glanced at Rick. "Maybe you were right to be hard on him."

"Homeboy is whupped!" The tech made a whipping sound and gestured with a lashing.

Rick stood. "Okay, okay, enough hanging out. Go do some algebra homework, nardling."

The tech's shoulder slumped. "You know what, man? I have to say something. That's completely uncalled for. I'm really not taking this abuse—"

The tech's head bucked back and his forehead split in a wide, vermillion opening, pieces of white and red spinning overhead in a ghastly cloud. Rick sprung forward and caught the young man before he struck the floor. Blood ran in torrents from the shattered face as Rick lowered him to the ground, his other hand withdrawing his weapon. Dean shifted over on his hip and attempted to gain his feet.

Armed soldiers in black helmets and riot gear flooded into the room. The lead officer with a silver star on his helmet edged up, assault rifle covering the room. His voice sounded confined to a radio behind the tinted glass of his helmet. "Which of you is Dean Fulsome, the Slaughter Man?"

Rick lifted his gun and aimed for the soldier. "We're happy to tell you, but first, how about you go fuck yourself?"

"Me," said Dean. "I'm Dean Fulsome."

Rick gave him a sidelong look but didn't lower his gun.

"You need to come with us."

"Like hell he does," Rick blurted.

Dean lifted his hand to calm his friend.

"You're in violation of Firecracker System 23 transportation ordinance. This membrane transport caused a system-wide failure across our networks. You have to serve audience with the mayor."

Two soldiers approached Dean. They were surprisingly gentle as they brought him to his feet. Then, in contrast to this, they roughly handcuffed him.

"Can I get some clothes at least?"

"The robe will do," replied the lead officer, still in a stare-off with Rick.

"Why did you kill this kid?" Rick asked.

"I'm not authorized to answer your questions, mercenary. The mayor's office will answer inquiries."

"The tech had nothing to do with the membrane transport problem," Dean explained, head spinning. "It was an outsider."

"The owner does not allow techs to engage in personal calls during a transport. This problem could have been addressed much earlier."

"But kill him?" Dean looked at the still body. "Who is this owner?"

"The Firecracker Lady doesn't need to answer to Limbus scumbags. Save your stories for the Mayor of Moon City. And if I were you, I'd explain it well if you wish to live on."

Rick slowly lowered his firearm. "Do you know who we work for?"

The lead officer took Dean by the shoulder and tugged him forward. "Limbus cannot place guilt on anyone else for this breech."

Rick holstered his gun with a snarl. "Dean, I'm going to get to the bottom of this. I'm going to City Hall too. Meet you there." He narrowed his eyes at the lead officer. "I know how execute-horny you regional squads are—"

"Coming from you, that's hilarious," quipped the lead officer as he pulled Dean up the ramp.

"Execute this man without due process and you will pay dearly for it!" shouted Rick.

The lead officer stopped, helmeted head whipping back. "You will threaten me then?"

"Hell yes I will. First me, then later my brother, and you *never* want to meet him."

Dean shook his head. "Don't get into it, man. We'll get it handled. Contact central office. Get Tasha to call City Hall. I'm sure she'll smooth this over."

Rick looked at him reluctantly. "I will. I'll get you out." He pointed at the lead officer. "Get this man some Constalife at once. He's just arrived here."

They escorted Dean outside. He stole a glance over his shoulder. Rick staggered back and considered again the corpse of the young membrane tech sprawled on the floor. He bowed his head and ran his hand through his sooty hair. Then the doors to the transport station closed on the solemn scene.

Chapter 5

.

Moon City Hall might have been more of a spectacle under different circumstances. Dean could feel the effects of membrane travel and the strange orbital conditions of his surroundings weighing down on him like a drunken gorilla on his back. The regional police acted like the flippers and he the pinball forever bouncing left to right. He took in some of the ornately carved hallways of stone with flecks of gold throughout. Electric torches burned bright behind sapphire prisms fixed overhead. The light through the prisms scattered geometric patterns over the rocky contouring, feeding the gold flakes in the rock and making them a universe of embedded stars. The sight dazzled him, literally, and Dean almost collapsed while admiring the galactic surface of a winding stairway the police led him down.

"Keep him together," said the lead officer to another.

"Who cares?" said the other.

The lead officer shoved the other into the wall. "I do. The mayor does. Do what is told to you and I won't explain why you went trigger happy on the tech."

Dean opened his mouth but the lead cut him off, "Shut up, Fulsome."

"Whatever you said, Commander," said the other reg officer.

"I'm going to change out of the armor," said the lead. "Tell his honor I'll be there shortly."

"You mean that? You'll be there, right? You're not going to the casino again, right?"

The lead stiffened. "You have a big mouth, cadet."

"Sorry, Commander."

"Get this man to the mayor and shut the everlovingfuck up."

"Affirmative," replied his subordinate, who promptly slipped his hand under Dean's arm and began to guide him on.

The lead officer disappeared into a crowd on the next floor. Lines of unruly-looking individuals waited in queues before a series of counters with receptionist windows, also sapphire glass. A general mix of humans and aliens alike milled around. Dean recognized some of the alien species, from the dauntingly tall Asedgi who looked like humanoid giraffes, to Fanglions whose feminine bodies flickered with white-noise skin, and then there were the Shadow Dragons who were slow-moving gargoyles with psychotic visages. The humans present were actually more intimidating; they appeared tribal or ganglike, some dressed similarly in bright colors with striking symbols, hair punkish or shaved bald, both women and men—they all reminded Dean of the gangs in that old 80s movie, *The Warriors*. On screen, those people almost seemed comical in their exaggerated gang regalia, but faced with this sort in real life, Dean felt a bit uneasy, and the feeling didn't get better as the grimaces and snarls and scarred faces considered the newcomer in his sky blue robe.

"What is this place?" he asked.

"Tax office and Department of Motor Vehicles," was the quick reply.

"Oh, no wonder," he said.

They departed the crowd and passed a darkened office. A statue of an alien had been situated just left of the door. Its blank expression made other statues lifelike in comparison, but Dean realized it was a fine representation. The Deitii didn't make facial expressions. His guess was confirmed as he read the placard near the doors: OFFICE OF DEITII AFFAIRS.

The officers rushed Dean down another flight of stairs into a smaller area with one single office. He noted the crest outside on the wall, "The Honorable Mayor of Moon City, Jacob Blath ++"

The ++ alarmed Dean. He'd read in his briefing that adult Deitii males put the double pluses after their names to signify a coming of age, because of their longevity and no noticeable aging features from childhood to adulthood. The women Deitii put two zeroes after their names.

"He's a Deitii?" Dean asked.

The helmeted officer released his arm and knocked on the door. "Hybrid. Human and Deitii."

"Wow." Dean whistled. "Never heard of that."

"Now you have."

They waited a moment. Dean reached out and touched the metallic leaves of a potted plant near the door. "These things grow here?"

"It's fake, dumbass." The officer knocked on the door again.

"You could have had me totally going. Especially since I can hardly keep my eyes open… You don't happen to have any of that Consta-stuff?"

"Come in, please," said a voice behind the door.

The officer opened the door and guided Dean in. The office was humble. Packed bookshelves on the back wall with a single desk and another metallic plant sitting upon it. The mayor was a slender man with thinning, slicked-back, salt-and-pepper hair. His face held little humor and little sign of age in contrast with the weariness in his eyes. Dean wouldn't have guessed he was part alien. His lack of warmth or any apparent soul wasn't a giveaway. He just seemed like a prick.

"Your honor, Lead Officer Harth will be here shortly," the officer told him.

"Good, please shut the door. Have a seat," the mayor told Dean.

Dean didn't need to be asked twice. Completely exhausted, he flopped down into the purple wicker chair opposite the desk. He heard the door shut quietly behind him.

"Nice place," he told the mayor.

"Dean Fulsome, I've had time to review your file on your way down," said the mayor, tapping the screen of his notepad.

"That so? I've been on at least three dozen long campaigns. It took all of ten minutes to get here. You must have skimmed it."

The door opened again. A large, bulldog-faced man entered dressed in a dark suit with long-hanging white sleeves that looked like serving towels hanging over his wrists.

"I'll take a Miller Lite or a Heineken," Dean told him.

"What?" The man's face twisted in surprise.

"I thought you were taking my drink order. I haven't seen the menu yet."

"I'm a little tired already of you." The man puffed out his chest. "Do you know what trouble you're—?"

"Officer Harth, stand down," said the mayor.

The man looked visibly hurt that the mayor wasn't on his side, or at least wasn't in favor of beating the shit out of Dean.

"That's enough, Donaldo," the mayor said more calmly. "I'm okay. You can leave us. I'll call if I need you."

"But, Mr. Mayor..."

"Leave, Donaldo."

Dean waved at him. "Bye bye, Donaldo. Quack, quack," he added.

Donaldo's face inflamed but he crisply shut the office door behind him. Silence ensued for a few moments as the mayor tried to regain his composure.

Dean folded his arms. He didn't need this. He'd come here to help these assholes. He'd put his relationship, his heart, in jeopardy, and he wasn't in the mood to get the strong-arm treatment. Aliens the size of F350 pick-up trucks had chased him around this galaxy. Humans could be rightfully scary in their own right, but his conversation with Sandra had left him too tired and depressed to let anything affect him at this point.

"You were going on about reviewing my file," he assisted. "Was it a good read?"

"Stow the smart-ass, Fulsome," the mayor muttered.

"My apologies. I get cranky when I see an innocent, young membrane tech get his head blown off for no good reason."

"What?"

"One of your regs took an innocent life."

"We will look into that."

Dean's fatigue got the better of his mood. "That's really big of you. I'm sure it isn't the first time."

"Is that what you think?" The mayor looked up at him and his eyes thinned under his tremendous brow. "That we'd do something like that so randomly?"

Dean shrugged. "I've seen a lot of shit, Mr. Mayor. Very little surprises me these days. I reckon I'm beyond jaded at this point, even so much that I really don't have the time or the room in my soul to debate you and your people's morals. I just need you to tell me why I'm in your office ahead of schedule and why you carted me off like a criminal when my company has sent me here to assist our man in the field with *your* problem."

"There is a reason for everything. Even our Lead Officer isn't privy to everything... I'll get to the technician in a moment," said the mayor, glancing back down at Dean's file on his screen. "Let's talk about you a moment."

"Oh yes, please."

"You were involved in the poisoning of the Princess of Ganymede. You've directed operations for Limbus, Incorporated, Solar System division, for four years now. You're a very hands-on director. You seem to take tasks that could otherwise be delegated to subordinates—like the Zetú refuge migration."

Dean swallowed and tasted something raw in the back of his throat. It might have been an aftereffect of the membrane transport or it might be the itchy intuition that this conversation was headed to an ugly, hateful place. If that were the case, though, Dean at least could be resolved with detesting this man thoroughly.

"Yep, I've been involved in a lot."

"But the Zetú exodus wasn't a Limbus related issue."

"Not sure I see your point in bringing the Zetú up, Mr. Mayor. I've done a lot in four years. They were only a small part in that time period."

"It's my prerogative to bring them up. I can bring up whatever I feel like in my position, in this office, *anything*. I can and I will, especially when questioning a man who comes into my city and works for a company that may be sympathetic to Freedomist Elite."

Yep, thought Dean, this was all about some racist politics between these people and the Zetú. He should have seen this coming. This man made him sick. The Zetú were the most decent alien species Dean had come across in his travels, a far sight kinder and gentler than human damned beings. Regardless, Dean put on his poker face. "Mr. Mayor, Limbus, Inc. backs no political parties through media or through financial contributions. For the record, I opted personally to save that convoy of Zetú. They were my friends and I owed them a large favor. It wasn't a directive from Limbus. We are an employment agency. I was actually written up for the action and also lost my... position over it."

"Sure you did."

Dean couldn't really scoff at the contradiction; he knew for a fact that Limbus played many sides to many political factions, and did indeed make campaign contributions. Yet, they made them to opposing sides for a myriad of reasons, most of which was to keep control of whatever the hell they really controlled behind their big iron doors at their original headquarters—a place he'd still not been and few others he knew had.

"Are you saying my contracted associate should leave this city? My superiors would be upset, but I also cannot remain here if our services are unwanted. The killer is still roaming the caverns as I've come to understand. If you don't like my friends, Mr. Mayor, and that somehow presents a problem with how I manage our contract here, I can certainly leave."

"*Friends*?" The word was bitter on the mayor's lips.

Dean nodded. "I know for the Stone Turtles that might be an uncomfortable concept."

The mayor snarled but it looked strange on his flat face. "That you'd even call the United People Under Stars that insulting nickname shows your allegiance!"

"Oh, calm down," said Dean. "Really, before you burst something. I have allegiance to me, myself, and my girlfriend. That's where it ends. The job is just a job. So I made friends who you'd never have dinner with. Doesn't mean I'm inviting them to the ball and forcing you to slow dance."

The mayor got up and looked out the window with unease. "We do need your presence here. I share blood with the Deitii, and if I'm not seen being proactive about stopping this slaughter, it won't just mean my removal from office. I'll be strung out and burned alive. Regardless of how much I need you Limbus people here, I cannot be visible in aiding someone connected with the Zetú—that would streamline the whole being burned-alive process." A disgusted chuckle escaped the mayor's lips.

"That does seem like a pickle."

"The contract will need to be paid through a third party—you don't have to worry about your... services."

"Well don't get all choked up on me there, Mayor. I'm the project manager of a peace-keeping mission. We are here to save lives, not just take the one."

The mayor lifted one of his miniscule black eyebrows.

"Hey," said Dean with a smile. "How do you like that? This guy knows a bit of rhetoric too."

The mayor sat back down. "I told you I'd explain the technician."

"I'm listening."

"How do you explain frying our network systems? Slipping past a membrane like that exposes code you could sell. The tech working there had to be working with you or someone else to make that happen."

"He seemed pretty surprised and out-of-sorts. I don't think he was involved. Pretty snap judgment of you guys too, killing him like that. Is that how things are done around here?"

"Sending a message to our enemies is priceless, Fulsome. Even if the tech wasn't involved, whoever set that up—"

"Don't look at me."

"It's hard not to look at you. The Zetú would love to get their hands on our intelligence."

"The Zetú are at war. And not with you. They don't have time for your power games. You have nothing of importance to them and you damn well know it, so quit scapegoating."

"Lower your voice to me."

Bitterly, Dean did. "Look, they didn't do it. I don't think the tech had any involvement either. Me? I got the Quantum Flu from that collapsing membrane. I could have bought the farm. That's an awful big price to pay for something our programmers back on Earth could easily do remotely."

"Perhaps."

His phone vibrated twice. That meant Sandy had texted him. He didn't want to even guess what it said. He felt like passing out. They hadn't given him any of that medicine stuff and he wasn't sure how long he'd be able to stand; the atmosphere was dense like being underwater, and his bones felt like they were composed of gelatin that had begun to lose its form.

He took a deep breath despite his discomfort and continued. "I'm here to aide in the apprehension of the Moon City killer and to facilitate your election. Those are my operatives."

"And yet you don't back political parties."

"We are interested in the partnership for the neocrystals from the Midnight Sea. We could give a good goddamn about your beliefs and your place in office."

The mayor's suspicion had begun to wane, but he still visibly, stubbornly clung to it. "Why not make a direct deal with the Miner's Association?"

Dean sighed. "No need to rock the boat. You're popular, and now that I know you're related by blood to the Deitii, that makes quite a difference too. They have one hundred times the voting power of any other citizen on this moon as I understand it. They have to live so they can vote."

"Indeed." The mayor folded his fingers together. "I do not share that privilege, being only of one Deitii parent, but they do like me. They trust me."

"Of course they do," said Dean. "And the miners like doing business with stable figureheads anyway. Otherwise they're skittish in agreeing to terms. Limbus, too, likes stability in their chosen partnerships."

"Seems as though you've thought this through."

"No, I have other, smarter people do that for me."

The mayor shut off his screen. "We will keep you and your contractor under surveillance. As soon as we have a body, you can expect a confirmation statement from a Moon City business to make a payment on our behalf. I don't ever want to see you coming back here though. Is that understood?"

"I'll try to resist the temptation. Thank you for your hospitality, Mr. Mayor."

With a glare, the mayor pushed a button. "Officer Harth, come take Fulsome down to the city clerk's office."

The door opened a moment later and the henchman stood there, stone-faced.

Dean shot up from his chair. "Donaldo! Boy, did I ever miss you."

The mayor pointed for the door. "Get him out of here. He gets his papers and within an hour make sure he rolls out of here in an unmarked vehicle in parking structure B, in the back, out of sight. Don't wander off to the casino. Make sure."

"Of course I won't sir," said Donaldo. "Right away."

Dean followed the lumbering henchman outside into the narrow hallway. He could tell the car was going to be about the only support he'd have from here on in. He glanced at his phone and brought up Sandy's text.

Not happy. We really need to talk about this arrangement.

Dean's heart sunk.

Yes, not a very good start to this assignment at all.

* * *

Dean had no idea where he was going. He'd been given directions and also been asked to repeat them to the mayor's people, but he'd forgotten everything. Each bone and all the fibers of his being were in conflict with each other. He'd received a call from Rick to meet him a few blocks down from City Hall, but those few blocks felt like tunneling through a mountain with a toothpick. The streetlights bent and wisps and tracers of light crossed; the street lifted and joined with the carved buildings in the cavern walls; someone honked and shouted angrily at him; Dean laughed—couldn't help it, for he was more tired than he'd ever been in his life and also had the feeling that if he fell asleep, and managed not to have a fatal car accident, he would still never recover from the slumber—he'd dream forever and never revive to the world of the living again. As he twisted the oblong-shaped wheel to the vehicle, which was centermost in the car rather than being right or left like back on earth, he had a vision, a ghostly one, of Rick waving to him, smiling, and then fear in his eyes that widened them, made them cartoonlike and unnatural.

"STOP! SHIT!" he yelled.

Dean blinked and drove his foot down onto the brake pedal.

It must have been a hallucination brought on by his severe exhaustion because it looked almost cartoonish. Rick vaulted into the air like a mythical being and sprung off the bumper, landing on the hood, half a foot from the windshield. Back home that might have collapsed or at very least left a healthy dent in the hood, but these vehicles on Moon City were all Fanglion models, and the metallic surfaces oscillated in waves with the impact. Despite this buffering of the material, the speed Dean had been going could have still killed someone, and this fact wasn't lost in the wide eyes of his friend, who peered down through the windshield.

"You rat-licking crap-sponge! You could have killed me, you know? Ho-ly shit! Did they not give you Constalife?"

That was an interesting last thing to hear before Dean's forehead smashed into the steering wheel and darkness poured down.

* * *

Dean woke upright.

In a tavern.

"What in the hell?"

"Take one more," said Rick. He pressed a yellow, diamond-shaped pill into Dean's hand. Something intense pulsed at the pill's core, a radiation that wouldn't reach its half-life before the end of all universes. "Stop ogling and suck it down," Rick said with a soft irritableness. "Use your beer, good sir."

Dean looked at his drink. It was half full, but he didn't remember drinking any before this moment. He lifted his weary eyes to his colleague, who took a long pull off his own beer, which had a rich cinnamon color.

"Got you some cheap lager," said Rick, wristing the foam off his upper lip. "I'm saving for my kids' college tuition and I didn't think you'd notice anyhow."

"That's good. Where am I?"

"Boy, you are jacked up," said Rick. "I don't even have kids."

"What am I doing here, Rick?" Dean straightened his back and tried to get a grip on the spinning room.

"You remember my name now. That's a good start. Take your third pill and I'll tell you."

"Third… pill?"

"Yes," Rick said with a sigh. "As in this is the next pill after *the second.*"

"I," Dean began, "don't even remember taking one pill. I don't even remember walking in here with you!"

"Sure. And you probably don't remember that I made you eat a whole Crato hotdog either?" Rick pointed to the empty plate full of sauce and bits of bread. Dean stared at it in horror. "I'm always doing that to my friends, forcing them to try new things."

Dean could taste a sweet meaty flavor in his mouth. It wasn't unpleasant but was foreign at the same time. "How… long did it take to drive here?"

"The drive wasn't anything. And the hike? Well, it wasn't far from where you tried to run me down with your government car."

"What?"

"No worries. That was a joke." Rick took another sip. "At any rate, your temporary accommodations are upstairs. Take the stairwell to the left of the john, behind the bar."

"They roomed us at a bar?"

"You'll get word from the Limbus crew where your hat will hang soon enough. If they treat you like me, you'll be moved from this armpit of the moon to a much more appropriate butt pit. Now take your last pill or I'm gonna cram it past your teeth."

Dean popped the pill in his mouth. It ignited his tongue, his throat, his stomach, and spread through him. Made him feel…

Awake.

Like never before.

He felt like he'd be coherent and full of energy for an indeterminate amount of time.

"Careful," said Rick with a long drink of his beer. "It may feel like you'll never need to sleep again but that's a bad thing. You need to find a normal balance on this moon. With the first dosage you'll get insomnia. You'll be lucky to get ten hours of sleep."

"Ten?"

"You need about twice that much here."

"I see."

"You'll get used to it… until you need to leave back to Earth and then you'll be all jacked up again." Rick laughed.

"Thanks."

"You are welcome, my friend. You are welcome!" His grin faded.

"I thought you'd meet me at City Hall. Where were you?"

Rick's eyes narrowed. "I'm sorry, man. They wouldn't let me through. I knew you could hold your own. And I knew they'd need your boots on this moon and eventually cut you loose in one of their ridiculous Fanglion sedans."

"The political environment is more hostile here than I thought."

"Didn't you read the briefing?"

Dean picked up his beer. It felt good that he could hold it and bring it to his lips with a coordination not afforded to him only moments ago. "Yes I read it. I'm thorough."

Rick chuckled. "Of course, you're the Slaughter Man! So why is this all so much of a surprise?"

"It's… not. I just—" Dean groped his leg and felt the shape of his cell phone in his pocket. "Shit. I just need to handle some things."

"Hey, man," Rick said with a quick drink. "I gotcha, I know. Where's your girl live?"

"Southern California."

"That's great. I called my nephew yesterday… or was it… the day before? Shit, it's too much time here to figure out. But anyways, I called him to say happy birthday. He lives in Bakersfield."

Dean gripped the phone in his pants pocket, his nails biting into the fabric.

Rick picked up on his uneasiness and smirked. "Finish your drink. Then ask Rex at the counter to give you the key to your room."

"I knew that," Dean snapped, recalling that instruction from his file.

The mercenary leaned back in his chair and licked his top front teeth. They were bright white and well cared for. His eyes suggested he'd met an end to his patience with his friend. "Dean, I know you've been through some stuff today, but let me remind you that earlier, in this same day, I had to apply cellupatches to five places where my organs were pouring out. Do you know how that feels?"

Dean opened his mouth but was silenced.

"No… you damn well don't. Because you're a program manager and aren't in the field being sliced, diced, carved, and filled with holes day in and day out, and I know that's not what you signed on for and that's fine. Congratu-shitting-lations, but a little gratitude for me scooping my intestines off the ground and running to your aide would be highly appreciated at this moment. Especially when I bought you a dog and a beer on top of everything else!"

A loud clap startled them both. A man leered down at them like insolent children and regarded each with a critical look. "The Firecracker Lady cannot abide by such clamor in one of her houses."

Dean leaned forward to tell this man what he thought of him and anyone who called themselves the Firecracker Lady, but Rick slammed his hand over his forearm and shushed him. "Yes," he told the man, "Sorry, we didn't know this house belonged to her."

The tall man gave them a serious looking over before relenting. When he was gone, Dean ripped his arm out from under Rick's hold. "The hell is this shit?"

"We don't want to play around with her right now. Okay? It wouldn't be good for either of us."

"And here I thought you were a badass."

Rick moved his pilsner away with the back of his fingers and leaned in. "The days are long here, buddy. Be careful not to get into too much shit before your head hits the pillow."

"Look who's talking," Dean replied with a well-meaning grin.

"I'm heading back. I'm fried and tired. We can catch up later today."

"Isn't it almost night? What about the morning—?" Dean stopped himself as he realized what he was saying.

"Got a while to go before morning. It's not for hours. Night is very long. You'll see. Take your Constalife. Follow the dosage."

Dean licked his lips, hating every moment of this new assignment. He just wanted to be home with his woman. "Want me to drive you back to your place?"

"No," said Rick. "I'm walking. Just head up to your room. I'm sure Limbus left you some files."

"I'm sure you're right."

Rick clasped Dean on the shoulder. "Let's reboot and I'll call you for a rendezvous later."

"Be safe," said Dean, patting his friend's hand quickly, feeling a bit awkward for being so sharp earlier.

"Always," Rick replied and pulled away, making his way through the tavern to disappear out the front door.

Chapter 6

I never made it back to the Deitii corpse in time. The reg police had already collected it and ruined my chances of finishing the meal. So instead of wasting time being angry over that, I continued a different hunt.

I reached the façade of the mercenary's apartment building, which housed a series of tinted, oblong black windows in the side of a massive boulder. I held his LIMBUS, INC. business card and took a large sniff of it—of him. Yes, this was the place. I slowly smiled and tucked the card in my back pocket. I checked the fourth floor and one of the windows flashed in my enhanced vision. The ghostly tracer images of the mercenary's movements through the apartment I saw clearly through the walls. The room at the end of the hall... of course.

"I would have thought Limbus could afford better accommodations for their contract killers," I said under my breath.

I walked to the front entry way and tugged on the double glass doors. They didn't budge. There was a small guard window set in the stone façade just to the left. The guard behind the glass was busy playing a puzzle game, Returno, which looked like a silver and black boomerang version of Earth's Rubik's Cube.

"Excuse me," I said to the guard, who looked up at once, annoyed.

"Yes, can I help you?"

"I've forgotten my key."

"Looks like you've forgotten more than that, buddy." He sized me up suspiciously. "That door is chip-set. You can't get in unless you've been chipped."

"It's my girlfriend's place. It's my first time visiting. She said she'd leave me a key."

He snorted. "You must have the wrong complex."

"No, this is it. Maybe I misunderstood her?"

"She can buzz you in if that's the case." His eyes lowered back down to his puzzle for a second.

"Darn," I said with a smile. "She's not here. She sent me to get some things from her place."

"That's no problem. She can buzz you in remotely from a phone or computer."

I bit my lip momentarily and turned away, trying not to let my frustration affect my mood. "Thank you for your help," I told him.

I walked down the street in the blinding sunshine cast down through the open cavern ceiling. This area was extremely sunny, as was everywhere outdoors on Moon City, save for the Midnight Sea on the opposite hemisphere. Large umbrella shade posts were common fixtures constructed by tax dollars, and this street had plenty. I wanted to regroup and figure a way into the apartment complex without too much fuss. I was nearly immortal now, but that didn't mean I wanted attention and setbacks. I still needed more of the Deitii children.

I walked to the nearest shade post and ducked underneath the black frond canopy. A skinny, runt of a kid leaned there against the pole. He nodded approval at my seeking shade. At once I knew he was wiser than a lot of other street urchin brats.

"I get tired of all the light on this moon," he told me. "The caves are not *real* dark though, you know? It's like being locked in a closet during the day. I went to the other side of the moon, to the Midnight Sea. Now *that* was true dark."

"Never been there."

"You from another system?"

"Nope," I said. "Been here all my life."

"What? Wow! That's crazy. I'm eleven and I've been to the ocean here like twenty times. Do you live in this complex?" asked the kid. "I've been here forever. I didn't see you move in."

Interesting.

"The chip they gave me stopped working and that guard is being a jerk. He won't let me in."

"The chips always work."

"Mine must be broken."

"They never break," the stubborn boy insisted.

I glared at him and he softened. "They're strict here. Like my parents. They're strict too. They wouldn't like me talking to a stranger. They think everybody is dangerous."

I folded my arms. "I moved here a day and a half ago," I told him. "Hey, if you can let me in, I'll go to my place and give you five Ganymede coins. It's all I have right now."

The kid canted his head and narrowed his eyes. "You a pervert or something? Why would you give me so much? That would pay for three star-shuttles to the Midnight Sea."

"I have plenty of money. I'm tired and I just want to go to sleep in *my* apartment, you know?"

"If you have so much money, why do you live here?"

I swallowed my impatience. "I have money because I don't spend it on lavish apartments. I don't part with my money easily. If my stupid chip worked, you can bet I wouldn't be handing out money to the likes of you."

"No need to get nasty. I'll let you in. Follow me."

I walked behind the child, a bit wary and wondering if I just shouldn't start eliminating every problem here, snuffing out so many flames like this and like that... For all I knew, the mercenary would make his way back here soon. I could smell his wounds, hear his restless heartbeat, and I knew he wasn't far, but thankfully, his scent was not intensifying, which meant he was staying put somewhere... and what was that astringent odor...? Oh yeah, alcohol... The man was having a drink.

Good, have a few. Give me some time to find out more about you.

"You promise you're going to pay me?" the kid asked, not looking back.

"I swear to God," I replied with a snort. "But are you sure you want to spend the money on all those trips? For some dumb ocean? A big, bacteria laden puddle?"

"It's not dumb," he replied indignantly. "And I've swam it a lot.

Never got sick once."

"Most kids would use the money on something more valuable."

"Like what?" he asked me.

"Shit if I know. Bubblegum?"

He scowled over his shoulder. "Don't be condescending."

"That's a big word."

The kid stopped and turned to face me. "My mom says that to my dad all the time. He's a mechanical engineer."

"That explains it." I gestured for him to move on and he did, shaking his head.

We approached the double doors and the guard's voice promptly piped through the intercom.

"What are you doing, Carl?" The guard's voice sounded dry and, if possible, even less warm than before.

"This is my friend. I'm taking him inside."

"Yeah?" The guard looked at me critically. "What happened to your girlfriend, buddy?"

I bit my lip hard for a second, really considering breaking that window and pulling the stupid man through the broken shards neck-first. "She's a friend of Carl's family," I explained. "He's bailing her out, since her phone is broken and she can't leave work to buzz me in. All these questions are really ridiculous. This isn't a military installation. And you know, I will be reporting this incompetence with the chipsets."

"You're the first one it hasn't worked on."

We ignored him and the kid named Carl swiped his wrist in front of the glass doors and they swished open without hesitation. I walked inside the apartment complex at his side, the door briskly shutting behind. The lobby was made of rock and a small waterfall spilled down the centermost wall. Blue strobe lights flashed behind it, making the water appear to move in bizarre, random increments. A stainless steel elevator at the far end of the room pulsed with the blue reflection.

"What was that stuff about your girlfriend?" the kid asked.

"A lie. When my chip stopped working, I made up a story in the hopes of him letting him in. I had to stay with it."

The kid let out a big laugh. "Fat chance. That guy has nothing else to do. Keeping someone out probably made his day."

I made for the elevator. "Sure. I'll meet you back down here."

"Oh no, no. I'm going with."

I gave him a critical look. "You'd go into a strange man's apartment?"

"Hell no, but I'll wait in the hallway," said Carl. "I'm not getting ripped off here."

"Smart." I nodded in genuine approval.

Great. Little bastard's like a wad of glue between my fingers.

I followed Carl to the elevator and the door parted automatically. We got in and I pushed the button for the fourth floor. We rode up quietly. When the doors opened, we stepped into the hall. The mercenary's reek made me dizzy as I directed my attention to the door at the end of the hallway. Briefly it flashed silver across my vision. I had to get rid of this damned kid or he'd know I was breaking in.

"So which is yours?" he asked.

I dropped my hand on his bony shoulder. "I'm so sorry. I forgot."

He backed away suspiciously from my touch. "Forgot what?"

I patted my pants pocket and rattled the change inside. "Been a long day and I'm so absent-minded. I put some of those coins in my pocket this morning. Sorry for making you come up here for nothing."

I reached into my pocket and pulled forth the promised coins. I'd been saving them since childhood and there were plenty more where that came from. I had no vices, so I hardly had need for much. Carl watched me spill the coins into his outstretched hand, where they rang musically.

"Quite a payday," he mused. "I don't even think my dad brings this much home."

I offered him an impatient smile.

Carl turned halfway from me. "Yeah, the C.P. kind of screws Dad that way. He says they do it to all their engineers."

In that moment, I wouldn't have been surprised to hear the slurping sound of my own guts spilling to the tile floor. "What... did you say?"

Carl was still intent on his haul and only slightly looked up from the shining currency in his palm. "They screw their engineers."

"No," I said with a swallow. "Where does your dad work?

"The Commerce Polity. Why?"

I had to get control of myself. Revenge was a petty feeling and I wasn't petty. I was more than this. More than anyone, anywhere.

"Nothing," I replied. "Never mind. Here take one more."

I extended out one more coin, and Carl reached forward to retrieve it. I couldn't stop what happened next. My hand closed around his and I saw his mouth open to scream. I pushed my other hand over his mouth to silence him and force him against the wall. I could feel engorged blood vessels and a drumming heart inside the child's body. They were pulsing, pounding. I heard their terrible beating and picked up on every neuron firing as silvery snaps across his young brain. Just from their electrical recipes, I could distinguish the memories there. I saw a quick montage of flashbacks from Carl's life: his obsessive-compulsive father scolding him about his laundry basket being too full, his mother crying because she burnt something in the oven and Carl lovingly hugging her in response, his bullying by other kids at Moon City Primary School. All the times spent alone in the enduring sunlight, wanting darkness, wanting peace. Many tears. The words, almost hypnotic to my sensibilities, crossing his lips and his thoughts: THERE IS NO GOD. THERE IS NO GOD.

I couldn't believe it.

Tears actually lifted in my eyes and spilled from the corners.

"You... don't believe in me?" I asked him, not understanding the level of heartbreak from the idea. Carl struggled to escape but my hold was powerful enough to secure a few grown men.

"I'm GOD reborn," I told him with a measure of sadness. "Didn't you know that? Couldn't you tell?"

Carl bit down on my finger and blood promptly spilled through his teeth. I didn't budge and hardly felt it. Dread filled his little brown eyes.

"Of course you don't believe in me." I couldn't contain my wrath. "You are spawned from the C.P.'s ilk. You. All of you. Walking, talking trash."

Carl shook his head violently, trying to tear my finger off. It wouldn't go. It hardly bled anymore, it was healing so quickly. I pulled him forward and slammed him back against the cavern wall. "You really don't believe in me, do you? You wouldn't ever love me, even though I'd watch over you. I'd make sure you were never alone in the endless sunlight again. Tell me you love me. Prove it and I'll always love you too."

I slipped my hand around Carl's throat. He was quiet but locked eyes with me.

"I love you."

"You don't mean it," I said back.

Carl squeaked. "I do."

"Bullshit..."

The young boy began to sob. "I love you, but you're hurting me."

Saline crept into my nostrils from his tears, from his terror, and I realized I'd lost control. My frenzy subsided and sanity restored itself—or had I finally been sane for the first time? I wasn't so sure yet. I released my hold on the child, and I cleared my throat shamefully.

"I'm sorry. I—I was in the Ganymede wars," I lied, "and sometimes I see things that aren't there. I go a little crazy. Please forgive me. I didn't mean to harm you."

Carl rubbed his throat. "I'm okay. It's okay."

I took a step away from him, and he took the opportunity to bolt down the hall.

"Hey! Kid! Come back! I said I was sorry!"

He pushed the elevator button. I started after him. "Stop!"

"You're too young to have fought in that war. I'm calling the regional police!" he yelled.

I sprinted hard. The elevator opened and Carl jumped inside, pressing buttons. I reached out for him. The door pinched the tips of my fingers and I withdrew my hand with a growl of frustration. I wagged my hand for a second, the combination of Carl's and the elevator's bite finally reminding me about pain.

"Shit!" I whispered.

There was no time. I turned quickly and charged down the hall. As I approached the last door, I pulled free my bone knife. I took a long breath before reaching for the mercenary's door.

* * *

It took some time to get into the apartment. Time I didn't have. I stared inside the mechanical tumblers and sprocket innards, impatient and panicked. Lifting my X-ray sight, I scanned the room, but saw only outlines—my hold on the power had faded significantly—usually I would have more consistency with my abilities, but when I was in starvation mode it flipped on and off like a sputtering power plant, coming to life and then dying again from moment to moment. Until I had a full meal again this would be how it would be. Then I could sustain myself for weeks, for the digestion of Deitii DNA caused exponential growth in power and sustainability. The mercenary who slept in this apartment had denied me that and caused a large bump in the road to my destiny.

I fought harder to see more inside. A man like this might have set traps.

Beads of blood formed at the corners of my eyes.

"Shit," I muttered, wiping it away. I couldn't wait long. The regional police were probably on their way. I put my knife in my tunic pocket and considered the pad where the resident swiped his wrist for entry. This was a simpler locking mechanism than the front doors downstairs—the metal catch, which I could plainly see, was only an eighth inch thick. I'd broken bricks with my sight before, alone in my apartment, late at night, lonely, but loving on my new power. That was after a full meal and less than an hour or so. I'd spent so much today and was running on empty.

You have to, I told myself. You made it this far.

I pressed my teeth into my lower lip and stared at the catch inside the door, looking at every atom at its center—then I narrowed my eyes, focusing harder until the atoms began wiggling and struggling to escape my vision—they needed to make room for the path I forged through them. Many of them reconnected stubbornly, but I kept on, until I heard a loud snap inside the door...

That wasn't what hurt me though.

It was keeping the small piece of metal separated, in suspension, and not letting it shatter. The whole point here was to enter the apartment undetected. I could have just punched through the door, but then the mercenary would know I'd been here and what good would that do me?

No.

I had to reunite the atoms, and that meant after I pushed the door open with the toe of my shoe, I had to account for every atom that had been displaced. Taking them all into my frail mind, I shut my eyes and drew them together. I ignored the blood rushing from my nose, eyes, and beneath my fingernails.

A louder snap.

The door shuttered in its frame.

I sighed.

I tasted my bloody vomit.

There was no time to regain myself. I slumped briefly in the threshold and used the bottom of my tunic to wipe away the blood from my face. I was woozy and stumbled into the apartment, heeling the door closed behind me.

The apartment was a simple one-bedroom, one-small kitchen, one-living room, one-bathroom-type deal—not too different from where I spent most of my time downtown. All the furnishings were drab grays and browns. A can of baked beans sat on the kitchen counter with a spoon inside. An empty Tres Exis bottle accompanied it.

"So this is where a Limbus assassin hangs his hat. You woke up here today, thinking about killing me... Didn't you?" I moved into the kitchen area and promptly began opening drawers, mumbling through my search, "Screw that. Screw that. Screw that. Screw this."

I got to the last drawer and sighed. "And fuck it all."

With a gasp of annoyance, I made for the bedroom. A whiny siren went off in the distance and I rushed back out to the living room and then into the kitchen. From the inner pocket of my coat, what I called my alchemy collection, I withdrew a couple overlarge pills. Quickly, I found the one I needed. It was lime green with a biohazard logo on the gelatin near the black lettering HCN 100%.

Now, where to put it?

I searched around for something that would smash, crush, or melt this capsule and let out the love inside.

The siren grew louder. Closer.

"Shit..." I said, out of sorts. "If I was hydrogen cyanide gas, where would I want to be born?"

I noticed a small tear in the carpet near the front door. Fast, I grabbed the capsule and got down on both knees near the hole the carpet. I tried to fit the capsule inside the hole, but my eyes caught something else at this level, something far more interesting. Across the adjoined kitchen-living room area, near the small bathroom, was a trash incinerator. A messy stack of documents had been piled nearby.

I took the capsule and walked on my knees to the incinerator. I opened its door and saw the burnt shreds of documents inside. With a glance back to the stack of unburnt documents, I pulled open the incinerator door all the way.

I smiled. "Lots of docs to burn. Lots of opening and closing this door. My gift to you. Of course this is just for what-ifs, my friend. I'd rather send you to hell and witness it."

I placed the capsule inside the incinerator and tucked it into a corner. Then I rested a half-burnt piece of paper over the top. Closing the incinerator, before I could stand, I noticed a name on the document on the top of the stack.

RICK AGATE.

A photo of the Limbus mercenary was right next to it. This explained his smell to me, that undeniable scent of greatness that was an ambience in his blood; the greatness wasn't his, but he bore a resemblance to it.

"Agate," the name formed in my mouth. I had been correct. That was who he'd been on the phone with. His brother was no doubt Christopher Agate. *Splendid family line, Rick... You are his sibling. Brother of the Gem Stone Warrior. Impressive.*

"Shit, I hope *that* son of a bitch comes to avenge your death," I said to myself, excited. "That will be some real good times."

The siren blared its loudest yet and the sound of heavy vehicle doors slamming outside got me to my feet. I went to the window in the living room and looked out. Three squad cars parked below and regional police stormed out with their robotic-looking body armor that had unsettled me since childhood. I hated those fuckers.

"Okay," I said simply, "I've had too much fun here. Time to go."

I went to the front door and opened it a crack to look outside. At the same time, I slid out my knife, hoping to use it as much as possible in silence. The next moment, I ducked into the hall, closed the door, and it locked again behind me. I put the knife against my pant leg and made swiftly for the elevator. My vision opened up and

I could see down through the floors of the apartment complex. Clusters of regional police stood in the lobby, some piling into the elevator and some flooding into the stairwell.

"Marvelous," I whispered.

The elevator opened on the second floor and the police covered the corners of the hallway, rifles shouldered. The others on the stairs came up to join them and posted at the exit. The stairs were probably the easier play, and I moved for the exit. I went halfway down the hall when an apartment door flung open. A half-dressed woman with drugged-out eyes crashed out into the hall with a hockey stick in her hand. The door slammed shut behind her and she leered at it in absolute rage.

"Bastard! Lying, cheating filth! I hate you!" she screeched and slammed the hockey stick into the door.

I halted before trying to go around her. I didn't have time for this. Without grace, I avoided the stick being winged into my face. The strung-out woman attacked the door again and the end of the stick shattered into splinters, leaving the end sharp like a spear.

A voice came from inside the apartment. "Police are downstairs, you dumb ass!"

The woman pounded her frail white fist into the door. "You think I give a good goddamn shit? They're probably here for you!"

If only.

I glanced through the floor as the police progressed through the second-floor hallway. I lifted the knife, ready to carve a path through this idiot. The druggie had no idea how close to death she was and continued another barrage of attacks against the door. I reached out quickly and snatched the broken stick.

"—the hell?"

I pulled her with the stick and sent her stumbling down the hallway.

"Prick!" she yelled.

As I approached the stairwell, I looked over my shoulder to see if she would follow. She had turned toward the wall and pressed her forehead against it, possibly crying.

I opened my vision once more and saw two regional police on the floor directly below, posted not far from the stairs. Carefully, I peered over the railing to the bottom floor. I considered the fall and whether my feet and ankles could take such an impact after all these events today. I edged out and slowly sheathed my knife inside my coat. I took time breathing, concentrating, looking at that distant stone floor below me. My heels lifted off the ground, my calf muscles tightening. I rolled my neck and breathed through my nose. There was no turning back.

I put one leg over the railing. The stairwell door crashed open behind me with an accompanied banshee-like scream. The druggie woman charged at me. "You don't lay a hand on me mother—"

She reached out to strike me, and on impulse, the next was a series of fluid movements— I grabbed her wrist; I took her by her small, wasted frame; and I threw her over the railing. A long scream echoed in the stairwell and then stopped as her head struck one of the railings on the way down. Her head struck another, most likely killing her before her body made a tremendous thud on the ground floor. Normally, I wouldn't flinch at something like that, but my eyes caught a glimpse of her spine snapping and her skull shattering, sending fragments into her brain that burst in fountains of blood. I winced a little. My shoulder ached from tossing her over the side too.

The regional police abandoned all efforts on the second floor and raced to the stairwell in response to the scream they'd heard. I watched them gather below to investigate the broken body. I returned to the elevator and took it down to the lobby. Once the doors opened, I didn't get far before several regional police accosted me.

"What is your name?" asked one who stood before me, dark face shield an inch from my nose.

I took a moment and then said, "Rick Agate."

The officer to my immediate right glanced at a data pad strapped to his wrist. "He's on here as temporary resident. Came down from the second floor though and the squad cleared every room. There is no photo file on this though. It was declined by LIMBUS, INC."

I heard a snort through the first officer's face mask. "Typical. Well, I don't care what Limbus feels is best or what our squad feels is a 'thorough search' of the second floor. We need to detain you until we find our person. Your height and build are too inconvenient I'm afraid. Please take a seat over there. Hang tight." He pointed to a silver, fabric divan in the corner of the lobby. I nodded and placed my hand over my coat, securing my knife underneath. Let them do their police things. I needed to think anyway and really didn't want to use any more energy than was required.

The police would glance at me from time to time and check their data pads, but I chose to stare down at my hands and keep them from shaking. When the elevator door opened and the kid, Carl, walked out, all my attempts to calm down failed. He spotted me right away and went to the police. I shifted in the uncomfortable divan. Carl pointed my way and one of the officers nodded. A moment later, he was walking over.

Shit.

I slid my fingers around the handle of my hidden knife, getting ready to punch a nice hole in this cop's exposed throat. The elevator door opened again. Two police walked out with a man in custody. He was a younger man with his hair painted silver and in devil horns. A long, red goatee stretched down his bare chest.

"Ain't nobody selling brain diamonds anymore!" he blared. "Are you people jacked in the head? I wouldn't stoop to that, you bastard shit-lings!"

The officer coming my way had stopped and looked over his shoulder at the commotion. I tensed with my knife. Waiting.

"What's the problem over there, officer?" I asked.

He didn't look at me, but said, "Been after that one for a bit. Works for the Firecracker Lady. Heard of her?"

"No," I lied. Everybody had heard of her. She owned nearly everything on this moon for the past ten years.

"Good thing for you," he replied and turned around to face me. "And your little friend over there vouched for you."

"Friend?" I looked at the kid suspiciously.

"Yessir, the rug rat over there."

"Oh, Carl," I said. "Yeah. We're... buddies."

"And his father works for the good ole Commerce Polity, so he's gold with me and my family."

I tried not to let my dark emotions surface over this. "Of course he is," I replied and locked eyes with the kid across the lobby. The boy smiled amidst the screaming drug dealer being hauled outside.

"You are free to leave on your business. Have yourself a good

Beyondnoon," said the officer.

"And you, officer."

I stood there for a second, a bit stunned by the outcome. The kid approached me slowly and folded his arms, a glint of determination in his eyes.

"You must think I owe you one," I said.

"Nope."

"Good—"

"You actually owe me two." Carl grinned.

"Is that right?"

"I overheard those regs talking about the girl who fell down the stairs. That was Barbara Stannish. She was a tweaker, but she climbed up and down those stairs high as a kite ever since I can remember. No way did she fall down. Seems like maybe someone created a diversion and gave her a little push. The regs aren't that dumb. They're thinking it was Devil Horns, but that's just because he's the bad guy they came for and it makes it so much cleaner to think he's the cause of all evil."

"So you weren't the one who called them here?"

"The regs show up five times a day to this place. I didn't have to bother and besides… you aren't the first grown-up who has tried to kill me. I work with murderers every day."

"You're a weird one."

"No," he said, leaning forward and whispering. "I'm smart. You see, it's me who's selling brain diamonds. Devil Horns over there actually buys more drugs than he's ever sold. I've made a bit of money off him myself."

"Thank you for the slice of your life," I told him. "Now, I'll be going now. I guess we both share dirt now, even if I don't care what you tell the regs. I could kill everyone here."

"I don't doubt it. You're the Moon City Killer, after all. I knew that by how you moved—like a God. You're him."

"You don't want to live very much, do you, kid?"

"You're wrong about that," he said. "I want to live by the Midnight Sea, forever. I just need the money."

I turned to leave. "It's nice to have dreams."

"Just one more thing that might strike your interest, or maybe it won't. I've got about forty-three regular customers so far. My dad lets me play in the warehouses near the CP's main factories. Lots of raw materials there to refine into my product."

"Good on you."

"Over ninety-eight percent of my customers are Deitii," he said loudly. "And I know where a bunch of them are living right now."

I stopped cold just short of the door and glanced back at Carl. "Is that so?"

Chapter 7

Dean certainly hoped these accommodations were temporary like Ricky said. He'd roomed in his share of seedy, rundown joints during his short tenure at Limbus, Inc., but the hall of rooms over the tavern looked like a shanty town where mildew, moss, and rust went to die. Like many places in Moon City, the floors and ceiling were cavern-stone, but rather than vestibules cut from the rock itself, the "hotel" was a series of plank board shacks all connected by a stringy black moss that bore clumpy, vomit-green flowers. Several gas lanterns hung from iron rings in the walls, a few propped up on the floor after their rings corroded to dust. Dean glanced at his room card—not even a key—just a card with the number 38 printed in faded, orange ink.

As he lifted his gaze, he hopped up as he nearly tripped over a man sitting outside room 36. The man's head was shaved and badly scarred from cranial surgeries. Dean had seen it before. Brain diamond addicts, or Noggins as they were most often called, had little choices of recovering, but those with money could triple their neural pathways and stay addicted and alive longer. Whatever money the man had was clearly gone. He sniffed dryly and licked his parched lips before loading his tongue with silver and purple crystals.

"Gonna blast off right here, eh?" Dean asked. "Ain't got your own room?"

"Smells like shit in there," the man said and swallowed the drug with a drowsy smile.

"No housekeeping, I guess." Dean chuckled and made his way past.

"Careful of my cat," the man instructed sternly. "Watch out for Butterball!"

Dean could hardly make out the lump of fur circled up near the man. "Sure thing." He took another look at the man and was reminded so intensely of his cousin Weston, also an addict, but no longer in this world to get high.

With a heavier heart, Dean walked over to room 38 and opened the thin plank door. There was a latch on the inside, thankfully, which Dean utilized right away. On the floor was a mattress, a wicker basket for clothes, a small chest with a padlock and key for belongings, and, oh, there was definitely a shit smell in his shack as well. Dean got the feeling the odor originated from the ugly moss hanging through the cracks in the planks above, rather than actual shit, but six of one, half a dozen of the other. It was revolting and would take a while to fall asleep.

He opened the chest and noticed several changes of clothes, shoes, the usual package of Limbus binder full of business cards, and a stack of touch-docs. There was also the weapon box that Dean and only Dean could open with eye and thumbprint. Rick or someone else employed for the company had probably staged everything for him. Dean let the lid to the chest fall and he sighed.

Night had just begun and it would be some time before he could sleep, thanks to the Constalife, but Dean still felt this awake-time as unnatural, like being underwater with scuba gear for years.

He sat on the mattress. His knees hurt and he wanted to strip out of the starchy, green garment thing they provided him at City Hall, the snazzy get-up that all prisoners get to wear—but once again, the day was far from over and he had a long, overdue call to place.

"Hi, sweetheart," he said to Sandra when she answered.

"Dean, it's late. I waited up."

"I'm terribly sorry, hon. I didn't have a watch yet. Just got my equipment now. Every day here is three and a half Earth days. I gotta figure what times of the day I can call you."

"You sound weird."

"It might be this longevity drug I'm on."

"No," she said. "I've heard you this way before. Someone died, didn't they?"

"You want to hear about it?"

"I've waited a month back here, at least give me a story."

"Fair enough," he said, "but then... phone sex?"

"Dean."

"Okay, yeah," he laughed. "I'll lay it all on you."

And he did. He told her everything—even how terrified he was as his body almost failed him against the Quantum Flu. With Sandra, he never had to hold back. That was one of the reasons he loved her so dearly. He could be vulnerable and she would let him. She wouldn't tear him down and call him less of a man. That was the sort of thing, he imagined, that had made him clam up so much over the years: his ex-wife wouldn't abide him being emotional, not in the least—such displays were solely her right, not his; men had to be stone. They couldn't let anything touch them. Dean wasn't big on putting his feelings on display though, but he felt safe with Sandra. He knew he could break down and she'd be there to pick him up and put him back together. That's why he couldn't lose her.

"I'm so glad you're okay," she told him when he was through. "Even if you're in that stinky shack."

He laughed. "Yeah, I'll get over it—well, probably not."

She laughed this time. "I know you're probably wondering what my decision is about hibernation."

"No, no," he replied quickly.

"Well let's talk about it when your assignment is complete. Okay?"

"Sure."

"There's really no reason to jump off that bridge yet."

"Of course not," he added.

"A month is definitely not enough time to make such a big decision. You're the love of my life, Dean, and if—"

A scream penetrated the silence outside in the cavern hall.

"What was that?" Sandra asked. "Was that... a scream?"

"I don't know. I'm going to see."

"Careful! Call me back!"

He hung up and leaned forward, opening the chest. He took out the weapon box. Looked at the eye scanner. Put his thumb over the imprint band on top. The lock clicked over. They'd given him a Splitter pistol. He took it and sidled up to the door, peering through the slats in the planks. Another scream rang out. It was the brain diamond addict.

Dean inspected his weapon. The splitter had only half a charge—not like he'd need much more to take down a tripping Noggin.

The screaming didn't sound like drug rage though. This man was in trouble. Dean unlatched the door and stepped out. The Noggin grabbed his skull—blood poured from his nostrils. Dean had seen this progress to a massive stroke. He tucked his gun in his jumpsuit pocket and knelt near the man. His orange cat, while trembling on its old legs, was alert and meowing at its companion.

The man's body arched and he let out another scream. Dean looked around, but nobody else came out of the shacks.

"Just you and me, pal." Dean ripped off a sleeve from the man's rotting clothes and wadded it up. "Put this in your mouth and bite down," he ordered.

The man squirmed and hummed a discordant melody. "Up... yours."

Dean forced his jaw open and stuffed the fabric inside. "Bite down, asshole."

The Noggin was through fighting and with blood-stained teeth, bit down. Dean turned his head sideways and pressed on the side of the man's skull. He could see the purple discoloration in the neck where the huge clot had formed. Without meds, this was the only way, and still a piece of the clot could get loose and cause a mini-stroke.

"Hold on," he told the Noggin. Dean reared back and drove his fist into the bulging vein in the man's neck. A muffled cry of pain escaped the Noggin's mouth and the fabric fell out. Dean struck again. Harder each time. After five good ones, he felt the hardness in the neck. Still wasn't quite there.

"Hey, man, no—"

Dean hit him so hard this time the Noggin pinwheeled sideways and the cat scrambled out of the way.

"Enough, goddamn you!" the Noggin grumbled and grabbed his neck. He'd bitten his tongue and his mouth was cherry red.

"Do you feel numbness?" Dean asked through labored breaths.

The man stated at him with incredulous outrage. "No. I'm pretty much not feeling fucking numb!" He grimaced in pain and scooted back to the wall of his shack.

Dean sat near him, getting his breath. "Play with fire…"

"Don't lecture me," the man snapped. "I've had clots go away on their own before. You ain't no hero."

"Fair enough." Dean got to his feet, overcome by weariness.

"Wait, man."

Dean turned. "Yeah?"

"I do appreciate… the gesture."

Dean nodded. He was about to return to his shack, but stopped, feeling the conversation wasn't really supposed to end here.

"How'd you come to be here?"

The Noggin rubbed his neck and glided his other hand over his cat's back. "Some guy souped up on something. He attacked me. Tried to kill me. He moved crazy fast, and he was fierce. Strong as hell. I caught him sneaking out of some place near the lumber district. Luckily something—someone—spooked him. He knocked me out cold and I ended up here. Downstairs said I got a whole week paid, so I decided to hang out until the rent ran out. Not so much for the room, but I wanted to meet whoever saved me. Whoever he was, he probably wanted me to shut up more than thank him though. And as you can see, I shut up great."

Dean smirked. Ricky had saved this guy from the Moon City Killer, and stashed him here to protect him. *I've really got to revisit his briefing more thoroughly.*

"Sorry I woke you up," the Noggin added, noting Dean's pensiveness.

"No worries, pal. Look, I got a few business cards. You wanna clean-up, get a job, Limbus, Inc. hires."

A dark grin crossed the man's face. "Limbus, yeah I've heard of your company. I might be better off OD-ing."

Dean laughed. "You could be right, but probably aren't."

The Noggin bobbed his head. "Leave a card outside my room then."

"My pleasure. Tell the recruiter you met Dean Fulsome."

"Ah, the Slaughter Man, eh?"

Dean swallowed dryly. "No, just, okay, I've got to go."

"Thanks again, Dean," said the Noggin.

He glanced over his shoulder. "You and Butterdick have a good night."

"It's Butterball!"

"No it isn't," said Dean, shutting his door.

Sandra was probably waiting for his call back, but he had to call Rick. It took six rings before he answered. They exchanged comcodes before talking. Ricky sounded tired and annoyed.

"Already need me? You haven't even settled in yet."

"What's with the guy you put up here in this here fancy establishment?"

"Oh, the Noggin," said Rick. "You met Chipper Saude. Lovely fellow. Evidently, he can eat five pounds of brain hash a day and still sing the alphabet to his orange tabby."

"I don't remember reading a statement about a witness to the Moon City Killer. The guy you saved him from… That's him, right?"

Rick paused and cleared his throat. "Yeah, that was the first night I got a bead on the Killer. Saude almost screwed it up."

"Why is there no witness file then?"

"Because he didn't see anything of value. Put the drug abuse aside, Saude didn't get a chance to see anything but a very powerful man kicking his ass. I even posed as another Noggin to see what he knew and eek some other info from him, but it was a waste of time. Not to mention a waste of money on the room for a week. Anyway, I'm not writing anything up because there's nothing to write up. I hate documenting bullshit."

"I hear you."

"Chipper Saude is one of the many dead-ends I faced for the last two weeks—many of which will not see the light of day on any Limbus-bound file."

"Because you're embarrassed."

"Kiss my ass."

"Only if you shave it first."

"Gross."

"I agree," said Dean. "Look, I'll go ahead and note my discussion with this Chipper fellow and I'll interview him one more time."

"Be my guest. You're a far more patient man than I."

"Speaking of, I have to call my fiancée back."

"Of course you do—hey, in a couple of hours meet me for Last Dinner in the banking district, a place called Inner Cell. It's not far from your hotel. I want you to try this burger there. Ask the bartenders downstairs."

"10-4."

"Later."

Dean ended the call and sat on his mattress for a few minutes. He wanted to talk to Sandra, but he didn't have much to say after he made little of the event out in the hall—she'd pick up on that right away. He battled with how much he should tell her at once. Then he could hear his boss, little Tasha Willing, piping up from the recesses of his mind. "Why don't you ask her about what's going on in *her* life, dumbass!"

Dean smiled. *Yeah, thanks Tasha.*

He dialed Sandra.

Chapter 8

I returned to my room in the lumber district. It was miserable hot here. I hated this place. It reminded me how the Commerce Polity had screwed me just as it screwed my entire family. Sure I'd been given a job, junior woodworker, then journey man, then apprentice, craftsman I, II, III, IV, and then I'd been a foreman. Briefly.

The day I held a Deitii's head under a band saw just for the hell of it—that had been the day my destiny unraveled, just like so much coiling alien flesh—that rind peeled away to show the fruit that had always been the nourishment I'd never found. Sort of like that kid Carl and his fascination for the Midnight Sea. He needed it. And I needed this.

I sat in my kitchen, hating myself for never throwing away my mother's checkered tablecloth and using her mason jars to store my reserves of spinal fluid. None of it was as potent as drinking from a still-living Deitii, but it certainly kept a vigor for several weeks. I tried to drink from it sparingly—especially since if I overdid it, I'd lose track of my day and be in a haze—I'd know more about the universe than I did about my own life. I'd forget my name. I'd forget what I ate for meals. I'd forget every place my legs took me from the morning to the blackest night. Once, I forgot to take my Constalife, a routine that became innate, second-nature, for a lifelong Moon City citizen. But I didn't need the drug when I had the power of God's ancestors imbuing my every muscle fiber and blood cell.

How long had it been since I'd drunk from my jars? I inspected each one. My lack of memory made me paranoid because this wasn't the first time I'd questioned where my reserves had vanished to. The first jar was almost entirely gone and I could have sworn it was full yesterday when I checked. But the lack of remembering how much I'd really drank went to show I had indeed indulged quite a bit. The more I drank, the less I recalled. When I came back to my reserves it never seemed like enough... always more. My feeding had been cut short today. I should have reached a higher level of awareness than I'd been permitted and that was also throwing me off balance. With Carl's roster of potential feedings, I would be well on my way to solving that problem however. Well, that is, if the kid could be trusted.

I realized I'd begun to grip my mother's table cloth in my fists. On my third feeding, a Deitii youth out of the Bleeding Caves, I got the clarity that there would come a time where I would reach a supreme state and I would no longer need to feed. I would become everything. I would know everything. What would that do to a bitter, violent man like me? Would I become a loving, benevolent being? Or would I destroy everyone who didn't serve my will?

If they did not love me, if they did not believe in the existence of my power—that I was their master—would I conquer all the universes and lay them to waste? Or would I watch quietly from a distance and be amused for all eternity? The order. The chaos. The love. The indifference. The passion. The Hatred. The Wars. The Peace. The Fighting. The Fucking. The Dying. The Living. The Births. The Murders. The Building. The Creation. The Imagination. The Decimation. The Destruction. The Ignorance.

The human race itself would be enough to watch for millennia, but then there were the trillions of other races out there in the cosmos. Some beings would need even closer watching, because of their proximity to my power and insight and how they heightened those toward my own. Nobody would be allowed to cross the threshold of power that would be mine. That would be the riskiness in watching all established creation, rather than killing everything and starting anew. I'd have to make that choice. Or watch for a time and learn.

Then destroy.

All of this excited me. I was tired of waiting. I needed to see more. I couldn't stay a mortal much longer. I deserved much more. That mercenary out there was only a man. I should have been able to kill him. He should have died at my hand. He should have known my power.

I spun off the top of the mason jar and put it to my lips. Drank. Drank my fill. Drank to feel the cold bite of the spinal fluid. Its silent fingers worked into the tissues of my throat and beneath, dropped into my bloodstream, awakened something magnificent in my heart, something I believed to be a ghost who pulled its eyes open just a crack more with every feeding, and my mind was that ghost's home, and while I could not fully hear its voice yet, I could taste its dreams.

I needed more than dreams.

I needed the ghost to pull its eyes open.

Forever.

Then its eyes would be mine.

Waiting for it to all wash over me, I regarded the three other jars before me. The fluid looked different when I was under the influence. Usually a pale fluid, it was now neon blue and rippling. Looking at it made me think of my mother, back when I'd liked her, maybe even when I'd actually needed her. I wanted to wrap my arms around that neon blue because it knew I was the one. It believed in me; it would cradle me and put all my fears aside because I was the most important person in the galaxies.

I needed the ghost. I need my new mother.

What in the hell had I been waiting for?

I likely wouldn't remember my next actions by tomorrow, but they were foremost in my mind at the moment. I reached forward and spun off the other three lids. Drank each down. Every drop. Only pausing after the second jar to take a few much needed breaths of conditioned Moon City oxygen.

I finished the third jar.

Before I could even wipe my lips, the ghost's eye flung open.

With the rest of me.

And the city.

I couldn't read their thoughts, but I had a sense of the two million souls living on this rock. Humans and aliens alike, I knew the essence of them—the intent of their lives. I recognized people I'd worked with in the mill, like an old mole or scar you rediscover on your body after years of neglect, but I didn't care for those people when I knew them and certainly didn't care for them now. It was difficult to separate everybody, even though the individuals were represented—it was much like distinguishing millions of shades of blue, staring at one long enough you would begin to understand the uniqueness of the color, but it took some doing and I wasn't attuned enough yet to do it instantly. They all glowed with similar fires, except for one. He was special. I knew his color well and could smell him. His odor was much like it had been this morning, yet I could smell the raw, charred smell of the undershirt he hadn't changed since our encounter. He was a tough man. Most people would treat 2nd degree burns, but he hadn't bothered. I smelled no ointment, or pain. That was the deepest smell of all... pain. And he must have had an amazing ability to just ignore it.

I liked him.

But had to kill him.

It's fine. I would make some other creature that had the same force of will. Killing him had to happen. Unfortunately, the mercenary had not returned to his apartment. I knew now I couldn't count on him ever going back there and springing my well-laid trap left in the incinerator. The document remaining in his living room may not be worth returning to burn—he wasn't stupid. He knew I'd probably tail him there somehow. I couldn't wait to see if he went back. He needed to die. Especially now, with how I perceived him— this mercenary was special—he was related to Christopher Agate, who was a legendary killer, but not superhuman... so Rick was different. I couldn't put my ever-growing mind around it yet, but I would. He was important, or connected to someone *very* important.

Rick was near the banking district. My vision flickered, blurred, splintered, until it all came into focus. Someone in a suit was handing him a fine, translucent slip—my eyes narrowed—it was a trace deposit. Rick was being paid off for something.

Probably something bloody.

I licked my lips.

They tasted of Deitii.

I tried to concentrate on the man handing over the payment, but I didn't want to lose focus on Rick, now that I'd found him. His clients weren't a concern of mine anyhow.

I took my knife off the table. I imagined cutting the mercenary's throat from ear to ear. I stared at the blade, and to my absolute wonder, blood began perspiring from the steel. It dripped down the edge and forked off in vermillion pathways. I stared harder, willing it to come forth. Scarlet blood of my own creation spilled from the tip of the knife and rushed over my hand. It was warm. I stopped the flow and cleaned up the mess. This was no hallucination.

I'd taken the next step of godhood.

I could create.

I stood at the table with a grin.

Rick would have the pleasure of seeing what my next creations would be—and the power of the Deitii grew within my body each passing moment.

As I locked the door of my apartment behind me, I imagined how much of a hold it would have on me by the time I reached the banking district.

Chapter 9

Without anything meaningful left to do, and Sandra sleeping soundly galaxies away, Dean dressed into his clothes Limbus had left him. It was their standard garb, a white button-up and black slacks and belt, with running loafers—a little dressier than Dean might have chosen on his own, but he'd grown used to the look and the role he served. To think, he'd almost lost his job after he slipped away on Grettish-5 and joined the Zetú refugees, after explicit order not to get involved, and that choice even followed him here. Limbus didn't like their people going off the grid. Either they were let go, or, Dean had heard, it could be worse...

But the Zetú were his friends. That was what had mattered.

Tasha understood that and had gone to bat for him. So if Limbus, Inc. hadn't made him disappear he'd be back working in slaughterhouses in Southern California, or maybe they'd have stashed him on some far-off planet, doing who knows what.

His phone rang.

"Dean," rasped Ricky.

Dean sat up on his mattress. "Rick, what's wrong?"

"He's here, Dean, brought a wall down, and I almost bought it. I'm still in the banking district. I'll... handle this, but I need you to stay put. Don't meet me as planned."

"Like hell."

"Dean, really, I knew you'd say that, but I'm serious. Please, stay put. I got this."

"I'll be there soon."

"You stubborn—"

Dean hung up and reached for his weapon. It slipped neatly into the deep right pocket of his slacks. It didn't matter what this man was or had become, Dean would be damned if he was just going to hang out in this smelly shack while he could be helping Rick. What if he was able to help? He couldn't live with another family of demons wrestling in his mind. And he couldn't bear to retell that story to Sandra—the story of him coming all the way out here to be a coward slinking back into the shadows.

There was a big problem though; he didn't know where the hell to go. Dean rushed back downstairs to the tavern, taking less care to avoid the foul black moss in the stone stairway. Once he reached the ground floor, he dashed to the bar.

The bartender was a thin, bald man with a faint mustache, dressed in black overalls that hung on his frame making him scarecrowesque. He took a step back as Dean nearly crashed into the wood framing around the bar.

"I need to get to the banking district, quickly. How do I get there?"

The man had a bottle of some blue booze in his left hand and his other was raised to his throat. "I—"

"Come on, which way from here? Streets? Left, right, what?"

"I—"

"Spit it out for shit's sake!"

A regional police officer put his hand across Dean's chest and pushed him away from the bar.

"Perfect," said Dean. "Hello, officer, can you go tell the mayor we need to get some people over to the banking district? What are you waiting for?"

The reg cop flipped up his visor and smiled.

It was the mayor's goon, Donaldo. "Sure I'll tell him, Fulsome. You might not want to draw a lot of attention to it though."

"Shit." Dean charged past him and heard a chorus of laughter behind him. Tasha would get an earful about how uncooperative this mayor had been, and this borderline harassment—no, not even borderline! She'd brought him in to help on the political end, but there wasn't even a chance with these people.

Dean arrived at his vehicle parked along the street. He glared at it. A lot of good it did him. He didn't know where the hell he was going.

"Where you going?" asked a voice from behind.

Dean was almost jovial seeing the dingy, gaunt form of the Noggin, Chipper Saude, again. "Hey do you know where the banking district is?" he asked.

"Oh yeah, my company headquarters is there," he deadpanned and petted his cat behind the ears.

"Please, I don't have time for jokes."

The Noggin's face fell. "Chill, guy. So yeah, it's not far. Head straight down that way until you get to Freefall Circle and make a right. Take that to Ivevest Avenue, go left. Banking District's at the corner of Ivevest and Loinage Boulevard. It's probably like two and a half miles out."

Dean pulled open the driver side door. "I owe you, friend."

"Nope, we're square."

Dean plopped down in the seat, turned the key, and stomped the gas. The loaner car actually picked up quick and accelerated to sixty mph in a few seconds.

"Sweet," he whispered with a laugh, but his heart was definitely not in it.

* * *

Dean didn't have to even search for the banking district; all the wooden structures were either partially consumed by angry blue-red fire or fully engulfed. He spotted Rick hunkered down behind a vehicle that resembled a Palomino truck mixed with a type of monstrous diesel contraption. The mercenary calmly loaded shells into a long sniper shotgun rifle. His neck looked like it had a wound from earlier that had scabbed over, but he was otherwise looking stable.

His own weapon pressed to his thigh, Dean got out of the car and hurried to take position near Rick. His friend rolled his eyes at his approach. "Told you not to come," he said, shaking his head, and crammed another shell into the rifle.

"I'm a rebel," answered Dean. He glanced over the side of the truck and noticed a flood of people swarming out of a large building in the center of the district, which had only just begun to grow with fire.

"I think he believes I'm still in there with them," Rick said thoughtfully. "I think, anyway."

He edged up and took a look over the truck bed. He cracked a grin and thumbed the safety off his rifle. "Check it out," he whispered. "Top floor."

Dean cautiously looked over but could only see flames on the roof.

"Can't see shit."

Rick chuckled and poised the rifle over the edge of the truck. "Our killer is up there. He's not looking this way, which I sort of love."

"How in the hell can you see him?"

Dean watched as Rick looked through the sight. He couldn't believe the man wasn't sweating from all the surrounding fires. Dean was already drenched and he'd only been out of the car for a few minutes. He was about to ask how Rick managed to remain so frosty when the mercenary squeezed the trigger and let out a hoot.

"Hot damn! Got the bastard in the same shoulder from earlier! Buckshot nearly took his arm off. Should have been his head. No head means good night. I hope."

Rick laughed and screamed a second later as something struck his cheek and clattered in the street. Dean's eyes darted to the knife spinning over and coming to a stop near the tire of his vehicle. He turned around and noticed the wound in Rick's neck had been re-opened and poured blood fiercely now.

"Bastard tit-for-tatted me," yelled Rick, sinking down and pressing his palm into the wound. His hand came away with a great deal of blood, but the wound didn't look bad at all.

Even so, Dean had a bad feeling.

"I'm calling support," he said and grabbed his phone from his pocket. "Mayor has to send medics—"

"Don't bother, man." Rick looked up to the dark cavern ceiling above. "What a crap day."

"Quiet—" Someone came on the line. "Yes, hello," said Dean. "Can I have the reg police emergency response...? This is Dean Fulsome. I'm contracted... What do you mean you're disconnecting?"

More blood erupted from the wound. It was surprising that Rick didn't seem more pale, but he was a badass and he'd experienced his share of hemorrhages. Dean knew blood though. He'd watched it with interest all those years he spent in the slaughterhouses. He knew the different flows, like some musicians knew exact notes when they heard them—perfect pitch, he believed it was called. He had perfect flow—he knew Rick wouldn't live long. The rush was too quick and the blood too vibrant.

He didn't have the courage to let on about this though, even if this man was brave enough to accept his fate.

"They're on their way."

"Sure they are," answered Rick.

"Hey, stop it, okay?"

"How'd he throw that knife so far, so accurately?" Rick mused. Blood spilled over his lips. "It's like he sees everyth—"

Something caught in Dean's throat, but in the next moment, he realized it wasn't his own throat, it was the man's before him. A knife had gone through the car window and entered the back of Rick's neck, the blade protruding out just below his Adam's apple. He let out a coughing sound and his hands instinctively went to his neck. Dean reached for him, but the look of shock in his glassy eyes went dark—instant death, in the next moment.

That's when Dean heard the sirens. "Help!" he screamed and scrambled to his feet. He could see the cruiser's headlights filling the cavern inch by inch. "Please! My friend is hurt!"

The next seconds were hours. Long images without color. *Help him. He's bleeding.* Dean studied every pore in the reg police officer's face, not because he wanted to, but because it felt like he was asking for help for ten thousand years.

"Who?" the man kept asking.

It took Dean a while to snap to it and turn to point out Rick—but when he did, there wasn't a body, only a long wash of blood across the ground.

"He was there a minute ago."

"Dying?"

"Yes!"

"Well, doesn't seem to have been dying enough to remain put."

"He was taken."

"Dragged off in the time it took you to run over here. Not likely," said the officer. "Nobody is that quick."

Dean looked at the blood. It did look smeared and trailing off. "We have to follow him!" Dean shouted and grabbed the officer's shoulders.

"Take your hands off me. Who do we have to follow?"

"The Moon City Killer!"

The reg cop's lips thinned and he shrugged Dean's hands off him. "We have to respond to the fires. Excuse me, Mr. Fulsome."

"Wait! This isn't a Limbus thing! Why aren't you going after him?"

The officer hurried off to the buildings. A fire brigade truck pulled in before him. Dean sank to his knees. His breathing was all he could hear and all he could concentrate on for the next full hour.

* * *

Dean pressed his head into the steering wheel, laced his fingers together, and put his hands against the back of his head. The pain in his sinus had spread through his entire skull. He didn't know if the migraine was a remnant of the Quantum Flu, this unnatural sleep (no sleep) cycle, or if it was left-over trauma from just seeing a friend's life claimed without a spare moment to process it.

A knock at his passenger window made him thrash backward in his seat. He didn't have time to be pissed at whoever scared the shit out of him—despite the huge grin on eleven-year-old Tasha Willing's face.

"That just never gets old," she said through the glass.

"Goddamn, Tash," said Dean, unlocking the door. "Do you even know what happened?"

The little girl was as calm as a seasoned corporate executive, and dressed in a smart pants suit to match. Her smile could be disarming or calculating-cold.

"He was a mercenary. They get killed sometimes. Relax, Dean."

"He was a friend, to us both—and his—"

"Body is missing, yes," she finished and opened her binder to look at the project documents.

"So you know what happened?"

She put her finger on the line of text and tapped. "Was he dead?"

"He got a knife all the way through the neck. Signs point to a solid *yeah*."

"Well who took the body? The Killer?"

Dean hissed through his teeth. "Aren't you supposed to have the answers here? You're the one who's been through every universe ten times."

Tasha sighed. "I'm only here... Well, let's just say I made this trip because I knew you'd need to talk. You're fragile like that."

Dean had never been told that. In fact, he was anything but fragile, as Sandra, his ex-wife, and the few women he'd dated could attest to. However, comparing him with the hardness of Tasha Willing, she might have a point. Still, he wasn't going to let her railroad him here. "At least you got the Golden Transport. You're here and gone and don't lose any time on Earth. Me? Shit! I've come out here, wasting decades, and probably screwed up my one chance for happiness, just outta being loyal to you."

"To me?" Tasha raised her dark eyebrows.

Dean took a long breath. "Fine, to Limbus freaking Incorporated. And now our contract killer has himself been killed and the mark is still running around Moon City."

"What's your point?"

"I thought it was obvious. The whole project needs to be shitcanned."

Tasha stared at him, bit her lower lip, and shook her head in disappointment.

"What?" Dean asked. When she didn't answer right away, he asked again with more urgency. "Goddamn, Tasha, what?"

"This project will move forward, Dean. We plan to open a recruiting office here and contract with the Deitii. We desperately need them and their council. They have skill sets that will be well-utilized within one network of client companies—but we need this serial killer dead. No more Deitiis can fall to murder. You have to put an end to all of that."

"How?"

"Track him and get rid of him. Isn't that obvious?" asked Tasha.

"Me? You're crazy."

"No, I'm staggeringly sane."

"I'm not a hired killer, kid," said Dean, not trying in the least to hide his disgust at the idea.

"Don't call me kid." The young girl with the ancient eyes frowned and shook her head. "Imagination wasn't ever one of your strong points, Dean. You worked as a Sticker—"

"I know what I did, okay?"

"You'd stand on the line in the slaughterhouse and kill hundreds of cows a day. That's where I found you. Covered in shit and blood."

"So what?"

"So what?"

"Yeah, *so what.*"

"So you know how to slit a throat. You know how to make a kill. Stop pretending this is different. Find this pain in the ass and END him."

"I never signed nothing saying I'd do that sort of thing."

"If you're going to argue with me," Tasha pointed out, "no double negatives."

"Shit…" Dean whispered and scrubbed at his face.

"Look, there's no time to send for another contract. You can go back now and lose decades and lose your fiancée…"

Dean stiffened at her nerve. "I thought you and I were friends."

"Sure we are," Tasha replied. "And if so, why the hell aren't you helping me out here? You knew me before you knew *Sandra.*"

"Careful, Tash, you're sounding jealous."

"Screw you."

"Oh good, I've finally gotten under that concrete skin of yours."

"Hardly."

"This is some stupid, stupid, *stupid* shit. Are you really that hard up? Isn't there anyone else in Moon City who knows how to handle him or herself? I'm not going to live for two minutes going against that monster. He killed Rick Agate! One of the best there is. It's throwing my life away, and though I might not be worth a Golden

Transport, I'm at least worth more than this ridiculous suicide exercise."

"You have no confidence."

"Give me a Golden Transport return to Earth."

"Can't happen."

"It has to."

"I can't—" Tasha pursed her lips. "I could perhaps arrange that, I suppose, if you can complete this task. In the meantime, I will send out a request for proposal to our network and try to get another merc moonside within a week."

"Get Chris Agate. He'll want to know about his brother."

"He already does. I called him before coming here."

Dean was flabbergasted. "And?"

Tasha shrugged her padded shoulders. "He's busy."

"Son of a—" Dean calmed his language. Even though Tasha was technically an advanced age, he still couldn't curse to the face of someone who looked so young. "The best assassin in this galaxy can't take time off to avenge his only brother? Chris Agate is probably the *only* person who can put this dog down."

"No, there's also you," said Tasha with a wide smile and a wink. When he said nothing, she popped open the car door.

"What do you mean, there's also me?"

"You're the Slaughter Man, after all."

Dean groaned. "Maybe with a lot of help, but the city won't give me any support. I'm blowing in the wind here."

"Well, now that's something I *can* help you with," said Tasha. "I'll be visiting the mayor next."

Dean chuckled. "Good luck."

"You too," she answered, not seeming to catch his sarcasm or perhaps just not addressing it.

"Golden Transport," he called after her. "If I get this done, you make it happen. Promise?"

Tasha smirked. "Would you believe me if I did promise?"

Dean's shoulders slumped. "Why don't you ever cheer me up?"

"That's not in my job description," she said.

"See you soon," he replied.

"That's the spirit."

And with a single chuckle, Tasha started off. Moments later, Dean lost all track of her; she was gone.

His phone rang then.

Sandra.

She must have had insomnia. He wanted to let it go to voicemail, but he couldn't afford more disconnection than they already had. So he answered, and they talked—but he didn't tell her about his objective now and what it could actually mean to them if he survived.

If he succeeded.

Chapter 10

I felt the heaviness of the mercenary's body—it was unusually substantial, solid, like transporting a small, dead planet. I had no other theory than that he was not from a normal bloodline, which was accurate because Christopher Agate was the closest thing to a god this universe had seen.

But he wasn't a god.

I was.

Or would be.

I nudged Rick Agate's body toward the edge of the cliff. Staring up was Black Kiss Falls, the abyss between Shinlow's Caverns and Battle Column Path where I'd peered below so fondly as a teenager. I never could tell if the answers for life were down there in the dark, or the answers for death, but it was a beautiful nothing, a place I still enjoyed.

I pushed harder on Rick Agate. My strength was waning a bit from starting all the fires and demolishing the office building with my bare hands. It had been necessary to draw him out and pin him down in one location, but the price on my energy had been high. I needed more Deitii to drink, but as usual, I couldn't recall how much I'd had earlier, so more was relative.

The mercenary's body flipped over. A thin line of blood dribbled from the knife wound. The man didn't even bleed like others—very curious—I would make a point to seek out the other Agate brother when I had the clarity of all universes in my mind. They weren't human like others. I derived Christopher must also be different, just due to his vast success in the killing arts.

I retrieved my knife and slid it back into its sheath. With a grunt, I pushed again and Rick Agate's body pitched off the side of the cliff, his body being swallowed by darkness, only a whisper of wind rushing around him.

"You'll see your brother, soon," I said, slowly backing away from the ledge.

I thought I heard a voice. A shout. The wind possibly... but I could take no chances. I leaned over the cliff and peered through the darkness, my eye sight carving through the black. I found the body at the bottom, hundreds of feet below. There was no heartbeat. Blood puddled at the head, from the eye sockets, the ears, nose and mouth. One leg was twisted around in a disturbing tangle. The body was still.

Whatever I'd heard, it wasn't Rick Agate.

Standing there in the silence, I thought back to all I'd done today to be rid of this man. The chase through the Bleeding Caverns, planting the poison gas capsule in his apartment, bringing the whole business district down in ashes. It was all so... good. I'd never lived with such focus and purpose, outside of maybe becoming unstoppably strong and wise in all ways. The mercenary had given me something to use all the power on. I liked that and once more longed for the dead man's brother to come find me. If Rick Agate had been sweet, Chris Agate would be ecstasy.

"You look happy," said a voice from behind me.

My body moved in flashes, a series of motions that felt like the flipping pages of amateur animation, with long stretches of absent images—I turned, then I was in the air, I was standing before the person, I had them on the cold ground with my hand surrounding a small throat.

Carl's eyes widened as my grip tightened. He must have thought once I recognized him I'd loosen my hold. The fact that he wasn't a stranger made me even more inclined to wrath. I considered killing him and sending his body into the Black Kiss along with my last victim, but I did ease my hold.

"Talk," I told him.

"Have new," the boy said, coughing.

"You have my attention," I replied.

"Had to follow... you." Carl's eyes turned back into his head and now I released his throat altogether, allowing him to gain back his breath.

"You are determined for me to choke you to death today, is that it? You ought to know better than follow me. If I need you, I'll find you."

Carl continued to retch and cough and rub at his throat. "Thought... you could sense... everyone. Figured you'd know I was here."

"Obviously I cannot sense the Deitii or I'd be feeding right now. It works only when I'm focusing, only when I'm reaching out. Don't ever sneak up on me again. Now tell me why you are here."

Carl sat up and I backed off, hunkering down at his side. "Remember when I told you about that list of Deitiis I have?"

"Yes."

"You said you could only use some, because you need younger Deitii only."

"Children," I said, the word actually tasting good on my tongue.

"I have something better now than that list. I just pocketed a new contract with the Mayor of Moon City. Nobody knows this, but I learned from my guy in the Firecracker forum—"

"How did you get such a connection?" I demanded. Carl was just a boy. That I was suspicious he'd have any liaison with the Firecracker Lady's black market group should have come as no surprise to him; it was synonymous with Carl telling me he could drink a four-hundred-pound lumberjack under the table—the forum was not a place for most adults, let alone children.

Carl swallowed uneasily. "You aren't the only one I follow. This rat knows his alleys, knows his sewers. Remember my dad's in the Commerce Polity. They're all on the take for the Firecracker Lady."

I snorted. "It would make sense. I'll entertain this. Tell me what you have."

"So nobody but me and the forum knows about this, not even the Firecracker Lady herself, but the mayor owns a camp for refugee Deitii children. The council of Deitii are aware and have secretly endorsed it in the past, but now… with you out on the streets, they are actually paying him to keep them safe."

"Why have the camp in the first place? They could keep them safe elsewhere."

"They don't own anything anymore. Firecracker's got everything. The lot of them are broke. I can't even sell crappy product to them anymore because they never have anything but Moon dollars."

Which aren't even being printed or distributed electronically anymore.

"Okay, and so the mayor, why would he bother keeping the children on city property?"

"To get good with the Deitii—their voting power is—"

"I know about their vote worth," I snapped impatiently, "but the mayor is a half-breed Deitii himself. He doesn't need to persuade them. They always blindly vote for Deitii candidates, even those not of full blood."

Carl's eyes narrowed. Despite everything, he actually had the nerve to be brash with me. I reserved my admiration for a moment however. "Look, I don't know or care why the hell the mayor's got a refugee camp. That's not why I'm here to tell you about it. I'm here to make a deal because I know where the camp is and what security he has utilized. All I want is enough to build a house by the Midnight Sea. Everyone else can go to hell."

"Tell me more." Saliva built in my mouth and moistened my lips, thinking about how many children the mayor could possibly have.

"He spares no expense to keep them happy. I managed to get a supply job for my contact who the mayor entrusts the camp to. I'm bringing in ten wagons a day loaded with drugs, food, water, and Deitii liquor. The mayor's paying for all of it out of pocket, plus my courier fees. If you were to pay me more than my current deal, this is all worthwhile."

"You must really want to retire in the Midnight Sea."

"You have no idea."

"So you'll show me where the camp is?"

Carl nodded but lifted one finger. "But you also need to get rid of the Master of Arms at the gate. He's my contact and who I made the arrangement through. I don't want him going back to the mayor and telling him I gave away the location. The mayor doesn't know who I am, doesn't want to know, but he will if the Deitiis are taken."

"Don't worry about him."

"I *will* worry if you leave the Master of Arms alive."

I smiled at the boy and he nodded slowly, understanding my intent.

"There is something you need to know though."

"What is your payment?"

Carl was taken aback and stumbled over his words. "I... two... no, six thousand," he said. "And five hundred," he added.

"Sixty-five hundred?"

"That's fair."

"There's more to be had, you know," he told me. "I have more Deitii contacts than just this and what I gave you on the list. Just in case you're thinking—"

"I won't kill you, boy. Just stay true to your word. Now what was this other thing you needed to tell me?"

"The Master of Arms is a Grettish Friar, and he has three apprentices onsite with him."

The Grettish Friars had been entrusted with Christopher Agate's first trials of combat training during the Emerald Scenario. They were the next best thing to dancing with Agate himself.

"I will pay you ten thousand for this information," I told Carl.

"Ten?" the boy said with eyes overflowing with disbelief. "Why?"

"Because you've made me very happy." I patted his head and offered my hand to help him up. Carl took my help and we both got to our feet.

"I need the money first," he said, straightening his back.

"You'll get it when I give it," I replied. "You will not follow me. You will wait down the street from City Hall, at Rockslide Road. I will be watching this time."

The boy studied me, touching his bruised throat. "I wondered if you'd torture me to tell you everything I knew. I planned on that maybe happening, you know."

"Yes, I know. You're less impulsive than most adult humans I've run across."

"You are human too."

I looked at him, deep in the eyes. "Shall we go?"

A light smile touched his lips. "I'll follow your instructions."

"Good boy. I will see you in an hour."

Carl mumbled his consent and I left him there in the shadows. I imagined my floating smile was the brightest thing in the caverns at that particular moment in time.

*   *   *

I watched his honorable suckwad from across the street. I'd thought many times about ripping his every bone out and driving them all into his eyes, nose, and ass. Considering his past presidency at the Commerce Polity, this was one of the persons who'd ended my once-life, as it were, and it would be nice to afford some special hate on him with my new strengths. But there were more important matters at hand.

The mayor shook the hand of some old bureaucrat and gave him a limp, expressionless smile. It was a shadow of his Deitii heritage.

I thought about eating him. He was half human though. Sucking out the mayor's spinal fluid would amount to sniffing a weak yellow lager compared to a Deitii child, where a single drop would feel like all the tanks of a large brewery emptying barley-wine not just into your belly, but saturating all fabrics of your past, present, and future. Adult Deitiis were half as potent as their children, but mixed race Deitiis, such as Mayor Twinklepuss up there, were even less.

And I didn't have to taste a mixed race to know that—I could smell the flaccidity of power in the air across the street from the manor, which was huddled like a coward next to City Hall. The fact he'd put the camp in the regressive cave in the back of the manor's property made him look as arrogant as a house cat on a golden throne. This was doing nothing to help my abhorrence for him.

I focused on the gated area around the stone manor, which resembled a demented, lopsided human skull. I could not see the Grettish Friars, but I did smell them, especially the Master of Arms. It was a campfire smell, an ocean smell, a blood smell, with back-notes of rose broth. I gripped my knife handle and giggled. Damn, I was ever so excited! This had been such a fun day.

I took another look at the mayor (Turdheart). The other man had left, but I think there may have still been a servant in the house. I couldn't pick up on that person yet because of how invested I was in the mayor. He'd sat down in his elegant "look how important I am" leather chair, had taken off his loafers and was dragging off his pants.

I asked myself then—would he know? When I came up behind him and made a beautiful incision from his mid-back to the base of his skull, would he know what he did to my life back when he worked for the Commerce Polity?

Probably not.

I had a wife then.

I had a child coming.

Now they were both ashes.

But I don't dwell on the sad human being I might have been—that would be foolish. Zeus never attempted to be a human. He just fucked them.

Repeatedly.

I moved out into the street, my blood quickening. The Grettish Friars could strike so hard with their galaxy glass scimitars it would take you out of every dimension, all of your variations... gone.

I stopped in the street for a second.

Would I mind that?

Not at all, I hated what life was and—

No.

No, wait. I couldn't have it more wrong.

In all other possible dimensions, my son had been born. He'd gotten to live. With my newfound sight, I'd glimpsed his different variations. This was the only reality in hundreds of thousands that he'd never been born. I was stuck in a reality where I'd never get to know him. And if I ceased to be, in all other possibilities, he would lose me just as I'd lost him. He was not even ten years of age yet. And he loved me. In every dimension... he loved me.

And I loved him. In my own way. Though I'd never know him in this life. In this reality, I would be made into God, but never a father.

I had to remind myself I was still transitioning. I was not yet the God of all, and I could taste the sharpness of those scimitars at this close distance, their edges intent on cleaving the cloth of space-time-spirit, which was a layer few besides me and several others in the universe had ever seen with our own eyes.

I fell into the shadows at the base of the manor. The clicking of razorroaches in the garden made me smile. Such a prestigious location in Moon City and even the roaches still knew where to find the best filth.

I was on the other side of the manor, but it was clear from the movements of the master he was anxious—he sensed me, although he couldn't yet place what I was. This was amusing, but I had a mayor to disembowel first, so I moved on through the stone walls, disassociating my molecules. As I reconnected on the other side, I swiftly vomited into a fake plant near a dark corridor. My stomach always lurched when it reconfigured, and the wood polish smell of this place didn't help. However, that I'd only had to vomit once was a sign I was improving on this skill. Soon I'd be able to ghost my way through unlimited surfaces and depths.

There was no time for self-congratulatory pats on my back though, and I headed from the sweeping stone stairway that led to the study. The mayor had moved into his bedroom. I felt a sudden exhaustion in him. I walked each step without fear, but careful not to arouse the Friars to my whereabouts. I stopped halfway up. I felt the other denizen of the manor in the room with the mayor. I pinched my senses tight and fed upon the image: a luxurious bed, long tan legs, a thatch of blonde public hair, a slight stomach with a wide slit of belly button, two loping breasts with areolas like bright red splashes of paint. The face was made up to look pretty with liberal amounts of product—too liberal for a common woman. This was a prostitute.

Her profession didn't give me pause. That any woman, or any man, for that matter, was laying naked on the bed of a half-breed Deitii didn't make sense. Hybrids weren't born with sex organs. But not only was this woman naked there—I could smell the mayor's ejaculate trickling down her left leg.

He was human.

Completely.

And like that, I understood. This was the reason for the Deitii children camped here. The Deitii knew the mayor wasn't really who he claimed to be, but if he cared for their children in a time of terror such as these, they'd keep playing along with the idea he had blood-ties. And they would keep quiet, now that there could be a scandal that may strip them of their extra voting power when the powers that be decided this voting inequality had proven to be easily exploited.

"Vexy," said the woman to the mayor. "You don't have to go through that whole chivalry thing. I'm a whore. I can walk."

The mayor, Vekinsku, a name he obviously chose as a Deitii front, waited on the phone with his finger pointed up in the air and his flaccid human penis pointed to the ground. "Yes, she'll be waiting curbside in fifteen minutes. Thank you."

"So soon? I could have done something else too... You were pretty fast and the time's not up."

"I'm good," he told her, ending his call with a sharp stab of the finger. He tossed the cell phone on a gold emblazoned nightstand—the hard rattle showed just how exhausted the man was, and it was only marginally post-coital exhaustion.

"Better get dressed. Taxi is on its way."

"I appreciate that." The woman dabbed her thigh with the bed comforter when he wasn't looking. I decided then I wouldn't kill her when she came down the stairs. "So," she continued with a bored lilt to her tone, "you found that Moon City Killer yet? Chewing up a lot of Deitiis, that one."

"Can you keep your mouth closed?"

"You know I got banned from Firecracker's circles, so who could I really work for that would make a difference?" She snickered.

I could sense his relief at being able to release some of what bothered him. "Limbus got involved. They've sent two people here to help us with the situation. You don't have to worry about walking the streets at night anymore."

"I ain't worried. I ain't Deitii. But why Limbus? Last time I was here, you told me you hated them."

I could hardly focus on the conversation now. *Two* people from Limbus were here. Who was the other? I hadn't sensed anyone else—shit—I hope whoever it was, he or she went to Rick Agate's room and found the hydrogen cyanide surprise I left in the incinerator. That would make this nice and efficient.

"Yes," the mayor droned on, "and there was also that thing about Limbus strong-arming us on trade rights. That caused massive layoffs at the Commerce Polity. People lost jobs. Lives were ruined. I tried to work with Limbus, but they don't give a damn—their agenda is theirs alone."

Those bastards... I gripped the banister so hard the dense polished wood buckled under my grip.

"Dicks," the prostitute commiserated.

"They'll get a present from me. If this mercenary and program manager they sent happen to survive the killer and finish the job, they won't be surviving my people. That'll be the gift I send back to Limbus for all their trouble."

"You're hardcore," she laughed.

"No," he said thoughtfully. "They know they deserved it. I don't even believe they'd retaliate."

I let go of the banister. Like hell I'd let Moon City take the remaining Limbus crony. If they were responsible for me losing my job—and Angelica—and the son I'd never know in this life, the vengeance was mine. This whole time I thought it was only the corrupt Commerce Polity, but it went deeper. Limbus didn't make my lover overdose of brain diamonds, but she wouldn't have, had she known about the baby. After I lost my job, we had nothing. And Angelica embraced it, rather than fighting through it with me.

I went back through the wall. My stomach went sour, but I didn't throw-up. I did, however, taste blood.

The blood of Rick Agate.

The flavor returned to my senses, despite never laying my taste buds on it.

I associated the taste with Limbus, Inc.

It would be the taste in my mouth when I killed the next Limbus tool. I would rip that person's muscles off the bone and watch them scream.

For now though...

I clenched my fists and two thigh-high boulders shattered next to me in response.

... I would find my meals.

The Grettish Friars had unsheathed their scimitars and awaited my arrival with cold clarity. They sensed me and were excited. I wouldn't disappoint.

* * *

I slowly made my way into the recessed cavern area behind the manor. The large supply truck that Carl had told me about sat parked outside the gate. The Master of Arms would have the keys for tonight. Normally, he would drive to the outskirts of Moon Forge Valley to meet with Carl and load fresh supplies—tonight, however, was different. The supply truck wouldn't be leaving here empty; it would be leaving full of those who had once enjoyed the supplies.

Collecting all these Deitii children, sedate and high on brain diamonds, would be of little consequence. I could drive them out to my shack on the other side of Black Kiss Falls and harvest them, one by one. That would be the fun part to all of this.

I moved stealthily into the clearing of boulders outside the barbed wired, chain-link gate, which was wide open.

Of course it was.

The children didn't want out, and most passersby would not want in—not when laying eyes on the three figures approaching with five-foot-long scimitars with the finest galaxy glass for blades. I could see the stars, planets, and micro-cosmoses swirling through them as the Friars locked onto my position.

My knife, gripped firmly in hand, lengthened in response, my mind trying to protectively compensate for the weapons I faced. The Master of Arms took the centermost position. Each of the Grettish Friars stood over seven feet tall, but the master looked to be a full head taller than the others. The mass of these aliens was nothing sort of terrifying in its capacity for intimidation; they looked to be a ton in pure muscle weight, as evidenced by the broad rhinoceros shoulders and hulking arms. Their enormous bodies were mostly obscured by burnt trench coats, which seemed to hover over them, just above their black army boots. Glowing gray eyes peered out of the darkness under torn, rough fabric fedora hats. The only facial feature observable was the red-fleshed tip of their sharp noses that slightly pushed out of the void-like darkness that was their face.

They had a mouth though, somewhere in there. This I knew, because I could hear them breathing and smacking their invisible lips.

I was not a trained swordsman. The Grettish taught the art of such combat between the ages five and twenty-five *for their civilian citizens.* These were Friars—trained from birth until death. I could tell by the worn army boots and trench coats that these three Friars were not youngsters. And those scimitars—my lives across the dimensions would be nothing if they struck me hard enough and that galaxy glass hit bone.

Thought they were all apparently seasoned warriors, the two apprentices did appear younger than the master. I could taste their age, for it came off their skin like what I imagined spring blooms might be—though this moon had no true spring time. Still, their youth and its savory perfume emanated from them. They were still outmatching me at swordplay—there wasn't any doubt there.

I decided not to even entertain the idea and threw my knife a few yards toward them. Gray moon dust puffed up around the knife as it landed on the ground. One of the apprentices immediately moved to retrieve it. He picked the weapon up in the smoldering glove of his left hand. He pointed both his scimitar as well as my own weapon at me. The other apprentice, a female, rounded her master and approached the other apprentice to assist.

I thought for a second about my knife.

And how the handle—

Wasn't a handle—

Anymore—

How it was really—

The other end of a two bladed spear—

And then how it would shoot through the Friar's grip, slicing off his fingers and then piercing his breastplate and traveling into the female Friar's sternum.

Both Friars fell in jets of sizzling yellow-orange blood. The two-headed machete spear burst from the body of the female and flew for the master.

My larger opponent swung broadly and shattered the incoming spear into countless steel bits, which fell around him like homicidal rain. Blood from his students had sprayed across his right shoulder like some type of radioactive mustard. The Grettish Friar slowly considered the fallen at his feet.

"Don't take it too hard, friend," I told him. "I'm sure you taught them well. I just don't follow any rules."

The Master of Arms held his weapon high and twisted his body. I'd seen videos of Friars chopping tanks in half with those scimitars — so even if he didn't muster the power to wipe me off all planes of Time, I wouldn't enjoy what became of my body if he hit home.

The Friar moved with startling speed and resolve, gray eyes burning, a wicked fog shrouding malevolent suns. I chose to run straight for him, rather than retreat, and meet him body-to-body. This tactic surprised him at first, but he recovered swiftly and swiveled on his back leg to get a better angle for a killing stroke. I leapt into his chest, at once feeling the heat of the Friar's volcanic body under the trench coat. His giant arm encircled me, pressing me down, holding me in place to take hold of my neck and hoist me into decapitation range.

But I let my molecules wander.

And I passed through the Friar's body, just as I had the stone wall of the mayor's manor. I walked through the Friar, tearing his body apart with my every stride. The Master of Arms fell into pieces, large and small, an eruption of molten yellow flowing out in all directions. A thunderclap let out as the scimitar dropped to the stone floor. And the tinkling of something smaller.

Keys.

I was on my knees now, vomiting, and this time it was a good four times before I recovered. When I got my presence of mind back, I glanced over to the gate keys resting there in all the saffron gore. I grabbed them and stood. I thought about taking the scimitar as well, but besides it being ridiculously long in length, I knew I wouldn't need it. There would come a day where I could merrily eat galaxy glass just to enjoy the flavor.

Gods, true gods, need no fancy weapons.

I went to the interior gates and opened them. The area resembled a drug den with throw pillows and huddled, sleeping bodies. A blank-faced Deitii raised its head and looked at me quizzically.

I answered its question before it had the chance to ask.

"I'm here to set you free."

Chapter 11

The car had run out of fuel less than three feet from the business district and Dean didn't want to phone in any favors to Tasha so soon after their chat. So he walked. With much revulsion and fatigue, he swallowed another Constalife tablet, since the reminder alert had gone off on his phone. He couldn't find anything to be positive about, even though Sandra had instilled in him that believing good things brought about good things. He'd taken that to heart, because back when he'd been a sticker in a slaughterhouse in Corona, California, there wasn't a day that didn't begin negatively that didn't end the exact same way.

As he slowly made his way back to the tavern through the vacant streets of some outdoor cavern mall, he thought about calling his fiancée. He missed her more by the moment, and the choice to come here, rather than fight the brass of Limbus, Inc., looked like a colossal mistake now. At the time he'd made the choice for the exact same reason. If Limbus tossed him out on his ear or relocated him in another star system, he'd never see her again. His master plan had been to rearrange her life to fit his own. *Sure, go into stasis sleep. I'm worth it. Right?*

"You're an asshole," he muttered to himself and turned the last corner.

"Heh?" a transient said from his shadowy huddle.

"Sorry," he mumbled.

"What'd you call me?"

Dean stopped and thought about telling the man he looked like a bag of shit with eyes, but stopped himself.

Pull it together, Fulsome. You aren't exactly sending out the positive vibes here.

By the time he arrived back upstairs in the dank, foul-smelling corridor of black moss and apartment shacks, he found the Noggin asleep with his cat, Butterball, on a burlap sack. The man shivered as his eyes raced under the blemished lids. The tabby's coat rose and fell peacefully. Dean mused that after losing his friend tonight and being assigned the suicidal task of dispatching a superhuman killer, this could be that positive imagery he sought after.

He went into his shack and grabbed the blanket off his cot. He went outside and rested his blanket on top of the brain diamond addict and his cat. He returned inside and a charcoal-gray envelope had fluttered to the ground near his cot. He absently retrieved it and tore open the envelope. A thin piece of printer paper had been folded neatly and typed in all caps in a perfect square in the middle—a signature Limbus-style communication

YOU WILL STAY HERE FOR THE NIGHT. CONTINUE TO TAKE CONSTALIFE SUPPLEMENTS ON SCHEDULE. THEY WILL NOT INTERFERE WITH NATURAL SLEEP CYCLES. YOU MUST BE RESTED FOR TOMORROW MORNING. WE WILL UPLOAD MAP COORDINATES TO YOUR PHONE FOR OUR CONTACT'S APARTMENT, WHERE YOU WILL RESIDE FOR THE DURATION OF YOUR STAY. CITY OFFICIALS WILL PROVIDE SUPPLIES AND FIELD PERSONNEL FOR YOUR PROJECT. ALL WILL BE AVAILABLE DURING MIDDLE MORNING.

They're giving me Ricky's apartment. Out with the old, in with the new...

The idea of how crazy that sounded made Dean go chilly inside again. He wanted that Golden Transport. He needed it badly to get back to Sandra, but in order to win it, he'd have to do what one of the most highly trained mercenaries in the galaxy had failed to do. It appeared, by the mention of supplies and other hired hands, that Tasha's talk with the mayor's people had gone well. Or maybe there had been no talking at all. Tasha Willings had a way of making things happen with very little effort. Dean wished she'd stick around Moon City a bit longer. He could use some of her rhetorical magic, for that he was certain.

He got down on his knees and rolled over on his cot. It was humid in the shack, so offering up his blanket hadn't been a big sacrifice. As he stared up at the stringy black moss hanging from the ceiling, he felt somehow farther away from home than ever. He thought it strange it just hit him like that, but it did. Going through membrane transport, aside from the horrible complications he'd gone through today, normally felt like walking through a short, overly air-conditioned hallway. It wasn't at all like taking a cruise on a starship for several months, where you could actually feel some of the journey. For that, Moon City might as well have been an extended alleyway behind the new Limbus office building in Sherman Oaks.

But he was away.

Far away from her.

And this would likely be his last hurrah anywhere. How could he have been so stupid?

He shut his eyes and tried not to think of the stink of the small room and the stink of his predicament. It riddled him with anxiety and self-doubt. He'd faced horrible things before in his short tenure working for Limbus, but nothing that would prepare him for such a foe. What would his game plan be? How would he use the men or women the city provided him for resources? Where could he even start to track this killer, who Rick had spent a great deal of time tracking? And had not given much in the way of debriefing on any of the information he'd turned up. Had Rick left anything behind in his apartment? Documents? Clues?

He knew he couldn't do anything about it tonight. He knew better than to go against what he'd read in the note. If he didn't get any sleep, for however many crazy long hours that would be, his equilibrium would still be off, and he wouldn't be able to function in this place like he did back on Earth. He had to convince himself he was going to bed a little early on a Friday night, and although he'd rather stay up, sleep was in his best interest. Because tomorrow would be better. Tomorrow, he would start fresh and go forward, stronger. So he let his mind wander to a hazy gray fog that deepened, and his consciousness soon slid under the mental gauze. He slept for a good fourteen hours. But his phone alarm was not what woke him.

He awoke to a labored, pained sound like something dying. It took a while to register the series of suffering meows. At first he ignored it, but then the cat's painful cries became so incessant, it simply no longer could be ignored. Nearly falling over himself, he got up from his cot, went to the door, and opened it. Outside, he found Chipper Saude, wrapped in his blanket, dead.

* * *

Dean checked his phone, too shocked to form an immediate plan. He had, indeed, slept for fourteen hours, but it really wasn't enough. Twenty was recommended on this godforsaken moon. He popped another Constalife pill, and once again considered the dead Noggin whom he had helped and whom had helped him in return. It looked like an overdose, yet, Dean couldn't buy it. People who got as close to overdosing on brain diamonds as Chipper had yesterday, usually took at least a week or so to climb up on the horse again. The mind was too spent. It would be like asking for more sex after a week-long orgy; even if the person had the will, the body was most likely closed for business. This was what Dean had learned was called "false recovery," for these addicts were not truly done with the drug, they were merely recuperating from its onslaught to their nervous system.

No. Somebody wanted Chipper out of the way, and Dean had a feeling he was the reason the target got put on the poor guy.

But there was something that didn't make sense about that. He was sound asleep, less than a yard away from where Chipper came to die and that was presumably where he'd also been murdered... so if his involvement with Dean, or Limbus for that matter, had got him killed, why had Dean not been taken out as well? That was truly a dark thought because anybody could have killed Dean—he'd slept like a drunk with nine tons of bricks piled on top of him—he'd been out cold, completely vulnerable.

He lowered onto one knee and dragged his blanket over the man's frothed-over mouth and then over his blood-blasted eye sockets. It could have also been another day in the life of an addict—

these sorts of things, when drugs and money were exchanged under the worst of circumstances, could lead to deaths like this.

Dean shook his head. *No, you're rationalizing away your suspicions. No dealer or other pissed-off Noggin would force Chipper to overdose. They'd have shanked him. Shot him. Beat in his head. Strangled him. But they wouldn't have wasted valuable drugs on him.*

Just then the register of Chipper's cat meow came through the fogginess of Dean's thoughts. He heard it coming from around the side of his shack. The animal sounded horrible, as though it were close to the end. Dean stood and his knees crackled. He didn't much care for cats. He was very allergic to them; he'd been bitten and scratched in the deepest part of his left thigh by his first girlfriend Amy's cat, Tigger, who had decided Dean was a tree it needed to scale. Aside from those instances, as a child, Dean's mother had convinced him that cats were demon serpents that had grown fur and cute faces to seduce humanity.

Well, he hadn't subscribed to that last one, but he still would have rather avoided cats if at all possible.

But the sound of its call.

He had to see if the animal had been injured. He could take it to another person here or in the tavern. He could get it some help, at very least.

Dean slowly stepped around the shack and stopped short of the puddle of rich, red blood. Sprays of crimson decorated the base of the shack, just where some black moss had begun to make its slow ascent of dominance. Dean stepped around the pool about six inches in diameter and tracked his eyes from the bloody paw prints to a small tarp that twitched and shuttered with every labored mewling.

"Holy shit," he mumbled and moved toward the tarp.

Dean got there and, not enjoying suspense all that much, yanked the tarp off. The cat's eyes darted up at him from inside a leather satchel. Dean recognized it as the one Chipper had next to him when they first met. The buckle had been latched and the cat had been trapped inside when Chipper put it in there. Dean hunkered near the bag and fingered the buckle. Numerous tan and orange hairs had embedded in the cheap felt interior liner at the fringe of the opening.

The cat hid inside.

"Smart," he said and opened the buckle and the cat burst out and ran away, meowing as it went. He wasn't entirely sure because the thing blurred like a small orange rocket, but Dean wagered other than being frightened, the cat wasn't injured.

The blood.

So what is that?

Dean took out his phone and brought up the apps. Tasha had already come through. He had the 3D printer and DNA sampler and connection to Limbus, Inc.'s contract lab, Borderon.

"Merry Christmas to me." Dean went to the 3D printer and requested a sample tray. The phone's print output device began to heat and glow soft lavender. Dean set it on the flat surface side of a bowling ball-sized rock near the shack. A squeaky meow went up from around the shack. Letting the 3D printer do its thing, he crept around the shack to have a look.

The cat sat near the blanketed form of Chipper's corpse. It turned its head and spotted Dean, letting loose a plaintive meow for assistance.

"Hold it together," he told the cat and went back to his phone.

The plastic sample tray had almost finished. It was about five inches in length and half as wide. Dean reached down as the printer clicked off and the element in the end of the phone ran its fan to cool down. He pulled off the slim cover and turned to the blood. He put his knee down on something hard and winced. Dean scooted away and had a look. A long, flat rock, shaped as a blade and wrapped in leather lace at the bottom, was half submerged in the gray dirt. The sharp end was caked in blood and dirt clumps.

Chipper's weapon? Had to be.

Dean felt a twinge of excitement. If the Moon City Killer had done this, he would already have a pointer on this as soon as the results came back. If he could get a good sample.

Speaking of...

Dean got closer to the shallow pool of blood. There was hardly enough for an appropriate sample. He would only get one shot at it.

The cat meowed louder.

He leaned over and carefully tried to fill the tray with blood only. No dirt. That might screw up the photo reading.

Meow.

Meow. Meow. Meow.

"Gimme a break, Butterdick," he whispered.

A bead of sweat dripped from Dean's hairline to his right eye. His hand trembled as he dipped the tray deeper. There was a small pink dash that was the fill line. The blood level rose above the line and he jerked back. The blood sloshed to the side. Dean froze.

Slowly he placed the tray on the rock and picked up his phone. He selected the molecular camera, lined up the tray in the brackets on the view finder, and started the sample image. It took ten seconds to acquire three thousand layers, which was sufficient, but Dean had run chemical and blood analysis before, and he knew that ten thousand was the sweet spot; he'd never had to run more than one sample twice with that amount of molecular imagery.

After another thirty seconds, he had the sample imagery.

Meow. Meooooooooow.

Dean sent the sample layer image to Borderon. Head buzzing, he reached over and looked in the satchel. Other than cat hair and a sliver of a wrapper from some Constalife-infused cat treats, there wasn't anything else. Dean got up and went around the shack. Butterball, still at Chipper's side, but now suddenly silent, glanced at him.

"Rough day," he said.

The cat just held his gaze.

"Who killed your dad, huh? Who did it?"

Almond pupils fixed on him. Not sorrow. Just a profound question inside them.

The phone chirped.

The results were in.

* * *

Dean tried Tasha several times before she picked up. He hadn't bothered to leave a message because Tasha never listened to them and made him repeat everything over in detail. He once told her to "Just listen to the message and get back to me," and she said, without pause, "Pretend I listened to it. Now explain it to me all over again." The young-faced ancient never lost an opportunity to make Dean fully aware of how busy she was and how grateful he should be when she turned her attention on him and his problems.

"So," she said and crunched on something, "your people should arrive today at some point. They will be meeting you at the apartment complex lobby. I got to tell you though, our budget is near exhausted now. If you expect to get Golden Transport out of there, it'll be your only way back. Any other mishaps at the membrane station and you'll be stuck there at Moon City for at least six months Earth time. We won't be able even to afford standard transport. There just are no other funds. The Zetú war has gobbled up all our resources in this quarter." She paused and added, "To a scary level. There are dangers outside the Grettish War Council. Terrorists are seizing ships and executing Zetú in horrifying numbers."

Dean was caught off guard. He couldn't even process this new information about his Zetú friends. It had misdirected him, and instead, he found himself feebly asking, "Wait, so Golden Transport isn't more reliable?"

"No. It's the same technology, but with interference, it can fail, just as standard transport failed you yesterday. Golden just sidesteps all relative time continuums. It was an attempt at time travel that ultimately didn't succeed, but it does alter a human's physiognomy."

Which is why you're an adult in a child's body…

"I can smell the wood burning, Dean. Other than your profound discernment over me being an old bat who hasn't had her period yet, why not tell me why you've called? Repeatedly. I assumed it was the support I'm sending?"

"It's not."

"We haven't discovered anything new about who sabotaged the membrane chamber."

"It's not that either, but let me know when you find something."

"Okay, can you just tell me what the hell this is about?" Crunch. Crunch. "Sorry. Pretzels."

Dean took a swallow of the smelly black-moss air and gagged a little. He looked forward to rooming at another location. Hopefully, if it smelled only half as bad as this place, he'd be happy. "I… ran a blood test. I believe the Moon City Killer was here last night and killed a drug addict outside my shack—room."

"How do you know?"

"I ran a test of some blood I found—the victim stabbed whomever it was attacking him. I ran it through our system. Borderon came up with no definable human results. Most of the DNA profile is Deitii. The system doesn't track that alien species, so there's no way to tie it to one of them."

"The Moon City Killer's body is obviously changing at the DNA level."

"But why would he kill this man? It doesn't make sense. It's a waste of his time, frankly."

"I don't know, but speaking of a waste of time, see you later, Dean."

"Tasha, wait I—"

His cell phone beeped as the call ended. Dean choked on what he wanted to call her and settled for mumbling, "brat," before putting his phone away. The next few minutes he gathered his sparse belongings. The reg police had shown up promptly after he informed the tavern owner about the murder, but the responding officer chose to have a few beers and flirt with the long-legged, big-bosomed brunette Noggin who haunted the table near the window, at least as long as Dean had been here (which felt forever). He had no idea when the officer would finally come up here to take care of Chipper's corpse, but he didn't want to wait any longer to get out of this foul-smelling slice of hell.

Butterball the cat raced up to Dean as he stepped around the body, shifting a backpack of all his items to his other shoulder. The cat meowed and glanced up at him, askance.

"What?" Dean demanded.

The cat nosed at Chipper's satchel and turned its face again to Dean. A long, almost inaudible meow followed.

"Going back to your safe place?"

Butterball flew toward him. Dean stiffened. The cat rubbed against his leg, and then hurried back to the satchel. Nosed it again.

"You want back inside? There's nothing in there."

Meow. Meow. Meoooooow.

"No, no, no, no, no." Dean waved his hands. "I'll tell everyone in the tavern about you, Butterdick, but I ain't taking you with me. Somebody will look after you."

The almond pupils fixed on him, seeming in disbelief.

"Ease up, damn you. I'm allergic."

Meow.

"I have to do something about my Zetú friends before they're all executed by the Grettish terrorists."

Meow.

"I've got to figure out how to kill somebody who is superhuman."

Meow.

"I've got to get back to the love of my life before she writes me off and forgets me forever."

There was no other meow, just a penetrating stare.

Dean looked around for a moment and shook his head, never remembering being so soft, and for the last possible species in the universe. "Okay, get in, climb aboard, Butterdick."

He leaned over and opened the satchel. The cat looked back as though to ask, "Is this what you want?"

"Get the hell in there before I change my mind."

Butterball darted inside and merrily made cat noises. Dean picked up the satchel, heavy with the animal, and slung it over his other shoulder. He had no inkling as to what in the hell had gone wrong with him, but he just accepted that the animal was his to care for now, until he could pawn it off to some non-allergic soul who actually *liked* cats.

As he left that horrible tavern though, he had to admit, it felt good to have somebody along for this ride. Especially since it might be his last.

* * *

After all the fuss about fingerprint signatures and documenting who he worked for, Dean was standing in the apartment that had belonged to his friend Rick Agate. The two-room apartment wasn't much to speak of, and the front door's knob had to be thoroughly wrenched on to open up, but it was leagues beyond the shack he'd just departed.

The first thing he did was toss an old can of baked beans into the incinerator. They weren't that powerful smelling, but Dean was certain that bacteria would find a home in their barbecued-cradled glaze before too long. Didn't matter if you were on a planet, moon, meteor, or asteroid—bacteria ruled. He would always fear and respect every colony of the microbugs.

And hate them for their disease and their smell.

He went to activate the incinerator and then thought against it. There were probably more things to burn and he only wanted to deal with the stench once, because his stomach was in sour knots right now.

Butterball ran into the bedroom. Dean didn't feel like exploring just yet, so he sat on the couch and looked at his phone. Maybe just looking at his newsfeed and Facebook would relax him to the point where he could start thinking about what to do next. He hoped these other "support" people didn't show up before he figured what that was.

His finger slid up the newsfeed. Limbus had neural interface where you could just mentally scroll through the feeds, but that was too creepy for him. He opted to keep his phone and do Internet surfing and social media lurking like the rest of his generation. Sandra was the same way.

Should I call her?

Dean checked his watch. It had been more than a day since they last spoke. She hadn't even sent him a text message.

Something is wrong.

He went to message her, but just before he could close out the intergalactic news feed, he saw it.

GRETTISH TERROR GROUP WASWAS has posted the latest Zetú slave execution.

A blond woman who looked like Washington, DC Barbie explained that "several ships had been taken, and it was debatable at this time if those ships had not been under the protection of All-Galaxies, Limbus, Inc., and Wewato LLC."

Dean tried not to blink as he watched as they ran footage of a Zetú slave having his limbs cut off. He was relieved it wasn't his friend Finny-Min, but the relief didn't quiet his horror or his disgust. He thought to call Sandra, but decided he needed to get his head on straight first. She didn't like weakness, even though she told him he could show her anything he was feeling.

None of that mattered. He loved her, but it was a shot in the dark right now that he'd ever get to see her again. He needed to stay focused and get this job done. If he could get rid of this Moon City Killer and get the Golden Transport back (and it didn't screw up during transfer), that would mean everything. He might even be able to talk Sandra into marrying his sorry ass. He almost wanted to call and tell her the possibility existed that he could be back as soon as this mission was over and not decades later. But getting her hopes up for something that might not happen would only make the outcome so much worse, and she'd also be terrified for his life because she knew him for what he was... He'd killed thousands of cows and many more aliens to boot, but he'd never been considered an assassin or a mercenary or a hired killer. He had his "victims" brought to him, more or less.

The Moon City Killer would not walk up to him like a stunned cow. He would not stagger into his own gruesome death out of stupidity and trust. This was beyond Dean's range.

But he had to figure it out.

Scratch.

Scratch. Scratch.

He turned to notice the Noggin's cat had taken an interest in the incinerator. It was scratching at the handle. It must have smelled some old food in there. Dean resolved he'd have to run the thing before heading out again. The cat would have to be the unfortunate one to bear the smell of burning old garbage. But it was a necessity; there weren't any landfills on this rock.

The cat stood on its hind legs and proceeded to paw more fiercely.

"Cut it out," Dean said and went to toe the cat away. "You're gonna get yourself toasted."

The cat turned its streaked orange-black face at him and meowed.

"Issues?" he asked with a laugh. "Guess you're hungry. Let's see what our friend Rick bought at the market."

Dean ventured into the small kitchen and pulled open a few empty cabinets before finding a few stacks of canned food. Spam. Black olives. And purple sword fish. Each can's label had the same gaudy text affixed beneath, *CONSTALIFE infused!*

"Only the best from your nearest terra cannery."

Dean found a clean bowl in the cupboard below the sink and went about serving up Butterball's dinner. Once Dean set it down, the cat happily gobbled up the lavender chunks of swordfish. Dean's eyes began to itch and water. He let out a tremendous sneeze into his wrist. "Gotta find you a new place, hombre, before you're the death of me. For now though, I'll leave you to your grub."

A text came in through his phone. He hurriedly went over to check it out, thinking it might be Sandra.

It was Tasha.

head to Stone Root Ale House. its the last place rick surveyed killer.

Dean hated texting but he thumb-typed a brief reply of compliance.

car was fueled last night + transported to the lot outside your hotel. your two support techs should arrive hotel late afternoon.

Dean gave his thanks but hardly felt like it. He needed support now, not forty-eight hours later or whenever the hell this place considered afternoon to be afternoon. At least he had the car back though, and the luxury of it actually having some fuel.

He grabbed his weapon, stuffed it in the back of his pants, and pulled his shirt over it.

"Stay away from that incinerator," he sternly told the cat, who ignored him. He grabbed the door knob and it took a bit of wiggling for it to disengage before he could open the door. "Only the best for Limbus directors," he muttered with a wet sniffle (CAT infused!).

They left the car exactly where he'd envisioned it would be left, parked as far from the front of the hotel as possible. Dean didn't mind the walk, however. It felt good to stretch his legs. His stomach was growling and his nose was all snotty from the cat. Other than those elements and being lovesick for Sandra, he foresaw another absolute shit day on this Moon City colony. He got into the car and it started up without any issues though, so he couldn't complain about his ride. For now at least.

His GPS located the Stone Root Ale House only three miles from the hotel. Most of Moon City's citizens had already tucked into their jobs by this time, so the streets were virtually empty.

The Stone Root Ale House could not be missed. A carefully hewn stone façade shaped like an enormous oak tree loomed above all the other smaller shanty establishments surrounding it. Dean parked alongside the curb, sneezed violently, and killed the engine.

After locking up the car, he headed through the open portal in the front of the tree shape. Stairs led down to a soft, orange glow. The walls inside had more sculpted stone configurations, these of twisting roots of various size and length. It must have taken years to craft it all. The descent wasn't as impressive, however; after about twenty stairs, Dean had reached the floor of the tavern.

Many of the chairs were still put up on the high-top black tables. A few people hunched over the bar, one smoking a cigar and the other chatting about something on the e-pad they shared between them. Dean decided to sit a few stools away but not look like he was being completely anti-social.

The bartender was a large, bald man in a green apron. From the sweat on his brow, he looked like he was finishing a shift, not just starting one.

"How ya?" he asked.

"I'm good. Good. How... are you?" Dean stumbled awkwardly, never certain about formalities.

"I'm fat and sweaty," the bartender deadpanned.

Dean cracked a smile and then went into business mode. "I had a friend of mine come in here not too long ago, asking about the Deitii abduction—"

"No you didn't."

"Excuse me—?"

"Until you buy some breakfast and a drink, you didn't know nobody, and I sure as hell didn't know nothing about no Deitii. We paging here?"

Dean pressed his lips together. His stomach growled as though to confirm this was an opportunity to kill two birds with one stone and then devour them.

"Sure, what's for breakfast around here?" he asked.

"We got steak hash and eggs."

"Lovely. I'll have it. With coffee."

"No coffee, or tea. Just alcohol."

"Eh, water?"

"It's used for cleaning cups that serve the alcohol."

"Can I just have water?"

"Can I just forget about that Deitii pal of yours?"

Dean winced. "Understood. Just breakfast then."

"Wrong answer."

"Shit, man, I don't drink this early."

"Now you do," said the bartender with a malicious grin. "And I think you want our most pricey, all-bells and whistles cocktail."

"Wonderful, bring it on. What's it called?"

"Its name changes from patron to patron."

"Is that so?"

"Yup," the bartender slid back and yelled through the kitchen window. "One breakfast!"

Dean could hear the cook grunt and the clatter of pans being withdrawn from cupboards. The bartender grabbed several bottles and began mixing up a drink without much ceremony. Dean watched, feigning interest as the bartender finished up and dropped one ice cube in the concoction. The dark caramel-colored drink was set before him and he immediately noticed a slight whirlpool in the center where the ice cube spun. The perpetual motion wasn't natural and he eyed it more closely. "Why's it doing that?"

"Double dose of Constalife in there, with Malo Macho Tequila — which is made from the prickly pears of our one and only succulent that grows here in Moon City."

"Is that what gives it this color?"

"No, that's the Dr. Pepper I added."

"Ah," said Dean and lifted the glass. "And what is this called that I'm drinking?"

"The Limbus Asshole."

Dean snickered. So, either he stood out like a sore thumb or this bartender wasn't as dense as he looked. He lifted the drink in cheers. "Many happy returns," he said and took a sip. It wasn't half bad. A bit too tequila-ish for his tastes, but not bad.

"So let's talk about the other night."

"Let's talk about it after your breakfast and all of your drink."

Dean swallowed down his bitterness for this man and sighed through his teeth. "Absolutely."

Thankfully, his food showed up not too long after. It was surprisingly rich and satisfying. The potatoes and onions were not greasy and they were seasoned with something like thyme, but with a uniqueness of its own. He didn't venture to ask where they got steak on this moon—he'd worked in slaughterhouses before and even from the best sources he couldn't think too much about it without feeling the draw to vegetables and fruit. It was all tasty though and his stomach rejoiced at having something solid inside it.

He downed the drink, just to get it over with, and hissed at the strength of it.

The bartender came back over after fixing a few beers for the e-pad patrons. "Wow. You were thirsty! Care for another?"

"You know I don't."

The man dropped the bill near Dean and leaned in, lowering his voice. "So I can't tell you too much, not that I wouldn't, but that I was pretty busy that night. The Deitii, the Killer, and the bounty hunter were all here that night."

"I already knew that."

"Did you know that several folks said the Killer smelled like burning smoke? Like hickory wood?"

"No, I hadn't heard that."

"Did you also know that we have surveillance up in every corner of this establishment?"

Dean glanced around, and in the stone ceiling, he saw small, black half-globes.

"I can pay—"

"Save it. I don't access to those feeds," said the man.

"Who does?"

"Surefire."

"Where are they?"

The bartender folded his arms. "You really aren't from around here, are you?"

"I know, it's obvious. Now, Surefire..."

"If you were a local, you'd know that Surefire LLC is one of the Firecracker Lady's many business endeavors—some would say a front for what she does better."

"Trafficking."

"From your lips, not mine."

"Do you think I can bargain with her to get access to the feeds?"

"What am I?" The bartender grimaced. "Your business advisor? How the hell should I know? If you want to take it up with her, go to her hotel on Carbon Lake Boulevard. You should be able to find it easy since it's the only high-rise building we got here on the moon. She don't just see anybody though, so you'll have to figure that out. Her people can be a bit... difficult in turning over information too. My advice would be to find some new damn clothes that aren't so Limbus-y and wipe that bewildered look off your mug. Elsewise they'll be seeing you as an outsider from a mile away."

Dean was shocked he'd gotten so much from the man in such a short time. Shocked, but thankful. "I appreciate it," he said and put down twice what the meal and drink cost. He took out his phone and locked in Carbon Lake Boulevard in his GPS.

"Nice having you in. Come by again if you get the chance." A long smile cut through the man's pasty, sweat-dappled face. "After all, friend, that drink's Constalife dose will keep you up for two days. There's plenty of time to drop in before you crash! Better get your affairs in order for your big nap, Limbus thug!" He laughed and the e-pad patrons chuckled along with him.

Dean couldn't respond. He could only think of a number his mind instantly calculated.

168.

That's how many hours two days on this moon would be. Ignoring the laughter and taunting, he pressed on up the stairs to the exit, wondering if he survived all that time, just how long he'd actually crash for and who would die during that time.

Chapter 12

I couldn't stop the shaking in my hands and in my forearms. After I killed the ten or eleventh Deitii, reality started flowing around me in a hurricane of glass and blood. I'd never appreciated the smell of their life fluid until I'd opened so many throats. It was a tart smell, like ripe cherries or one of those other solar system fruits I used to buy from the import-grocer in the Bleeding Caverns. I loved it, and currently, I was covered from my hands to my shoulders in it.

In the bedroom, I counted up to fifty-seven bodies. Being the resourceful fellow I was, I arranged with Carl to deliver a hundred yards of tubing, thirty more large specimen jars, a Githarian NoDeath generator battery to supply extra power to my spinal-tapping pump, and extra blades for my industrial food processor. I would be very busy today, tapping each body, withdrawing fluid, and harvesting, processing, and juicing all the brains. I might need to drink from some of my remaining source just to have the endurance to do all this in one sitting.

And in one sitting I had to. As much as I wanted to look for the other Limbus visitor, that would all need to wait. If the spinal fluid and raw brain matter wasn't preserved in a timely fashion, it would degrade to nearly useless material, and this was too damn great of a find to let it go to waste.

I paid Carl what I owed him, and was happy to do so. Never thought running into him would be such a find, but it had paid off. I also told him to keep an eye out for any other person who showed up at the mercenary's apartment. Chances were that whoever else showed up there today would probably be the man or woman I was looking for. I'd have the kid keep an eye on the Limbus lackey while I finished business here.

I wasn't a bit ashamed to admit my happiness. I even began to hum as I cored out one Deitii's skull and then went about pulling out pieces of its mind. Scratches covered the length of my bloodied arms from all their struggles. I'd gotten the aliens all into my house and padlocked the only door. Their screams weren't heard; it was beneficial to live on the outskirts of the lumber district. Nobody wanted to deal with all the sawdust and the scent of lacquer in the air all the time. The screaming, if it could even be heard over the booming factory down the street, would not have fallen on any residential ears, because other than me and an abandoned convenience store, there was nothing on the south end of Moon City.

It took a few hours, but all the bodies were tapped and the spinal fluid was pumping into the specimen jars, filling them at an astonishing pace. I refused to get too mesmerized by it all though, because I'd only so far unhoused and preserved fifteen brains. I had forty-two remaining, and after that I had to put their pieces in the food processor, mix up the preservation materials, adjust pH, and then bottle. I'd told Carl I needed him to empty my refrigerator of all food—his to eat or sell—and I'd also need help hauling the bodies back into the truck. They were all getting the same one-way ticket down the Black Kiss that Rick Agate had received. I'd call Carl later. The kid talked too much. Asked too many questions. He was useful though and I tended to like him as much as I possibly could like another human being.

I put my knife up to the pallid, cold temple of the next Deitii. Not even a new cut made and I heard a brisk knock at my front door. I paused and waited. I would ignore it.

Another knock came.

Followed by a voice.

"I know you're in there," said a familiar-sounding female voice. "Your truck is here. I'm not stupid. Hey open up, I need to talk."

I recognized her then. It was Mazina Frye. She'd worked with friends of my family, and we'd met at a sad attempt at a reunion.

Neither of us cared enough about our friends and relatives to hang out for the duration. So, a one-night stand happened. I just never thought it would turn into a seasonal thing. That was a strange time. I dated her a few months, all in the wake of losing my wife. It was also just before I first discovered the taste of Deitii. There was no question I was a completely different person back then, both spiritually and physically.

I couldn't get into a conversation with her. Who really gave a shit if she thought I was ignoring her? I didn't owe her anything.

"I have to tell you about your mother," Mazina said and knocked again. "It's really important. Come on, let me in."

Goddamn it. I didn't care what had happened to my mother, except that I wanted to know if she had finally died. I never consciously searched for her when I turned my eyes to the galaxy because I was afraid she'd be able to see me watching and feel validated by it. I would be so happy if I just knew she'd drank herself to death or one of her boyfriends pushed her down the stairs in some backstreet ghetto in the Outer Caverns. It would bring me peace and I wouldn't have to mentally block her out. I could resolve that that character in my life story had finally been written out, and good riddance.

"Come on, jackass," hollered Mazina with another volley of sharp knocks.

More than anything, I just wanted to know if Mom *had gotten what was coming to her.* I stripped off my gory shirt and shut my bedroom door.

"One minute," I called out, examining my gruesome arms. "I just got out of the shower. Let me put something on."

"Not on my account." Mazina sounded mischievous.

I went to the sink, turned on the faucet, and began scrubbing off all the stains. It took a while and Mazina made some nearly inaudible comment about me "taking a full orbit around the sun to answer the freaking door."

When I answered without my shirt, Mazina smirked. "Nice to see you."

"What about my mother?"

"Can I come in?"

"No. What about my mother?"

Mazina brushed past me. She was in a lavender strapless shirt, short black skirt, and black heels. Her makeup and clothing suggested streetwalker. I didn't remember her being so trashy. Insecure maybe, but not so slutastic. Her makeup was overdone and her long, brunette hair needed washing, badly. She sat on my couch and crossed her legs. I could see the razor burns around her bikini zone from where I stood.

"If you're trying to give me a hard-on, it won't work."

"Oh?" she asked with a smile. "Doesn't work for you any longer? I hear that happens to men getting on in age."

"Tell me about my mother so we can end this."

"She needs to meet you today. She'll be eating at the Passing Sun."

"She doesn't need to meet me for anything."

"You don't have to eat with her, just hear her out."

"Why'd she send you?" I asked, folding my arms.

"Because she knew we had a thing. And she paid me fifty bucks."

"Didn't know she had that much to spend."

Mazina arched an eyebrow. "There's a lot you don't know. She's turned her life around."

"Good for her."

"She doesn't want you to be angry with her anymore. She wants to start anew. Forge a relationship with you."

"This is the stupidest thing I've heard in a long time. Get out of my house."

"Really?" Mazina said and sat back, looking more relaxed now. "I recall lying in bed with you once and you telling me you always wanted someone you trusted by your side, that you wanted to teach and be taught. Couldn't you have been talking about your mother?"

"I was talking about someone I'll never know."

"Your son. Yes, you did talk about him a lot. I think because you needed a parent yourself."

"Did she pay you extra to philosophize with me?"

"No, that's free of charge."

I went over and grasped her wrist, pulling her up to her feet. "I want you out of here. Tell my mother she can take her new life and choke on it."

"Before you get all caveman on me—"

"You wish."

She laughed and put her clammy palm on my cheek. "I do need to tell you one last thing. It might change your mind about going to see her."

I grabbed her wrist and removed her hand from my cheek. "There is nothing you can say that will change my mind."

"Oh no? What about 3D ultrasound photos of your son you've never seen?"

I stopped and glared at her. "Why would she have those?"

"Your mother took her for the ultrasound and maternity photos—her boyfriend Ryan paid for the entire session. They were going to surprise you. Your mother was trying. Even back then, she was trying to reach you. I guess your wife understood. Why couldn't you?"

"Does this conclude the lecture?"

"After everything happened with your job at the Commerce Polity, you can tell why she held onto them."

I snorted. "Have her mail them to me."

"She won't," Mazina said. "She insists you meet her at the diner, around beyondnoon."

"They're just photos. They won't bring them back to damn life."

"No," Mazina admitted. "But do you really think they should be with your mother?"

"That part of my existence is gone. Just like you."

"We cared about each other. Don't think for a second there wasn't a connection—"

I smiled. "You were a flavor that passed across my tongue, Mazina. Talking about it like it's more makes me embarrassed for you. Now take your sad whore outfit, your bad perfume, and the rest of your lousy little self, point it over to that door right there, and march the hell out of my house. Never come back. Never think about it."

Her eyes blossomed at this, though she hardly believed my sincerity. "You're an ass—"

"Hole," I finished and shook my head. "I'm *so* much more than that. You don't really know."

Mazina staggered away as I released her wrist. She didn't look back as she left. I pulled the door shut behind her so hard my old childhood painting of the Midnight Sea hanging nearby shifted off its nail, fell to the floor, and shattered. It had been the first and last drawing I'd ever made for my mother. She'd accepted it with a kiss on my forehead. The next day I found it covered in peanut shells pinned beneath a bottle of Blakar whiskey. The wet ring from the bottle was still visible in the lower left side. I took the painting back and kept it with me ever since.

It wasn't important to me anymore. I left it there amongst the shards of broken glass and snapped wooden frame. I tried to put my mother out of my mind and return to what really mattered. My ascension.

Chapter 13

On his way to see the Firecracker Lady, Dean heard another account about the hostage situation with the Zetú. He couldn't believe the Grettish were putting them through the same bullshit over again. He'd give anything to be able to help them out. Finny-Min was his friend. Even with severe nerve damage to his spine, the Zetú accountant had prepared Dean and Sandra a five-course meal from some of the finest galactic cuisines edible to human beings. To think those Grettish bastards bore the responsibility for the torture that had caused that nerve damage made him hate them even more.

The last he had heard from Finny-Min, before the war ignited again, he had sent a transmission of his newborn child, whom he'd given the last name of Dean. It would have been an honor even under human circumstances to have a child named after you, but for most in the Zetú tradition, the last name of Gaga was mostly preferred. Their fandom of Lady Gaga had exploded across their cultures and around ninety-five percent held the Gaga last name, and that figure was rising. Finny-Min was just as enamored with the singer as the rest of his species, but he still gave Dean that unique pleasure to be valued even higher for his successful rescue campaign.

Now his old friend was in trouble and Dean could do nothing to help. He'd texted Sandra about it and she'd sent him a brief reply, *You can't help everyone hon.*

A lot of her replies had been short lately. Dean wondered if she'd met someone else, if she was pulling away already, falling out of love...

It twisted his guts. He had to get back to her. He had to get that Golden Transport.

Dean's thoughts fled as the high-rise loomed into view through his windshield. Stone and wood had been utilized equally to create a type of Neolithic empire state building. There had to be over a hundred floors and possibly others above those that could be distinguished by the rows of torches along the ledges of each. The Firecracker Lady wasn't a small-time criminal by any stretch; she was the type who robbed entire world banks while dining with the same planet's ambassadors.

The case file had told him to not engage the Firecracker Lady, even though she was already aware of Limbus's presence on the moon. Dean needed to see that surveillance footage though. If her people could get him access, it could lead him right to the Moon City Killer. If the Firecracker Lady hadn't been girlfriend to the president's son from the Fringer Corporation, she may have already sent her own people after the Killer. The Fringers went beyond the Freedomist Elite's racism for the Zetú. They hated the Deitiis as well, and Dean had read in the case file that they'd been trying to get the mixed-species mayor of Moon City thrown out until the Firecracker Lady convinced them to back down. The bottom line was that a dead Deitii was a good thing to both the Fringers and to any big-time crook who wanted to out-balance their electoral power, and that worked well for the Firecracker Lady.

Dean would have to make up a story. He couldn't let them know he was tracking the Killer. For all he knew, they'd try to stop him. After all, Deitiis were vanishing so fast they'd soon no longer be a problem for their enemies, and they probably didn't want someone getting in the way of all the free carnage.

Dean chose to leave his weapon in the glove compartment. He'd learned in the past that showing up unarmed to a place he knew he'd get patted down would increase his chances to negotiate a deal. It was a risky method, but it sent a message that couldn't be denied. He came in peace.

He got out and locked the door, turned around, and a large arm caught around his midsection, slamming him back against the car. Donaldo leaned over him, all smiles. The man was so up on Dean he could count the pores on his nose.

"The hell you doing here, Fulsome? I think it's past time I wipe the floor with your ass."

So much for coming in peace.

"You work for the lady too, eh?" asked Dean, not moving from under the weight of the man's thick forearm.

"Everybody on this moon works for her, even if they don't know it."

"Seems I've come to the right place then. I wanted to speak with her about a deal."

"You ain't got nothing she wants."

Now Dean chose to push the man off him. "I'll see about that."

"Like hell you will."

Another smelly strong-arm caught Dean's wrist. This one was uglier than Donaldo, if not as broad in the shoulders. Both men grappled with Dean and took hold of him.

"Not looking for a fight, people. Limbus can make this worth her time. I just need to see some surveillance feeds for outside marketing research. Demographics."

"That sounds like horseshit to me."

"I can put you in touch—"

"No, I won't be tricked by none of your friends on some phone call," said Donaldo through heavy breaths. They pushed him around the side of the sky-rise, down a sidewalk that led to a poolside area. Donald swiped a keycard at the gate to open it. A tall, strawberry blond woman lay out under a sunlamp near the pool. She lifted her sunglasses to the approaching men. Dean noticed outside of the pool of artificial sunlight sat a baby's crib.

"April, go fetch Jake and I some Ale bombers. I'll watch the kid." Donaldo waited a moment and then kicked at her lounge chair. "Get up and go. I said I'd watch her."

"You aren't going to fire a gun around her or—"

Donaldo took her by the wrist and guided her to her feet. The woman was in great physical shape but had a few scars on her torso. Dean wondered if those belonged to Donaldo.

"I ain't firing nothing. Just go get our drinks, yes?"

April huffed. "Sure," she said and stole one last glance at her sleeping baby before heading to a door that read CASINO on its glass panels.

When she was gone, Donaldo pushed Dean down onto the lounger and shut off the sun lamp. The baby, looking to be around ten months or so, twisted around in the crib, on the verge of waking.

"So, let's see now. Let me ask again." Donaldo cleared his throat and his assistant goon, Jake, folded his slender arms over his leather vest. "What do you want with video recordings?"

Dean swallowed a bad taste. Not only did it screw his chances of making a deal to tell these idiots, but he was under contract not to divulge mission objectives to others not in Limbus's employ or under contract. Tasha might pull the deal with the Golden Transport if he leaked such sensitive information.

"I told you what I needed it for," he answered.

The baby cooed then and Donaldo's eyes flitted over. "Look what you did? The baby can't sleep through bullshit."

He bent over the crib and picked up the infant. "Cute, eh?"

"Very. She yours?"

"Who knows?" Donaldo chuckled. "April's loose enough to trap an elephant."

Jake tittered.

Dean waited.

The big man set the child down on the damp concrete. He angled his face up to Dean. "She crawls just like her mom. Want to see?"

Dean shook his head. "Stop screwing around."

"Oh, I think this is important. I think you're going to tell me why you're really here on this moon, why Limbus is here."

"Why are you messing around with the kid?" Dean demanded. "It's *us* talking here."

"Hold him," Donaldo instructed his companion.

Jake took Dean around the midsection. His slender arms were far stronger than they appeared. Dean tried to break free, but it wasn't happening.

Dean grunted and shook his head. "You aren't going to let her go," he said, calling his bluff. "We can just sit out here all damn day, which is pretty long, but I'm not going to tell you a lie. I told you why I'm here."

Donaldo laughed. "You ain't heard the deal, Fulsome. See, this kid... she's going to crawl. That's what she does."

He gently took his hands away from the baby, who started off at once toward the edge of the pool.

"You tell me and Jake will let you go. Doesn't matter to me. April might get a bit cranky over this, but she's a slut, not a mother."

The baby increased her crawling pace. It was only a yard away from the pool.

"You aren't going to let the kid drown," said Dean. His heart thundered.

"Oh, why?" Donaldo said with a goofy grin. "Because I'm better than that? Because under this is a heart of gold? You'll have to ask all the people I've killed why they didn't happen to get that side of me."

"Bullshit."

"This is awesome," Jake whispered behind Dean.

Donaldo nodded. "Hell yeah," he said and turned around to watch the baby venturing closer.

"Are you through?" Dean asked. "This is stupid. I told you why I'm here."

The baby was within a few feet of the pool's edge.

"Wow, Fulsome, you're one stubborn bastard."

"Look—can you just pick the baby up? Let's talk."

"We are talking—whoa, I think it's about time to go over!"

The baby placed her hand on the tiled edge.

"Get her, you bastard!" Dean screamed.

"No, you get her," said Donaldo, "after you tell me."

"Christ!" Dean squirmed and Jake guffawed.

The baby let out a sound as it pitched over the side, followed by a silent splash.

"The Moon City Killer!" Dean yelled.

Jake let go of him and Dean plowed over to the pool. Not ever learning how to dive, he belly-flopped into the water and furiously swam down to the child. He took hold of her wiggling form and made quickly for the surface. Thankfully, he heard her coughing as they emerged. Donaldo reached forward and took her. "You're fine," he muttered and gave her a few slaps on the back. He eyed the baby closely like a damaged wrist watch. "Yeah, fine."

Dean dragged his body out of the pool.

"You did good, Fulsome." Donaldo cackled.

Dean glared at him as he shook his drenched sleeves and pants off.

"Jake, go see what's taking the chick so long." Donaldo gently put the coughing baby back in the crib. His companion hurried off with a childish spring in his step. After he disappeared through the casino doors, Donaldo closed in on Dean. "Your secret's safe, Fulsome."

"How's that?"

"I work for Limbus too."

"You *what*?"

"Keep it down dumbass," Donaldo cautioned. "I'm a plant here. You weren't supposed to come, but now that you're here, you have to know. The Lady's gotten suspicious of me. I had to give her something on the video feed that looked like her brand of thuggishness. She don't let outsiders in that easy, and if I brought you in cold, she'd not give you shit and she'd probably give me a harder look. Then we're both screwed. Understand?"

Dean tried to push down his loathing for the man with this new information, but it was difficult. "What about Jake?"

"Jake's a Sythe Android. I built him myself. He only speaks the words I give him to speak."

That explained the thin man's strength. "You couldn't have thought of something else? That was pretty shitty."

"Well, April and the baby are my androids too."

"You're a fucker."

"I can live with that." Donaldo slapped a big hand on his shoulder and pushed him to the door. "We got to keep up the look, you know."

"Was killing that tech at the transport station keeping up the look?" Dean asked.

"That wasn't me. That was one the mayor's crew. Didn't even know that was going down. He's not a decent guy, Dean."

"And the Firecracker Lady, what's she?"

"A piece of work," said Donaldo, "that's what she is. Just you wait and see. I'm going to get you in to her."

"How can I keep my mission a secret now? I've blabbed it over her surveillance."

"There's no audio around the pool area," Donaldo explained. "But once we step inside though, you're gonna be you and I'm gonna be the guy who almost let a baby drown."

April was on the other side of the door with two drinks in hand and Jake at her side. "What's going on?" she asked.

"The baby needs you," Donaldo said. He reached forward and squeezed her breast, making a *honk honk* noise.

Jake laughed like a mental patient.

The android woman named April glared at them both and Dean joined her.

"What?" Donaldo said to Dean, feigning shock. "I make my chickbots feisty."

* * *

Not in his entire life had Dean ever rode so long in an elevator. After a few minutes he was on the verge of asking Donaldo if it was broken, because he sensed no upward motion. This was a special elevator located behind the blackjack tables near the public restrooms, tucked in a secluded corner. Donaldo had used his keycard again to open it. So there were no other floors, just the top one, and in the elevator, the button only had the not-so-subtle thin drawing of a stick of dynamite on it. Maybe it was supposed to look like a firecracker, but it looked more lethal, and that made sense for everything he'd heard about this woman.

"We're almost there," said Donaldo. He folded his arms behind his back. "So tell me, what's up with Earth? I haven't been there in three years. Did that one jackass get elected? In the US?"

"Probably," replied Dean.

"Can't say that I miss it. I'm able to work with my robotics here and I'm valuable. I don't think I'd be that valuable back there."

"You'd be surprised." Dean stood there a moment longer, still dripping wet from the pool and his mouth hanging open. "How high does this friggin' thing go?"

"Four hundred and sixty-seven floors."

"I can't believe you with that robot baby thing."

"Hey, you don't know the half of it when it comes to me and robotics."

"I wasn't giving you kudos for your androids—"

"No worries. I deal with ignorant folk all the time."

Dean scratched his beard stubble with his middle finger.

Donaldo continued, "So I got to tell you something about the lady. Okay, Fulsome? You listening?"

"Nothing better to do. This elevator seems to be stuck on infinity."

Donaldo studied him for a moment as though unsure whether to process this as an insult or not. At last, he relented and turned to face Dean. His expression was the most serious he'd ever given Dean. "There are a couple things you should know before going to talk to her, especially since she knows you're the Slaughter Man."

This was so exhausting and pointless. So many grand egos involved. Dean hated that sort of thing. He tried to wring more water out of his shirt. "What are these things?"

"Don't mention her hair. Ever. Not ever. It's pretty. It's red in a completely different way than you'd ever expect. It's weird. It kind of--

no, shit, it does... turn on most people born with male parts--- but just leave it alone. Period. It's not a point of discussion."

"I'm insanely in love right now. You're not giving me anything I can't handle," Dean replied. "What else?"

"Be careful with your questions. She likes to do the asking."

"But wait... I have to ask about the surveillance. I need to ask about that."

"Don't phrase it like a question."

"That's silly."

"Tell that to the twenty Grettish Friars she's got posted around the room." Donaldo grunted. "Take my word for it. Less questions or no questions is better. Let her ask and you answer. You'll find that works best."

"Don't mention the hair and no questions."

"You got it."

"What happens if I do? She going to sic the Friars on me?"

"Something like that."

The doors to the elevator opened and Dean groaned, "Finally!"

"Hush up, man," Donaldo warned, immediately becoming more fragile than the man Dean had met at the pool.

"What? She doesn't like loud voices either?" Dean walked out onto a marble dais. "I'm beginning to think this Firecracker Lady has a touch of the bitchy."

"More than a touch," said a voice from across the room. The woman, in her early thirties, stood behind a counter of different bottles of liquor. Her face and body were in shadow. Several locks of her hair poked out into the light like radiant red razor blades, but otherwise only her moving hands could be seen. She was crafting a drink in a two-foot-tall fluted glass. There were layers of purple, blue, and red, but that wasn't the end. She was adding a thin layer of honey-colored liquor to the top. "So Morse told me about the pool downstairs. Don seemed to be having a bit of fun with you."

"He was," Dean answered.

"*Daisey duckle doo.*"

Dean squinted and shook his head, "What does tha—?"

Donaldo jabbed him in the ribs and he went silent, cutting his question off.

The Firecracker Lady sniffed. It sounded impatient. It sounded bored by their presence. "It's Fanglion for *The dumber dumb ass loses.*"

With a sniff of his own, Dean shrugged. "If you say so."

She took a deep drink from the tall glass, nearly emptying half of it. With a sigh, she set it down and came around the bar. "All vitamin and protein solutions, if you must know. I'm not into poisoning myself."

She stepped into the light. Her hair was in a smart, short, business fashion, a shade of red Dean had never seen before. It was like copper alight with a neon chemical fire, yet it looked too natural to be dyed. Dean was stunned. It wasn't even red... It was a brand new color his eyes were seeing for the first time. He immediately felt his body tense. He could understand why others found her irresistible, just for those spilling pieces of fire about her face, but Dean's heart belonged at the other end of the universe.

"How did you get—?"

Another jab from Donaldo silenced him.

The Firecracker Lady pulled over a chair from a small bistro table, turned it backward and straddled it. Even though she was dressed in a black business suit, it was apparent from its fit she was in extremely good shape. She didn't allow herself to be ogled, however; there was a regality to her that would not be denied, and her deep gray eyes were especially haunting and powerfully affecting anywhere they aimed.

Her lipstick was glossy black and it seemed to fit every word she uttered. "You're leaking water all over my damn floor."

Dean looked down at his clothes. "Yeah, well, that wasn't really how I'd planned this meeting to go."

"Yeah, you were put through the ringer. Look, I've got about a billion calls, texts, emails, and shitograms to answer, so can you tell me why you've chosen to show up here? I don't work with Limbus, you know. Never directly anyway."

Dean tried to suppress his shock that she also knew his affiliation. "I wanted to see if we could make an arrangement. I need access to surveillance from a few taverns in the lower district. It's for marketing purposes."

"Like hell it is."

"I have no reason to lie."

The Firecracker Lady laughed, but it sounded angry. Her eyes held him fiercely like a prey-hunting hawk. "I'm not some stupid broad who nods at something just because a man said it was so."

"You don't know much about me, but if you did, you'd know I'm not a charmer. I'm not cunning. I'm not trying to pull one over on you. I just need what I need, and I hope we can make a deal."

"A deal?"

"Yes."

She leaned back, amusement flickering in her steely eyes. "That sounds great, said the woman who has every goddamn thing she could ever dream of."

"Everybody has something they want and can't have."

"Not me."

Dean seethed. He was tired of people messing around with him. He glanced to the shadowy recesses of the far walls. The Grettish Friars huddled there, gray eyes glowing with silent anticipation. He looked back to the Firecracker Lady. Her body language suggested she was through, that she wouldn't entertain anything he would say. But he had to keep her. He had to see that Killer on those video feeds.

"You're wasting my time," she said, smacking both of her lips with a crisp resonance in the room. "I don't need to give you access to anything." She stood and shoved the chair away from her. "I've got to get going. This was nice."

"Wait." Dean straightened and cleared his throat and his toes curled inside his wet shoes. "Where'd you get that red hair from?"

Donaldo gasped and stepped back toward the elevator.

The woman slowly turned, eyes slits and face almost as red as her hair. "What did you... say?"

"No, I didn't say anything. I *asked*," Dean reminded her. "Where'd you get that red hair from? Did your mom mate with a radioactive clown? I mean I'm sure some people are into that sort of thing, but it must be hard with all the good samaritans dousing your head with buckets of water all the time."

Donaldo tried the door, but it was apparently locked. "Shit..." he muttered.

Dean locked eyes with the woman. She was actually very attractive, not at all clown like, and her perfectly straight, unusual fiery hair was one thousand shades of beautiful, but he knew exactly why she didn't like it mentioned. The Firecracker Lady wasn't an object. She was a presence. A force. And he picked up quickly that she'd rather see a man dead than have him comment on her most striking features. She didn't have time for sexist bullshit.

That said, she looked pretty damned offended, even if she hadn't called her Grettish Friars out of the shadows just yet.

"Well, will you look at that," she said with a twinkle in her savage stony eyes. "I see you needed my attention and you got it. Amazing. You've gone and amused me for a second, Dean."

"Aim to please," he replied.

"Fulsome, will you shut the hell up! I don't want to die, you bastard!" Donaldo throttled the door knob.

"Calm down, meatloaf face," the Firecracker Lady demanded.

Donaldo's hand fell away from the door and he went as silent and still as a statue.

The woman walked down and stood before Dean. He was several heads taller than she was, but her gaze held him like a vice. She made a circuit around him and hummed. "I deconstruct everybody I make a deal with, Slaughter Man."

Dean's head cocked in surprise and her silken black lips parted into a grin. "I know who you are. I know you worked as a sticker at a slaughterhouse on Earth, in a city called Corona, California. Your job was to shove a knife into the throat of range animals all day long. Is that right?"

"Something like that."

"Then you were fired for something unfair. *Boo hoo.* And Limbus found a contract for you with the Princess of Ganymede, which led to an attempt on your life. Namely, her trying to eat you, and then you incapacitating her with poison. You did me and the universe a pretty big favor with that little trick."

"You're welcome."

"Still," she mused, taking another walk around him, sizing him up, "you were probably more suited to continue working in a factory. You're a director of a large program in an organization that spans the multiverses. It's making that bald spot on the back of your head widen."

Absently, Dean stroked the back of his head. He maintained it was a cowlick.

She went on with a knowing onyx twist to her full lips. "I read all about your tenure at Limpdicks, Incorporated. Saying you're a fish out of water is an insult to the fish's ability to flop around. You are miserably lost. You have no delegation skills, you let subordinates and superiors equally walk all over you, *and* if something strikes your sense of duty, you foolishly obligate yourself to it as though there were such a thing as real friends in this life. Yes, I have a tendency to over-research my audience."

Dean opened his mouth and she silenced him by raising a manicured fingernail.

"Face it, Slaughter Man. You want something simpler for your life. You don't want interstellar travel and galactic politics and hunting down surveillance footage from a wild redhead on some distant moon—you want peace, and maybe you want a woman back on your planet or some other. Whatever it is, you don't want this. You're a decent, hardworking, loyal man who doesn't needs frills. You need a warm home, you need love, and you need to protect it. That simplicity, for many people, is wondrous, even beautiful."

Dean smirked. "But not for you, I wager."

"You wager right." She came around and faced him. She folded her arms under her breasts and stared at him a few moments before going on. "No, nothing about you is appealing to me. Powerful, ambitious men with money and staggering intelligence are the type who soak my drawers. You? You aren't even fun to look at."

"I didn't come to ask you out."

"That's where you messed up," she observed. "With me, a little more charm would have gone a long way."

"Well," he said with a long sigh. "Then I'm totally screwed, because I'm about as charming as a tongueless dog drinking out of a mud puddle."

She tittered and brought a hand to her mouth. Then she erupted robustly in laughter.

"With a face that could stop a clock," Dean added.

The Firecracker Lady had a laughing fit for a couple of minutes. Dean and Donaldo nervously joined along. As her chuckles tapered off, she wiped some tears from her eyes. "Okay, Fulsome, okay. You're not half bad. Guess I judged you too quick."

"I'm used to it."

She sniffed and her eyes went dead. "Still, my boys are going to need to carpet the floor with your blood and bones. Kill him!" She snapped her fingers rhythmically three times.

Burning, gray jack-o'-lantern eyes cut through the dark recesses of the surrounding walls as the large forms emerged, their burnt trench coats sweeping across the tile floor like roaming soot, their fedoras just concealing their gruesome faces with enough shadow to make their flesh indistinguishable. There were ten Friars on each side, and all of them hefted a large scimitar that raced with micro-cosmoses and swirling stars. The torches fed off the surfaces of the galaxy glass and blotted out the dark wielders. It all looked like pieces of a fantastic stained glass window converging to the center of the room.

Donaldo cursed under his breath and began fighting with the door again.

"Sorry, guys," said the Firecracker Lady, heading back up the stairs to her desk. "This was good times."

"How much is she paying you?" Donaldo yelled at the Friars. "I have bots and androids that are one of a kind. Priceless. Give me a pass and I'll bring them."

The Friars moved forward, undeterred.

Dean thought for a moment. Bribing them wasn't a bad idea. The Grettish were a selfish species. There was even a saying, "Don't Grettish the baby," which essentially warned against being extremely selfish as it related to the Grettish practice of selling their children as food to withhold invasion for the Princess of Ganymede.

It was likely these Friars were being paid far better by the Firecracker Lady than they ever could by Donaldo, expensive robots included. There was something that moved selfish beings even more than money, though.

Their lives.

The Friars lifted their weapons high, a bunch of ridiculously oversized demonic baseball players stepping up to the plate. Donaldo plastered himself against a wall, a form of defense that would not go the distance. The Friars smelled like rust and burnt leaves and roasting flowers. Dean stood up straight and cleared his voice.

"I wouldn't strike me with one of those," he warned.

They didn't lose a step and continued toward him.

"That's galaxy glass and I've only yesterday come through a membrane transport."

A snap of the Firecracker Lady's fingers halted the Friars. She regarded Dean through thin eyes. "So what?"

Dean cleared his throat and said an inward prayer to any deity that would listen. "There have been many recorded instances, a high percentage from what I hear, where someone using one of those swords ends up erasing themselves from all universes, rather than the other way around."

She licked her blackened lips with delicate amusement. "Because you've come through a membrane transport recently?"

"Correct."

"And why is that?" The Firecracker Lady looked impatient and annoyed. Her hand lifted again to snap.

"It takes a few Earth weeks for a body to regain all its original structure. Some of my molecules are still catching up to me as we speak. If you split me down the center with one of those things, it will cause a rift, and one of you"—he looked to the Friars—"will likely be pulled through it and wiped off all panes of time."

All the Grettish Friars turned to look at the Firecracker Lady. Some of them lowered their scimitars. She snorted. "Where did you learn this?"

Dean shrugged. "In a galaxy glass seminar for poor, dumb, ugly, blue collar assholes."

She once again exploded with laughter and nodded. "Very good, yes. Okay. You have my ear for a little longer."

The Friars had already begun to retreat to their positions at the wall, not needing any commands to get them moving.

Donaldo started giggling too. The Firecracker Lady stopped abruptly. "*You* haven't been through a transport lately though." Her eyes moved from the Friars to Donaldo. The Grettish warriors turned their boiling gray gazes on him.

Donaldo's laughter trailed off and he bowed his head.

The vibrant redhead returned to her desk. "Enough playtime. Tell me what it is you want with my video feeds, Slaughter Man."

Dean knew lying to her would bite him in the ass. Now or later. He had to be straight.

"I'm investigating the Moon City Killer."

She plopped down behind her desk. "That so? Seems an odd mission for someone… with your attributes."

"I agree completely, but it all pays the same. Limbus can't get another contract here right away and time is crucial for the Deitiis."

"Indeed. And you think you'll find this killer by reviewing my surveillance?"

"I do. For a fact."

"Well, my boyfriend is kinda content on having the Deitii population thinned. It's not in my better interests to have that stop. It keeps him and his idiot association happy." She folded her slender hands. "I like him happy. He's better in bed when he's happy."

"That seems to be reason enough to let the oldest species in the universe go extinct."

"Once again," she said, shaking her head, "that sense of duty."

"It's also what I'm being paid for."

"That's a better point." The Firecracker Lady picked up a mini muffin off a plate on her desk. She popped the whole thing into her mouth and chewed for a while. "Sorry," she said through chews. "Hungry as hell today."

"No worries."

"So." She dusted her hands off. "I'm a betting woman and I don't think if I strike a deal with you it will end up mattering anyway. From the reports I've heard about the Killer, you will not be long for this world, Mr. Slaughter Man. That's unfortunate because I could have grown to like you."

"Shucks."

"Bring me a mason jar of crocoshark venom and I'll give you full access to all feeds for a full day's review."

"Crocoshark?" asked Donaldo, throwing his arms up in disbelief. "You might as well just have those Friars chop us up right now."

"He'll be fine." She made a thin smile.

"What's the venom for?"

"A new product. Turns brain diamonds into what they are calling brainrubies or brushfire. I like the second name."

"Sure you do. So I'm off to get you something to refine your drugs?"

"Absolutely."

"How good is this stuff?"

"A drop on a teaspoon of sugar will keep someone high for two full weeks. Our weeks."

"Moon weeks?" Dean felt exhausted, aware once more of how much he'd dosed on Constalife.

"Yes, Slaughter Man, so you Earthers would be sky-high for about *fifty days*. It's a wonderful product, but I don't have the time to dance around naked about it. Head on out. Your friend there can tell you the where and how to find the crocosharks, and how to go about draining their venom."

"I'm sure… See you soon," said Dean.

"I bet," she answered and started to focus on some documents before her. She reached out and pushed a button. The door behind them unlocked.

As they headed out, she called out, "And, Donaldo…"

Warily he turned. "Yes, ma'am?"

"Get the vagina-bot, toy baby, and retardo-droid out of my building. If you bring any of your mechanicals back, it'll be the last thing you do. Nobody sets a foot in here who doesn't answer to me. Human, alien, or machine. You got that, shithead?"

Donaldo nodded and hurried out. "Thank you."

Dean ran after him. "So about this venom—"

"Outside," he said through labored breaths. "I'm not spending another second in this place."

Bounding into the elevator after him, Dean was hardly in the mood to disagree.

Chapter 14

I watched Carl gaze over the bodies of the dead. He didn't appear to be disturbed or even guilty that he'd essentially been the person who facilitated my killing and harvesting of the refugee Deitiis. No, the boy had a question in mind, and from what little I knew of him now, that question would be a practical one.

"So ask," I told him.

Carl's eyes flitted to me and he nodded. "This is going to take a long time to haul them all out to the trailer. Was there a time frame you were looking at? I'm just a kid and all."

"It takes however long it takes. Keep watch on the road. Factory is on mid-shift, so nobody should come down here. But we aren't taking chances. You make certain you're alone every time you make the trip from the front door to the trailer. You got that?"

"Sure."

"I shouldn't be long."

"I thought you hated your mother."

"That's right," I told him.

"So why go to the diner? It can't be about the pregnancy pictures, right?" He eyed me skeptically. "Those belly photos always just look like black and white smudges anyway."

"It's not the photos themselves," I explained, pulling on my coat.

"You're just in love with the subject matter?"

I regarded the boy with a measure of admiration. "Yes, that was my son, and in all other realities, he and I are together. I've seen it at times. He loves me. I love him. We protect each other. But I will never know that love. These photos are all I will have of him in this life, in this reality."

"Even as God?"

"Even so," I concurred.

"There's more to this though, isn't there?"

"You're too smart for your age," I said to him, "and you're right. The photos, while cherished, I could ultimately live without. It's the fact my mother has ownership of them right now. That bothers me. After thinking about it for a while, the matter bothers me *greatly*."

"So this won't be a long meeting with Mama?"

I ignored his joke and shook my head. With a beleaguered sigh, I stepped over the pile of glass shards from the painting that had smashed on the ground.

"You want me to clean that up for you?" Carl asked.

I shrugged and took the knob for the front door.

"Hey!" Carl hunkered down beside the glass remnants and pulled free the painting of the Midnight Sea. "This is great. How much did you pay for it?"

I smiled. "Nothing. Drew it at school, long ago now."

"Oh you're good." Carl admired it.

"I think you're just in love with the subject matter."

"Touché. Joke if you like, but I'm going to live there someday, my friend, someday," he told me, eyes not falling away from the drawing.

"It's yours," I said.

"I appreciate it." Carl gave me a grin that suggested he'd known it would be his the second he laid eyes on it. "I'll hang it across my bed."

We both looked at the drawing for a moment, then I patted his head and left. I headed for my visit with the walking, talking womb.

* * *

The Passing Sun Diner had to be one of the very few restaurants that would serve all three breakfast levels into the lunch hours. As I walked past the red-and-white leather booths, I spotted a variety of meals that would never appeal to me again. Breakfast staples were normally energy starters like blucoke wheat germ, ruffle grapes, moonflower seeds on lightly buttered hazel bread, or a steaming dollop of grits. Bi-breakfast usually included everybody's first dose of Constalife, and most chose to get their daily dosage out of the way by eating aromatic foods that would drown out the medicinal flavor, like bat-wing soup or fire rice curry. Tri-breakfast was an indulgence meal of pancakes or waffles, fruits, and sugar cheeses since nobody's appetite really kicked in until after forty-two p.m. and then the stomachs shifted to lunch-time items that included non-fatty meats and some dairy.

I hated it all. After tasting the real source of food within a Deitii's mind, I'd never be enticed again by these smells. Nobody would be. It was the difference between drinking mud and strawberry champagne. The ignorance was not endearing; it was downright revolting. I didn't envy the old men merrily shoveling hazel bread past their greasy lips, or the prim and proper ladies daring to have their bat-wing soup so late in the day. They were sorry sacks of useless life. They all qualified for inclusion in the category of pestilence and vermin.

And she who especially qualified was the sullen woman at the end of the rows of tables with her stack of half-eaten sugar cheeses and coconut waffles. That was the same thing she always ate for lunch. Nothing had changed at all. Looking at her made me ill, and I almost turned away. She hadn't spotted me yet. She stared off toward the kitchen, dejection in her eyes. I had the opportunity to read her thoughts, but I kept this meeting…human… and kept moving steadily forward, that folder slipped under her waffle plate my only guiding force. My eyes moved through the plate and layers of folder and I saw the image. It was indeed a 3D sonogram. My unborn son. My boy. How could she have kept this from me so long?

I tasted blood as I stood before the table. Gently, I pulled my teeth from my stinging lower lip, lest I bite straight through it.

"You have something for me," I told her.

She jumped, startled by my silent approach. I could see the long Moon City years around her eyes, but she hadn't aged poorly. I always assumed she would, with the brain diamonds and the

Fanglion vodka cocktails, and all the countless trysts she got herself into with strange men, both human and alien. I thought she'd finish the job for me before too long, but she'd gone and cleaned herself up. That sort of pissed me off even more than her keeping the photos from me.

Her pale lips hooked in a sad smile. "It is great to see you Dev--"

"He doesn't exist anymore."

She snorted in disbelief, and then straightened seriously, trying not to lose me. "That's fine. What do you call yourself now?"

"Busy," I answered. "Hand over my property. I will leave. You can finish lunch."

"I thought we might talk for a bit."

"Well you've never been great at thinking. I'm not surprised."

"You look really good," she said, sizing me up. "Vibrant. Your skin. Your body. You must be doing manual labor to be in such fine shape."

"Hand over the photos of my son. They don't belong to you."

"I paid for them. He is my grandson."

"Was," I corrected and felt a jab in my own heart that reflected in her green eyes.

I took a coin from my front pocket and thumbed it onto the table. She watched it vibrate slowly to a stop to rest silently by her coffee mug. A waitress approached me from behind. I sensed her, and before she could open her mouth, I turned my gaze to her.

"I'm not staying." A little put-off by my abruptness, the waitress nodded and circled back to check on another table.

"I don't want your money," my mother told me, "or need it."

"Yes, you've gotten on a better path. Good for you. So glad it happened after my childhood rather than *during*. Folder now, please."

"Are you going to hate me for your entire life?"

"Yes," I replied.

"Why won't you give me another chance?" Tears lifted in her eyes. "I love you. You were my baby."

"We both deal with our loss every day. You had a son. I had a son. In all other possible realities, he and I are best friends. This is the only dimension where I mourn him, rather than cherish his friendship. In all other realities, you do the exact same repugnant things throughout my youth, but when I have my son, I learn to love. In this life, in this universe, I don't get that. I have only my hate for you and the emptiness my boy left behind."

She cocked her head. "What are you going on about? Other realities. You sound like a Noggin."

I put a fist on the table and leaned closer to her so we were eye-to-eye. "I see all realities when I turn my eyes to them. I see the chances I could have had that I didn't, and I see every variation and every constant in all my other lives. My hate for you is constant. My love for him is constant. The one thing I cannot have is also the one thing I want more than anything else. I want to be with him. I have the blessing and the curse to understand that through my new powers."

"Powers?" she said with an uncomfortable swallow.

I reached forward and pinched the side of the folder and pulled it free from under her plate. She made no move to stop me. Terror replaced the tears in her eyes. "I'm going to sit on the throne the creator once sat upon. Soon. If you're enjoying your new life, I'd make a point of never *bothering* me again. You aren't my mother. I'm not your son. You are a reformed addict and whore. And I am God reborn."

She turned away from me with a gasp. The tenor of my voice had alarmed her so that she didn't realize her lukewarm coffee had begun to boil, her waffles to steam, and sugar cheese to melt into silken puddles.

"Glad we had this talk," I said softly and pushed up from the table.

With the folder clutched in my hand, I left her there, trembling. That was a perfect last image of her to take with me in eternal life.

Chapter 15

Dean had rephrased the question several times. "Where do I find these crocoshark things? And just exactly what the hell are they?"

Donaldo took another quick sip of some bright-green-and yellow-layered Constalife cocktail he'd gotten at a walk-up bar along Stonebone Drive. It was a busy place, reminding Dean of a New Orleans Bourbon Street populated with a majority of aliens over humans. The big guy was a bit shaken after the Firecracker Lady had outed his robots. He'd muttered several times that she *must be onto me about my Limbus affiliation as well.*

"Are you calmer now?" Dean asked. He checked his phone again. Sandra had texted him something very sweet about missing him. He wanted to read it more thoroughly. He wanted to know she was doing okay and what the company had her working on. If he couldn't get the Golden Transport, maybe he could meet her somewhere half way, if she could get an assignment—he shook the thought away. It would still mean she'd be risking years away from her family. He'd royally screwed up, taking this assignment. Why had he just said yes? Why did he let them roll over him? The Firecracker Lady had pegged him right. He let everybody take advantage of his good nature. He could be a wise ass at times, but when it came down to it, Dean could never really stick up for himself.

"Let me finish my drink and then we can talk," Donaldo told him.

"Sure," he replied. *What? What did you just say? Idiot?* "No," he said firmly. "I've already waited here, watching you sip that damn thing. We talk now."

"Okay, tough guy." Donaldo turned around from his drink, leaning on the crowded bar. "You're going to take a road just east of here called Riddleworth. Follow it away from the main cavern entrance. It's the farthest place in the main cavern system you can go, and the darkest, so bring light with you. There are swamps there. Man made. They hauled the water there from the Midnight Sea, originally to make shadowfish farms. They tried to create an entire ecosystem there but the crocosharks, buzztoads, and wolf bats were the only things that thrived."

"Sounds beautiful."

"Crocosharks carry pouches of venom under their jaws, whereby it can be withdrawn from holes in their teeth or by squeezing an utter on the pouch."

Dean snorted. "It has cow parts too?"

"I've never seen one of these things. I'm just going by what I heard. The venom serves two purposes, being actual milk for their young and a fatal venom to their prey. To humans in small doses, it's more like a narcotic. You get bit really good, though, and you'll overdose in less than ten minutes."

"Are there a lot of these creatures out there?" asked Dean.

"Nobody can really say. It's tough to get them to come out of the water because they gorge themselves on the buzztoads, which reproduce like rabbits on Viagra. There's no need to come to the surface most of the time."

"That's not going to make it easy."

"Use the rotten method."

"Explain."

"Go to the swamp after first dinner, when they're more active. Before you go, find some really bad-smelling, rotting food... It doesn't have to be much... and set it out on the shore. The crocosharks can smell better under water than a bloodhound on a breezy day. They love rotting food more than they love buzztoads. You'll see a bunch of warning signs around the swamps not to picnic in the area just for that reason."

"You're sure that'll work?"

Donaldo shrugged and took a swig from his cup that ended his cocktail. "Like I said, I'm sharing stories. Shit, I don't even know how you're going to slow one of them down long enough to squeeze out the venom. If you kill one even, I heard the venom degrades after a few minutes, starts instantly losing potency because the milk floods with other secretions to prepare for decomposition."

"I gotta milk the venom while they're alive?"

Another shrug. "Firecracker Lady doesn't mean to ever see you again." Donaldo clapped him on the shoulder. "Sucks to be you, Fulsome."

"Thanks."

"I do have some good news." Donaldo read something on his cell phone and nodded. "Yep, they're both back, and waiting."

"Who?"

"Your support. Tasha said you needed help with the Moon City Killer. I've got two individuals who I think you'll greatly appreciate — well, if you survive the crocoshark."

"Well, what are we waiting for? These people can help me in the swamp."

Donaldo shook his head. "No, they won't."

"Well, what the hell kind of support are they?"

"The best kind for killing, but they won't engage anyone unless it's the Moon City Killer or somebody getting in their way. That's how they were programmed, and by law, they have to be programmed that way."

"More robots?"

"They're SL-SHRs. Not just any type of robot, Dean."

Dean's chest went cold. "Where the hell did you get two Slasherbots? Limbus could buy this entire squad of mercenaries for just one."

"I helped develop them for the Fanglion. These two belong to me, and since Limbus got me the job with the Fanglion government, I allow them to be used in campaigns from time to time. For a price of course, and the fact Limbus has kept me out of a large Grettish criminal law suit I won't go into."

Dean threw up his hands. "You really can't get them to help me in the swamp? Really?"

Donaldo smirked. "Do you really want to start introducing variable targets to an artificial intelligence that operates like a contracted serial killer? If these safeguards weren't in place, you'd have my two robots out there doing far more damage than the Moon City Killer. He's after the Deitii. They would be after *everybody*."

"Well, maybe I don't need the Firecracker Lady's deal then. If the SL-SHRs can hunt the killer down, stalk, and terminate him, why should I even risk this trip?"

"You have to point them to something, Dean. They need a face. A smell. A name. They need more than you have right now. If you get those surveillance feeds, they'll be able to start their campaign for you. Trust me. They will come in handy."

Dean sighed and shook his head. "I just want a damn break already."

"Look, you've got time before first dinner. Come to my workshop. It's a few miles from here. I need to get you imprinted on SL-SHRs safety protocol system, anyway. In case you somehow get the clever idea of getting in their way of taking down the Moon City Killer, we wouldn't want you ending up in a pile of body parts."

"That would suck," Dean admitted.

"Great," Donaldo said with a smile and began up the crowded sidewalk. "I'll show you the way to my pride and joy. You're going to get a kick out of these two. You really will."

"I'm sure."

Dean followed him. His cell phone burned a hole in his pocket the entire walk. He really wanted to reach out to Sandra, but he needed to keep his eyes on Donaldo in the mass of aliens and human Moon City inhabitants.

* * *

Dean had seen an SL-SHR robot one other time in a pirate outpost on Mars. He'd only seen it from a distance, but recalled being surprised. He was expecting the Terminator, but the one he'd seen looked more like the robot from that 80s movie *Short Circuit*. When he'd joked as much to a younger logistics guy, he just stared at him with vacant eyes. "You know? Johnny-five?"

The vacancy grew. Dean had almost suggested one of the robots from the Black Hole as an alternative, but the guy clearly wouldn't get that reference either.

Donaldo's robots were far more intimidating looking, however, and for strikingly different reasons. They both were more representative of the original model of design that the Fanglions had been trying to replicate. They loved human horror movies. They loved them maybe more than the Zetú loved Lady Gaga. They even adopted Halloween as a national holiday, but it was more in celebration of the John Carpenter film than the pagan fall festival it originated from.

It was obvious Donaldo also had a thing for those types of movies because in his workshop there were posters of Carpenter's *The Thing*, King's *Carrie*, and Barker's *Hellraiser*.

It was no wonder that the tallest, most powerful of the two robots had been named Jazon Meyers. "Jason with a Z," Donaldo had told him rather fondly, as though programming the most complex AI system for a robot in the universe was less impressive than unnecessary phonetic spellings.

Jazon stood around six feet eight inches tall by Dean's estimation. The face was a round silver plate with holes in it and a grand two-foot-high red Mohawk sprouting from the top. The neck was a series of rods, not unlike the Terminator, much to Dean's satisfaction. The body was where the nods to movies ended, however. The chest was a triangular shield with reinforced blacktek armor bands running down to the hip area where some powerful, almost human-looking legs extended and sunk into a pair of hellish, black iron boots. The metallic muscle fibers of the legs, a substance called widowsilk, also composed the arms, all the way down to the elbows where they turned into machetes.

Dean knew a lot about widowsilk and galaxy glass. That's actually why he'd been on that Mars outpost, overseeing a shipment of both of the expensive, highly dangerous materials that had been stolen back from Grettish pirate groups. He'd seen the strength that could be employed by muscle groups formed of the widowsilk substance: entire block walls taken down by a punch delivered from an infant-sized robot. The fact that Jason with a Z had arms the size of a professional wrestler and machetes for hands made Dean feel like he was standing near a great white shark who hadn't noticed him yet.

Donaldo patted Jazon Meyers' pointed shoulder gently and went to a keypad on his messy work counter. "One hundred and ninety-seven kills over only a year of run time. Not too shabby, right?"

"Not at all," answered Dean and looked at the holes in the steel mask, wondering if the thing was watching him or not. "Tell me again how these things are controlled?"

"Functional directives," said Donaldo, typing. He checked his watch and silently cursed. "Shit, I need to get back to the mayor soon."

"You wear many hats," Dean said. "Who *don't* you work for?"

"I only work for one dude, and that's myself."

"What did you mean by functional directives?"

"God, really, I gotta explain?"

"You said I had time," Dean told him. "And I'd rather keep myself busy then stare at these things..."

The second robot was shorter than Jazon, but far more unsettling. Dean didn't even want to really take it in yet, since the larger robot stood only feet away from him.

"They are incapable of malfunctioning on their masters. The idea had been to ramp up the fear of all the marks, since traditional assassin robots could eventually be hacked and their AIs broken down and exploited. SL-SHRs have constant development of artificial psychoses that are all snowflake-unique. In other words, they cannot be hacked because their minds cannot be broken down. It would be like trying to translate a surrealist painting into plain English. They cannot be understood because their minds devolve and evolve rapidly with both staggering genius and staggering psychopathy. The one thing that remains firm in their programming, that is safeguarded in such a way that can never be undone, is their main directive to kill a single target at all costs."

"How can you tame something with a crazy mind?" Dean asked,

"Incentive. Pure, deep, beautiful incentive. Ask a drug addict to go out and do something painful to get a Santa-sized sack of their drug of choice and they will. The SL-SHRs are no different. They have pleasure receptors that activate during a murder, and the receptors fire even higher when the act is done in an unconventional manner. We give them the freedom to kill the target exactly as they please and it releases a torrent of reward center impulses throughout their bodies."

"Why do robots need an incentive?"

"These ones do," Donaldo put simply. "If you strip them of their psychoses, they become like any other artificial intelligence, which is easy to break down, but if you leave their minds to fester, the only thing that you can do to convince them to leave on a mission is the orgasm they get from an unconventional kill."

"Sick."

"They are effective."

"Yes, I've heard that." Dean stared at Jazon and swallowed. "Does it talk?"

"No," Donaldo replied. "And Mr. Loveman only whispers."

Dean's eyes moved to the other robot for the first time. He really wanted to leave now. There was something very hollow and unnerving in the mechanical thing. If Jazon Meyers felt like a wild animal a breath away from rampage, the other robot, this Mr. Loveman, felt off... like a demon in casual clothes, like the end of a nightmare that brings you awake, like a scream in the flesh.

And he did appear to be flesh. He wasn't metallic like Jazon. The flesh was a bright, translucent white though that was obviously a cover material for more widowsilk appendages beneath.

Dean found himself looking away before meeting eyes with the robot. "Aren't you afraid they'll go and kill you in your sleep?"

"Me?" asked Donaldo. "Never. The one directive they really can't misinterpret is to kill their master. They are programmed to be selfish, and if I die without instructions about their new master, they are ordered to employ suicide."

"And for people they help?"

"That's what I'm working on," said Donaldo with a few more taps of the keypad. "We have to imprint you into each of their systems. That way, they can't misinterpret you ever getting in the way of their mission. We've run into problems in the past with that. The SL-SHRs love to find loopholes in their programming so they can justify a new murder."

"Fantastic."

"They're cool. You're going to enjoy working with them."

"Why is that one called Mr. Loveman? I get the other name, but why that?"

"He named himself."

"How's that?"

"Beats me," said Donaldo. "I wanted to call him Chucky Kruger. I've never had an AI refuse to take one of my names. Even those with more freedom tend to give their name a low priority. Not Loveman. Within the first few hours after his awareness came online, he told me he only wanted a last name and it would be Loveman."

Dean examined the robot closer, still avoiding the eyes. A purple polo shirt. Baggy khaki pants with a hempen belt. Black flip-flops. Dean's eyes paused at the feet. They were astonishingly real. Mr. Loveman was humanoid in form, but the skin of his arms and face were obviously synthetic material, just not the feet.

"Oh, you noticed, huh?" Donaldo stopped punching at the keys for a moment. "He's a pushy son of a bitch. He pretty much extorted me for that upgrade. I'm just glad he only wanted it done on his feet. I guess the synth feet didn't look quite right in flip flops, the crazy bastard."

"Is that... real human skin?"

"Shit, I wish. Getting some borg-meat grown is cheap these days. That flesh's DNA-optimized *homo sapien superiorous*. He liked the sheen of their skin better than us Earth monkeys."

The Uber Human species was one Dean had never come across. They were nearly immortal, could heal from most injuries at impossibly fast rates, and averaged nine feet tall in height. "So how'd the robot get you to ante up for that upgrade?"

Dean finally lifted his eyes to Mr. Loveman's. They were two glossy, ink-black stars. His mouth was a single, straight line cut across the expanse of shimmering pale skin.

"He threatened to kill Jazon Meyers if I didn't upgrade him. He got around the main single-target directive by deducing that Jazon is not a citizen of any planetary region. I've since had to change the directive across all platforms to include damage and destruction of private property, so this won't happen again. All other star systems took the free update for their SL-SHRs. Loveman anticipated I'd do this, so he encrypted his property directives, and therefore remains the only type of these AIs in the universe that can kill other robots by choice. There's nothing I can do about that."

"How many kills do you have?" Dean hazarded to ask the robot.

A low, rattling whisper escaped the thin, straight mouth. "Seventy-eight over two years and seven months."

"So not as prolific as Jazon here."

"No," answered the robot.

Donaldo was furiously typing and moving code objects around on his display. "Loveman's a quality-over-quantity type, aren't you, Mr. Loveman?"

"Yes."

"I get the feeling he's not being completely forthcoming with that number, but yeah, he's killed some A-list aliens and humans alike, all types of interstellar celebrities, well-known drug kingpins, presidents of star systems, and the entire thirty seats in the Fanglion parliament. Jazon has some big-name kills as well, but his numbers are high because of private citizens he's interpreted as standing in his way."

Dean looked back at Jazon Meyers. He'd much rather work with the taller robot, which seemed more like a powerful tool to be used, instead of a demon let out of its box.

"Come on up, Fulsome. I need your handprint."

Doing as he was told, Dean walked up to the workbench and put his hand on the reader glass near Donaldo's console. The laser underneath scanned quickly from red to green. Donaldo typed a few other things and then clapped his meaty hands together. "Success, you are white-listed. Neither of these robots can ever harm you, even if you are directly in their path of the Moon City Killer."

"You sure?"

"I'm sure. These directives are outside their personality drives. Think of them as logical beings with a contained ball of crazy in their center."

"You're very reassuring," said Dean.

A breathy whisper with no air behind it penetrated Dean's right ear. *"Buy Sandra flowers."*

Dean jumped back and put his hand on his weapon. Mr. Loveman had snuck up behind him without a single sound. Those blank star eyes regarded him below a mop of short, jet-black hair parted on the side.

"What did you say about Sandra?" he demanded. "How did y--?"

"Oh, don't freak, Fulsome," said Donaldo with a chuckle. He scanned your cell phone. Probably read all your texts. He does that to me all the time."

"Well, tell him not to do it. Goddamn."

"Can't help you there. These things have more freedom than other bots. That's what drives them to be effective."

"You can send the flowers remotely," whispered Mr. Loveman. "Log on to 1800flowers.com or another website."

Dean gasped. "Donaldo, what the hell is this thing talking about?"

"You wronged her, Dean Fulsome," Mr. Loveman went on, interlacing his hands together at his stomach. "You left her alone to come to Moon City. She may never see you again. You should send her flowers through a delivery service."

"Knock it off, Love," Donaldo said, getting out of his seat with an exhausted grunt. He patted Dean on the arm. "Follow me. It seems you've had enough of our friends here."

"No shit," Dean agreed. With one more passing glance at the unmoving robot, he followed Donaldo out of the work area to the back. The big man sidled up to a trash can and observed the contents.

"This should do you fine."

"What now?"

"You got a date with a crocoshark, remember? This will help bring one up to the shore. Got to pay those bills."

"I should have stayed working in slaughterhouses."

Donaldo hoisted up a beige trash bag, the funk immediately wafting off of it. "Hey I forgot about that. You should share that with Loveman, he'd love to hear about it."

"I'll pass," said Dean, taking the revolting bag. "How long should I wait for these things?"

"Oh, I have a Mason jar back in the shop," Donaldo replied absently. "I'll go grab it for you."

"Don," Dean said with a sigh, "how long?"

"Oh, you'll know if it works almost right away. Crocosharks have a keen sense of smell. Everything I've been told, they'll begin emerging within minutes of the bag being dumped on the shore."

Later, miles away in a dark, frightening swamp with only the light of a single lantern and his cell phone, Dean would remember being told this, and he would look down at the pile of trash he'd dumped along the shoreline, kick some of its contents around again to hopefully dredge up a smell, check the time again, and silently curse at all the *No Picnicking* signs posted on the nearby boulders.

An hour had gone by, and but for the occasional splash of a buzztoad, the surface of the water had not stirred once. And an hour after that, when Dean left with his empty Mason jar to go back to his apartment, the silent state of the murky swamp remained completely unchanged.

Chapter 16

Dean flopped down on the couch and rested the Mason jar on his knee. He tilted it back and forth, looking through the amber glass idly. He'd tried to call Sandra on his way back from the swamp, but the call was full of static and ultimately was cut short. She'd mentioned something about going out with friends to dinner, but he couldn't make out any other details before the call dropped.

Butterball rested near his feet, purring in a small , coiled ball. Dean took another piece of toilet paper from the roll he'd brought over to the couch and dabbed the corners of his dripping nose. This cat was going to be the death of him before he even found the Moon City Killer.

He'd checked his phone again for more details on the hostage Zetú situation, but the story hadn't developed all that much since he last looked. He hoped that Finny-Min and his brethren had made it outside the warzone, that they weren't taken on that slave ship. If Dean concentrated on it too long, he felt like he might slip into some kind of pathetic despair, and despite never having his parents around to be disappointed in him as a kid, he somehow figured they might have been if he began to curl up into the fetal position next to Butterball the cat.

Suddenly, his phone rang and Dean jumped. He glanced at the number and his shoulders slumped. It was a Moon City number.

"Fulsome," he answered.

"Yeah, it's Donaldo. You back?"

"I'm back. Empty handed. Didn't you get my three voicemails?"

"I left my phone at home. Loveman and I went to the café for a bit."

"You take your SL-SHR along when you get coffee?"

"Nah," explained Donaldo. "I went for the moon crepes. Mr. Loveman orders the coffee."

"How does that work?"

"He doesn't drink it or anything. He just likes to watch the steam."

"Okay, can we just talk about the swamp?"

"Sure, calm down, calm down. What's up? Didn't the trash work?"

"Not at all. I was out there two hours."

"Oh, you should have come back sooner."

"Well, I didn't, you asshole, and now I'm stuck." Dean hissed a sigh through his hand and closed his eyes to rest them a second. "Is there any other way to get those surveillance feeds? Can't you hack into them? You're a hotshot programmer."

"I absolutely can do that, but I *won't*. I'd like to keep my balls attached thank you very much." Donaldo gave a nervous chuckle. "Look, Dean. I'm sorry. Why not try to find something else to take out there? I've heard rotten eggs can work."

"Where can I find those?"

"No clue. Start at every restaurant."

"Shit…" Dean fought the impulse to just hang up.

"It doesn't have to be rotten eggs. It just has to smell horrible. Take a bunch of garbage out there. Something will work, trust me. Maybe I just didn't have enough rancid stuff in the trash. I do eat out a lot you know."

"Thanks. I'll try that."

"Good luck. I know you can do it. I'm going back to the mayor's now, so we have to stop communicating. Text me 666 when you've gotten access to the surveillance. I'll send the SL-SHRs to meet you at that point. They'll take care of this problem once and for all."

Dean didn't bother saying good-bye and ended the call. He dropped the phone on the couch beside him and groaned. He didn't mind bringing more garbage out to the swamps, but what if it didn't work again? He had plenty of time and wouldn't be sleeping any time soon, yet he had the feeling this was a wild-goose chase, and his time would be better served hitting the streets and asking questions.

No. Those feeds have the Killer on them. What better source are you going to stumble upon?

He leaned forward and noticed the cat looking up at him, blinking sedately, content. Dean gently rubbed behind the cat's ears and he instinctively sniffled. "You are a sorry sack. You know that, Butterdick? Pooping in the bathtub, spilling your food in the kitchen, messing with the papers near the incinerator. Yep, you are one… sorry… sack."

The cat fiercely rubbed the side of its face on the back of his hand. Dean noticed a black flake stuck behind its left ear. "You got a little schmutz here."

He pulled it off the cat's fur and squinted to examine the black scrap. It almost looked like dried seaweed. Not like the turds in the bathtub which were small and brown and firm, so this wasn't shit. Thankfully.

Nothing better to engage in, Dean brought the flake to his nose and smelled. Instantly, he recoiled and flicked it away. "Yuck! Good god!"

He couldn't unremember the stench. It was that black moss from the tavern. The stuff that had been growing from the ceiling and floor like some devilweed.

Nastiest smell Dean had ever…

He was up on his feet then. From the kitchen he grabbed a garbage bag and immediately headed out the front door. He gave Butterball a quick salute of thanks and left for the tavern. The cat meowed a good-bye from where it stood near the incinerator.

* * *

The drive to the far end of the cave seemed longer this time. The boulders, stalactites, and torch-lit road hazard signs repeated in such a way that they felt hypnotic. Dean's brain sent impulses to him that suggested the need for sleep, but then something recalibrated internally that reminded him, *Oh, you're awake, buddy… You're awake and you're going to be that way for a long while.* As he reached the shoreline to the swampland, he heard a pinging sound under the hood of the car.

"Give me killer robots that won't kill, a car that won't drive, and a mission," he grumbled to himself as he parked and killed the headlights. Immediately, the surroundings went black. Only touches of light from the nearby anti-picnic signs gave any shape to the area. As he learned the last time he'd come out this way, he needed about fifteen minutes for his eyes to fully adjust to the darkness.

He sat there and scanned the area. He really hoped the bag of moss he'd taken from the tavern would do the trick. The smell had made its way into the car even though he put the trash bag in the trunk. It was such a revolting odor, one so acute in its misery that Dean could almost taste it in his mouth. He grimaced and took a swig of water from Rick Agate's canteen he took with him. Thinking about the mercenary got him more upset. This kind of thing, rolling around with swamp creatures, was more suited to Rick's type. Dean would have emailed Tasha this with a few pointed facts about his job title as well, but he knew what she'd say. *You used to wrangle and kill animals for a living, Slaughter Man. Don't keep belly aching.* Then she would go on to reinforce that it wasn't her job to cheer him up. If he needed a hug, he should find someone who didn't mind giving him one.

"Gotta love her," Dean whispered, and at that moment his eyes drank in the outer reaches of the motionless swamp, the strange gray lily pads and cattails, the lichen-covered pieces of waste lumber that had been dumped here years ago after a large construction project, the dark blue vines that grew from the water, spread over some boulders, and dangled off the sides like rotten waterfalls.

He got out of the car and popped open the trunk. The contents of the trash bag struck him like a giant fist to the face, so bad he even took a step back, gagging. He'd discovered the black moss when gathered together smelled even worse than it did spread out and growing naturally. It was so rank he'd had to throw his gloves away. Grabbing the bag and the Mason jar, he headed over to the shoreline.

There wasn't even a spare moment to hope it worked.

The response was immediate.

Not even reaching the shoreline, he saw three distinct, large ripples along the surface of the swamp. Unsettling faces lifted from the brine. They looked like crocodiles, but more aquatic looking with gray scales that color of shark skin. They had a dorsal fin on their back, and though their tails swayed in the water like a crocodile's, it had a caudal fin on them like a shark as well. The other telling sharklike trait was the arrow shape of their heads and the rows of triangular teeth brandished in their half-opened mouths.

Dean tossed the bag of moss to the shoreline. It spilled out in a heap. The crocosharks swam faster to intercept it. The one in the back closed in on the leader, opened its mouth, and soundly bit the neck. Even in the dim light, Dean saw the eruption of blood around the attacking creature's face and he could hear it rain down on the surface of the water. The victim thrashed for only a few moments before going still, and its decapitated head floated off.

Clutching the Mason jar in both hands, Dean watched as the animals crawled out of the water and nosed through the moss. Without much ceremony, the larger of the animals mounted the other, its black, jelly eyes rolling back into its head in an unsettling white. They lay there, breathing heavily as they mated in the disgusting moss.

Pretty kinky, thought Dean. He approached a few steps to see if they would move. When neither animal budged, he took twice as many steps and kept going until he was about a yard away.

Dean swallowed as he slowly lowered to his knees. Directly under the jaw hung a grayish-blue sack that folded in and out like a silent accordion retrieved from burning wreckage. Thin, amber cords hung out the bottom. He looked at them and rolled his eyes—*the shit I get myself into.*

He walked on his knees closer to the mating creatures, which continued to be in a motionless fugue state. Reaching forth, one hand poised to take the nipple, and the other holding tightly to the Mason jar, Dean found he needed to move even closer. He winced at the shuffling sound through the dirt and pebbles his knees made. This was hardly a stealthy ninja-like execution on his part, but so far the two beasts couldn't break from their ecstasy.

Dean took the thick, warm amber cord between his fingers and positioned the Mason jar underneath. He had surprisingly never milked a cow, even though he'd worked around cattle for a large part of his adult life. He'd been around ranchers before and had seen the process though. How hard could it really be? This was no cow but the concept had to be roughly the same. Other than pinching and yanking downward on it, what else did one really need to know?

So he pinched. Yanked. Pulled downward. And nothing happened.

A slight gurgling ascended from one of the crocoshark's stomachs. He hoped that didn't signal their lovemaking coming to a close. Dean pinched harder and twisted on the hollow, fleshy cord. Something dribbled out. He worked harder and the venom-milk sprayed into the jar. Scooting closer, Dean wrenched at the reptilian udder repeatedly for almost ten minutes until he heard only slow drips in the jar. The sack collapsed into an unsettling prune shape. The jar was just under half-full. Dean cautiously went around to the other side of the animals to work at the other sack.

The second attempt took longer to get going than the first and this one had more of a sulfurous smell escaping while he milked— then again, it could have been that moss he'd brought; he wouldn't have been surprised if the rancid odor had found its way out from underneath the bellies of the animals.

The jar was getting heavier in his hand. The second sack was far more engorged with milk than the first one, from the feel of it. Dean would have a full jar without any problem. A bit of the venom dripped off the side and stung his fingers.

Good enough, he thought, and from his back pocket he took the lid. Carefully, he spun the lid onto the jar and made sure it was tight.

The crocoshark's eyes bolted open at the sound. The creature on top whipped its massive tail out and caught Dean in the side, sending him sprawling into the swamp. The brisk salt water caught in his nostrils and his chin slammed into a submerged rock, making him bite his tongue, and blood flooded his mouth.

He couldn't tell what was happening, but he could feel the muzzle of one of the beasts turning him over and the sharpness of its teeth tearing through his pants. Dean kicked at the thing and it withdrew momentarily. Then another impact came from the side. *Its lover.* The jar slipped out of Dean's grasp. He lunged to retrieve it. His face broke the surface of the water and he saw the jar fling up into the air. A crocoshark leapt from the water, its head bumping the jar higher in the air and sending it back to the shoreline, most likely to shatter.

Dean slid his hand behind his back and pulled out his firearm. A crocoshark swam for him full force. He aimed for the head and squeezed the trigger.

It sunk below the surface before any of the shots could connect. Dean lost no time and trudged to the shoreline. The salt water burned his eyes and the darkness did nothing to help, but he spotted where he *thought* the Mason jar had landed. As he closed in on it, he saw the shape there, just a hint of electro-torch light playing off its shape. His eyes drifted to the sign that the torch illuminated and he almost felt like laughing. *Danger. No Swimming.*

Water thrashed behind him. Was it the crocosharks or his own legs pushing through the swamp? It was impossible to tell, but his mind began randomly spitting out possibilities. Maybe the crocosharks retreated after he fired shots. Maybe they were more afraid of him than he was of them. Maybe he really had connected with some bullets and he'd injured one of them.

Then something kicked into his lower back like the boot of a giant monster and sent him forward in a C-shape, some blasted away parenthesis that would never end an aside (and Dean wasn't a reader, so this meant he had been struck so hard it had momentarily changed his personality and turned him into the end of this). His weapon left his hand.

He slammed. Down.

His eyes popped black.

Silver whirled overhead. Little metallic butterflies spun around, coming in for a landing on the part of the brain that needed them most.

He vomited.

Only for a second.

Because the water broke behind him and shark teeth expanded to accommodate a large bite out of his head and torso. Dean was punch-drunk, but his instincts fired inside him and he charged for the shoreline.

His foot caught between two rocks. He tried to back up and release himself. It didn't work. His shoe was buried deep, beyond the laces. The crocosharks sped up, their long, reptile arms pushing the water behind them powerfully. Dean reached down and forced his fingers through to free his foot. A charged sound that followed with a crackle went off nearby and water spurted up. The jaws of the two fierce creatures spread open and the teeth looked like an infinity Dean never wanted to be part of. He pulled at his foot. It budged slightly, but not enough. It would take time.

Time he didn't have.

He prepared to use his fists against the creatures. Doubtful it would work, but resolved he would make them hurt before they took him down, Dean straightened his back and watched as the two crocosharks emerged from the water.

One of their heads exploded in a purple-red cloud of blood, bone, and gore. The other shrieked and descended under the surface immediately. The other crocoshark's corpse floated on the water, headless. Dean watched it warily as he pushed his fingers back down into his shoe that was lodged between the rocks. Something hard and cartilaginous shifted in his foot, but he broke free with a gasp of pain and relief. With a stumble, he continued toward the shore, limping. He was within a yard of the Mason jar when dirt exploded near his feet. Another shot had been fired.

Two men plowed out of the shadows, one with a handgun and the other with a high-powered rifle. They were both roughly the same height and had face paint on to hide their likeness. "The mayor sends his highest regards, Slaughter Man," said one of them.

Dean had to clear his hoarse voice. It didn't work well though. He still sounded like he had a cheese grater lodged in his esophagus. "I thought the mayor didn't want anything to do with my project."

"That has changed," said the other minion.

Dean watched as they picked up the Mason jar, examined it, and then after a moment exchanged a quiet spell of laughter between each other.

"The mayor gets off on crocoshark venom, I take it."

A snort returned. Dean couldn't be sure which spoke now, because of their identical garb, physique, voice, and gait, but it didn't matter. He knew they shared the same sentiment. "Some of the wealthy human delegates love it, and that's enough for us, Cowman."

Dean had never been fond of being called Slaughter Man, but compared to Cowman, he decided he might have to rethink that.

"Now," said the taller of the two. "Let's go get you set up for some more crocoshark milking. We got a trunkload of jars for you to fill. You wouldn't mind, right? After all, you're an expert now. Ain't that right, Luka?"

"Sure thing, Kalu," the other replied.

"Luka and Kalu. How long did you guys sort that one out?" Dean asked.

He heard a gun cock. "You know, Fulsome, it's easy enough to say one of the crocky-sharks chewed you into little pieces. The mayor ain't no fan of Limbus, Incorporated, so we won't have to explain much. Plus, neither one of us much cares to be out here with you for twelve hours. You drift?"

"No," Dean said. "I don't. Drift, float, or swim. You're telling me that I've got to milk these things all night and fill up the mayor's jars, but you don't want to be out here. Why not just say you got the one jar and I escaped? That sounds like a happy plan to me."

Luka chuckled. "Maybe, if those were the mayor's jars. They ain't. They're mine and Kalu's there. The mayor gets one for his delegates. He doesn't need to know about the others." He tucked his weapon in the back of his pants and turned around. "Now come on and help me unload the trunk."

"If I help you guys, can I keep a single jar?" Dean asked morosely. "I will cooperate if you can promise me—"

Luka whipped back around. "You're outta your damned mind, Cowman. You aren't getting one drop of this venom. You'll leave here with your balls hanging and your heart still beating. Be happy for that."

As Luka turned back, he made a muffled sound of surprise. The glint of something in the torchlight poked through the small of his back. Dean struggled to see what it could be when, suddenly, the dull metallic shape jerked up all the way through Luka's body, severing him with twine from the belly button through the skull. His top half split apart and hung open like a ghastly tree that had been chopped down its trunk. Blood vessels blew out squirts and mists and organs tumbled free. Jazon Meyers pulled free one of his machete hands that had punctured the left hip for leverage.

Kalu fired a shot. Dirt exploded near Dean's left foot. He wasn't sure what the man was aiming at, but he put his head down and ran for the cover of his car. Another shot rang out and the flash illuminated the dark scene for an instant. Dean saw Mr. Loveman slowly approaching the frantic man.

"—the shit are you?" he called out and fired again.

Mr. Loveman charged forward, caught the man's wrist and wrenched it sideways. Kalu screamed. Loveman snatched the gun out of his enfeebled hand and shoved him against the car. With a fluid motion of his left arm, the robot pointed the gun into Kalu's left eye.

"Wait!"

Mr. Loveman started firing. Each shot making his black star eyes flicker. He emptied all the ammunition in Kalu's left eye and squeezed the trigger a few times after the bullets had run out. With a sickening gushy sound, he pulled the barrel of the gun out of the sizeable hole in the dead man's head and let the body collapse to the ground.

Dean's heart thundered as he watched the SL-SHR drop the gun unceremoniously and head over to the Mason jar. He picked it up, observed the contents, and moved his body around, almost in a slithering way, to face Dean. Behind him, Jazon was hacking Luka into smaller pieces.

"They are dead, Fulsome," Mr. Loveman told him. "There is no need for hiding now."

Dean stayed put. "What the hell are you two doing here? I thought you couldn't help me."

"Master knew the mayor sent people to follow you. They were tailing you earlier and figured out what you were doing out here."

"Saving me isn't your directive."

"Without the venom, you would not have the access to the Moon City Killer. This is our directive," whispered Mr. Loveman. He shuffled forward in his flip-flops, his realistic-looking toes covered in soft, gray moon dust.

Warily, Dean came out from behind the car. "How long have you been here?"

"The whole time."

"You can help me with the mayor's people, but can't help me with the crocosharks?" he asked incredulously.

Mr. Loveman handed him the Mason jar, which thankfully had not shattered. "Neither of us could have helped you with that. We both love animals."

Over his shoulder, Dean saw that Jazon Meyers had begun throwing bits of human parts into the swamp.

"I've got to get the hell out of here." Dean shook his head, which felt about to explode, and went to the car.

"That's one pretty dress Sandra's wearing tonight," Mr. Loveman said.

Dean looked at him but the robot's back was already turned.

"Let us know when you have the surveillance feeds of the Moon City Killer," he added.

"Sure," Dean said, just to simply end his conversation with the creepy-ass thing. He opened up his car and plopped down in the driver's seat. He turned on his phone and saw Sandra had sent him a photo of herself. She was going out with friends and was in a red cocktail dress. She looked absolutely amazing. So much, that Dean was speechless for a moment. It bothered him that the robot had had its oily, black star eyes on her before he'd even had the chance. But it didn't ruin the love he felt for Sandra, it only showcased how impossibly far he was from her.

Dean resolved to be in a better mood. He'd lucked out back there. Now he had the venom for the Firecracker Lady and she would need to keep her bargain and give him access to that surveillance. He would, at last, see that bastard who had brought him to this godforsaken moon. Hopefully, Loveman and Jazon would make short work of him and then it was Golden Transport back to Sandra, back to Earth, and this would be the last time he'd ever leave the solar system again, without Sandra at least.

He sent Sandra a text telling her how very beautiful she was and to have a great time, but *not too great of a time haha.* Dean settled down on the couch in the apartment. He needed to relax a bit before returning to the Firecracker Lady. Although he wasn't tired per se, his mind and body needed some cooling off.

Despite realizing this, he was restless. He thought about tidying up those documents and throwing them in the incinerator, but Butterball curled up in his lap and anchored him there. He knew he'd be sneezing like a sonofabitch before long, but he let the cat rest for the moment. He scrolled through the intergalactic news feeds on his phone and almost at once wished he hadn't. The Grettish had posted an execution of a Zetú slave. A gathering of other slaves. His friend Finny-Min stood with his son, Dean, amongst the other horrified Zetús. The eyes of his friend expressed more than words ever could have, but had there been a translation, it might have been *will that happened happen to my boy next, or to me?*

"Shit… they're there." Dean buried his face in his hands and tried to squeeze away all the disturbing images flooding into his mind. "Finny-min and his boy. There's nothing I can do. God help me."

Chapter 17

The Firecracker Lady had a new outfit on—well, it wasn't so much an outfit but a bikini and hula skirt. Studying the Mason jar on her desk, she lit up a cigar with a match and puffed on it vigorously.

"I thought you didn't put poisons into your body," he said.

"I choose what I deem poison, Fulsome."

Dean stood there, feeling the eyes of the Grettish Friars on him, unsure if they'd go for the "I just came through the transport" bit again when deciding to split him in half with their galaxy glass scimitars. The image of Jazon Meyers with galaxy glass machetes flickered through his mind and he shivered.

"Takes a big pair to get a hold of a full jar of that stuff. I like you a little more, Dean. I might end up screwing you after all."

"Thanks," he replied drily. "But I'm engaged."

She tittered. "Oh, that's cute."

"I *am* engaged," he insisted.

"No, no, I meant it's cute you actually took me seriously."

Dean blushed angrily. "Are you going to keep our deal?"

His cell phone started ringing. The Firecracker Lady nodded through a puff of cigar smoke. "Need to take that? I'll wait."

With a snort, Dean mumbled thanks and answered the phone. It was his case coordinator, Charles Blu. As soon as Dean had seen who was calling, he knew he would have to answer. Charles could be very persistent; he was great at what he did but never wanted to venture outside of researching new contract opportunities back on Earth. If he had to deal with any extraterrestrials from other star systems, he had a mental block brought on by extreme xenophobia. After Dean calmed him down, he told Charles to just email the case file and contact information to him and he would take care of it.

"Sorry," he told the Firecracker Lady as he hung up.

"No, I'm the one who's sorry," she said. "I'm sorry I sent such a belt buckle into the swamp to wrestle with crocosharks."

"Hey, you got what you asked for, didn't you?"

"I bet you didn't even want to come to Moon City. This isn't your forte, going after offworld serial killers. You're no assassin. You got talked into this, just like that guy on the phone talked you into doing his job for him."

"Am I in therapy here?"

She narrowed her eyes and flicked the ash of the cigar into a white porcelain ashtray shaped like a naked man. "I don't have a filter for when things bug me about people. Was that guy your direct report? He was, wasn't he?"

"Yep. So what?"

"I'd fire his ass."

"Well," said Dean, "thankfully for him and his family, I'm not you."

"That's strikingly clear. I own half a galaxy and you're risking your ass to use *my* cameras. Yes, I do believe we are quite different beyond your peepee and my whowho."

"Risking my ass was my part of the deal. What about yours?"

"Oh, just settle down a minute. You're so hyper." The red coal at the end of her cigar glowed brightly for a moment as she pulled on it. "Can I ask you something?"

"I guess you're going to anyway." He sighed.

"Do you think I dress this way because I'm some slutty bitch on a power trip?"

Dean was taken back, but recovered quickly. "No comment."

"Well, of course not. You either pull out a white lie or you avoid what you really want to say. You're the strong, silent type, but you're also soft in the center. You don't want anyone to *not* like you. So you just let everyone mow you over. With me, as I said, we are different and I don't give two mumblyfucks what anybody thinks about me. But I'm giving you permission here. Answer my question."

"What question?"

"Keep up with me, Dean, the slutty bitch power trip question."

He grumbled. "No, I'm sure you dress the way that makes you happy."

"You're wrong," she replied. "I actually am slutty and a bitch and I love power trips. However, why I dress this way is only half that. The other half is my boyfriend likes this kinky beach blanket bingo bullshit. He and I are going swimming in the pool upstairs after I'm through with this cigar. Dressing this way does *nothing* for me, but I do it anyway. Why? Because I want his affection. I want to keep him happy. I'm screwed up."

"No you aren't."

"I can have any man I want and I'm wearing this ridiculous thing. I don't even like swimming."

"You aren't screwed up."

"Stop playing it so safe. I am screwed up. Years ago I fell in love with Surgeon Delta. You ever heard of him?"

"Who hasn't? He's almost as popular as Chris Agate."

"Never met Agate, but Delta ruined me for any other man—not by length or anything but how he'd get behind me and put his—"

"Do we have to talk about this?"

"Awww," she said through the smoke. "Baby's squeamish about boy parts?"

"Yes, in fact. I don't even look down in the shower."

She erupted in laughter. "There you go! That's what I want. Just tell me everything straight up."

"Fine then. So we are good now? Can I get my access to those damn cameras or what?"

"Of course, Dean Fulsome," she sweetly said and leaned forward, tapping her fingers across her laser console. "My people will meet you down in the casino and give you access."

"For a full day."

"That was the deal." She beat out more ash. "Oh, and if you know any freighters willing to smuggle that stuff off the moon, you let me know. I can give them a lovely percentage."

"Can't help you there."

She shrugged. "Who knows? You have to ask to get an answer."

"I'll let you know... and have a good swim with your man."

A sly grin. "Thank you. Just remember, Dean, neither of us has to do these things we don't want to. We choose everything."

"Agreed. So you keep wearing that stuff and I'll keep doing other people's work for them."

She stubbed out the cigar. "Until we're through with doing it, right?"

"Yeah."

He heard the door unlock behind him as she released it. "Goodbye Slaughter Man. I hope you find what you're looking for on those cameras."

"Thank you Fire—wait, what is your name, really?"

Her smile was sad. "That's only for Surgeon Delta to know. I think I'll keep it that way. No offense."

Dean bowed a little. "For the record, I don't find you bitchy at all."

She pointed to the door. "Enough feel-good straight talk. Haul outta here, dickface."

He left, grinning, somehow feeling privileged to be insulted.

* * *

The two men who escorted Dean to a backroom in the casino looked nothing like henchman for a crime boss as renowned as the Firecracker Lady. He might have known better, since she employed Donaldo, the geeky super robotics genius contained in an intimidating frame, but one of the henchmen was a bartender, the other a currency exchange clerk. Perhaps she just trusted him enough now where she didn't need to bring in the big heavies.

But then there were the consoles. Moon City wasn't a large satellite, but it was at least a hundred times larger than Earth's moon, and though the entire civilization was considered a "city" in this system, there were over a thousand counties and hundreds of thousands of districts. So the consoles... the screens that could be a window into all these locations... there were only three.

East. West. South.

Dean sat and looked at the keyboard, which was ten times longer than any keyboard he'd ever seen and with dozens upon dozens of strange keys.

The exchange clerk coughed into his hand. "It's Fanglion. We never use it. Just instruct the camera, date, time, location, reverse, forward, play. They all work. It's intuitive too."

"Good deal. Why isn't there a feed for north?"

"Nobody's out by the Midnight Sea—it's too far and not enough proximity to power grids."

"Fair enough. How do I engage it?"

"Com Cam Three Five—Dean here will be your master for the next seventy-two hours. Starting now."

Dean said, "Show me the Stone Root Ale House two days ago."

The image scrambled and revealed the tavern during opening hours.

"You can be more specific," said the exchange clerk.

"Show me when any Deitii enters the bar."

The time flew to later in the night. Not the night an earthling would have considered night, but around past second midnight. An unassuming Deitii entered, said hello to a couple of regulars, and headed for the bar. It was a child in age for their species, but if you're over one hundred years old, a human will sell you anything you want to get messed up on. It just made sense.

To us.

Dean watched as the child sipped on a lager and read some news on his e-pad. A man sidled up to him and struck up a conversation. The face wasn't in the shot.

"Is there sound?" Dean asked.

"Not at this location," answered the program.

"Show me just one second before he leaves that chair—the Deitii, I mean."

"Approximately forty-nine minutes later." The screen changed and Dean watched the Moon City Killer leave with the Deitii he would later murder and consume.

"Show me the human who left—show me any footage of him appearing in any camera since then."

An hour later, Dean almost wished he hadn't asked that question, because this surveillance system was comprehensive. Even if the Killer's shoulder appeared in a frame of some camera in some alley or street, it would show it, but since the man always wore a fedora, his face was almost always obscured. Dean began to think there might never be anything of value—even through the banking district fire and Rick Agate's death, there was surprisingly little footage to actually use from the camera's visual reporting. And still no distinct visual recording of the Killer's face that he could give to the SL-SHRs.

But then something appeared on the screen that was valuable.

A diner.

The Killer sat down. He still wore the hat and still had no direct look into the camera. But the woman he sat with did.

"Is there sound at this location?" he asked.

"There is," replied the computer. "Play?"

Dean smiled. "Please do."

* * *

He watched the exchange play out between the Moon City Killer and the woman who was his mother. It was Dean's fifth viewing before Donaldo called him back.

He put the phone to his ear. The big man sounded a bit out of breath still, having to leave the mayor's residence to get back to his shop.

"Okay..." Breathing, breathing, breathing... "Loveman..." Breathing, breathing, breathing. "Got some..." Breathing—

"For Christ's sake," Dean interrupted, "catch your breath."

Donaldo sucked in hoarsely and after a few moments sighed. "We have information on the woman, which includes several ex-boyfriend's apartments, ex-employers, and here it is... bingo, one estranged son, who lives by the franchise lumber factory."

"Off the beaten path?"

"Way off the beaten path." Donaldo swallowed some more. "Shit, gonna have a heart attack."

"Don't die yet, your SL-SHRs won't be any good to me," said Dean.

"You're all heart, Slaughter Man."

Dean ignored this. "You said lumber yard, eh?"

"That's what the data file contains. It's really recent too, up to just last month. Looks like you have your man. Mr. Loveman and Jazon will need a face, though. I can't send them to that house at the lumber yard without a confirmed target."

Dean shrugged. "Why do they need a face? The target is whoever lives in that house. Male, early thirties, strong build, dark hair. Likes wearing fedora hats."

"Doesn't work that way," Donaldo explained. "The directive is specific. Facial recognition is required."

"No chance there are any cameras pointed at this house?"

"No, but there are some at the lumber yard. You might be able to zoom in on it."

Dean activated the surveillance computer again. "Send the camera number from the lumber yard to the computer."

He heard Donaldo in the background asking Mr. Loveman to send it to the surveillance system.

"Address acquired, loading," the computer told Dean.

The image of a backlot full of lumber stacks came into view. Beyond a fence, in the distance, Dean spotted a small clapboard dwelling in the center of a series of boulders. A dirt road led there in a wide hook off the main thoroughfare.

"Zoom fifty percent."

The camera went past the chainlink fence and the image of the house still had startling clarity. "Six, no seventy percent zoom."

The house and the front yard fit into his screen perfectly.

"How specific can I get with this thing?" Dean asked the Firecracker Lady's casino lackey.

He was reading an e-pad without humor. "I asked it once to follow all the blond men in the city over six foot four and slim builds. I was here for a while."

"That's your type, huh?" Dean scooted closer to the computer.

"Sure." The man chuckled. "At very best, the male body looks like a stack of rocks glued to an aardvark snout."

Dean grinned absently, thinking of the command. "Computer?" he asked.

"Yes, Dean Fulsome," it answered.

"I want you to rewind this footage until a vehicle shows up."

"Rewinding."

The footage reversed, all the light sources varying only as nearby streetlamps were relit. Otherwise, there was no daytime or nighttime in the footage. Suddenly, the footage stopped as a large vehicle with a hauling trailer appeared in the shot.

"Rewind until the car door opens," Dean attempted. To his surprise, the footage rewound until a kid emerged from the car and the Moon City Killer stood at his side. For the first time, the man wasn't wearing a hat.

"Rewind until the front door closes," Dean whispered.

The kid and man reversed to the front door. The Killer turned, his hand linking with the door knob as he closed it behind him.

"Show me a frame at a time."

The Killer pulled the door closed, and as he did, he face turned straight to the camera.

"Pause!" Dean cried.

The Moon City Killer stared straight at him with unsettling, hollow eyes.

"What did you find?" Donaldo asked over the phone. It sounded like he was crunching on chips or something now, rather than dying of lung failure.

"Computer send image in highest resolution to Donaldo."

"Sending," the computer immediately replied.

After a moment, Donaldo hummed over the line. "So that's him, eh?"

"Send the SL-SHRs to the location," said Dean nodding. His heart began to race. "That's our confirmed target. That's the face of the Moon City Killer."

"Will do," said Donaldo. His voice lowered as he turned away from the phone, but Dean could make out what he said. *"Mr. Loveman, are you ready to have a good time?"*

Chapter 18

Originally, I wanted to count my remaining jars at the reserve location, but somehow, I knew Carl would hang around if I did. So I gave him the task of counting them for me. It gave me time to sit with the ultrasound photo of my little unborn boy.

This turned out, for me, to be an unhealthy stretch of time.

I could see my life in other dimensions, but I could not feel it. I could not feel *him*. He was my best friend and ally. I didn't have one of those here. Sure, people like Carl would come into my life, but I could never connect with them like I know my other millions of selves were so tightly connected to my son. In some dimension, he was named Easton. In others, Brian. I'd only seen one instance where he'd been named something else, and that was Miles. Out of all the dimensions, when I had the ability to see into them, I would watch the Miles version of my son the most. He had the least amount of flaws in that life, and also happened to be more dedicated to me than other manifestations, although they were all loving sons.

I dragged my fingers across the photo. A tear fell against the slippery surface of the image and it rolled down, leaving a thin wet trail. "Miles," I said, trying not to weep, "I wish you were here. I wish you could be my son *here*."

Hercules, I thought. Once I'm a God, I could find a woman and give her a child... but it would never be Miles. It might be a wondrous creation of mortal and immortal, but it would never be that boy I saw through the gauzy panes of dimensions and time and space.

I longed to see him then.

There was much I still needed to tend to, and another Limbus operative out there who tracked me at this very moment, yet it didn't matter. I would kill him or her just as easily as I killed Rick Agate. I wasn't concerned with that.

My boy. I just wanted to watch my boy, and imagine how a hug from him would feel, what would be behind it. The love he would know for me. The father. The son. The love between them.

I couldn't bear it. The tears fell freely now and I had to know. I had to see. I had to be closer to perfect than before. I had ten jars of the spinal-brain slurry here. I would ingest them all. And I would see him again. Miles. *I'm here Miles. I love you more than that version of me loves you. He doesn't appreciate you the same way because he has you. I lost my son. I lost my life. I'm becoming God to get over that loss. Don't you see what it means? How important it really is?*

Staggering into the bedroom, I saw them all lined up around my sorry, unmade bed. They looked like something one might see in a moonshine operation or brain diamond house. I knelt in front of the first jar and unscrewed the lid. All those planets fought over crocoshark venom when the answer to immortality and godhood lived in the Deitii children's minds. It was right here all along, and so few ever tried a taste for themselves. It was their loss and my gain. I would find all the Deitii, adult and child alike, once I reached the final phase. Then I would end them. I already knew now there would come a point where I would never need to drink from them again, but I couldn't afford leaving their kind alive to give someone else the same idea. They would need to go, just like any other species that crossed me.

Once I finished most of the jars in my reserve, I would reach that threshold. My body told me this. And these jars on my bedroom floor... would be my last push before the conclusion.

I was excited to begin.

The first jar almost gagged me, but I drank everything and licked the rim of any remaining particles. On the second and third jars, my stomach began to feel the initial bloat, and the walls of my house became transparent. Fifth, sixth, seventh, eighth... I was in the stars. I clamored around my bedroom, but I also strode in the cosmos, pawing through supernovas and newborn suns and filling all the emptiness with my presence, like a luminescent stone covering the hole that remained in the heart of an old statue created long ago and left behind.

I felt the lip of the tenth jar shatter under my teeth. I drank it down, glass shards and all. I dissolved them in my mouth before they had a chance to damage my flesh, which soon would be meaningless to my existence.

It would take me a few hours to gain control of myself, but my mind could roam as freely as it wanted to. First, I would visit my son, Miles, and check on his life. I could only go a few years into the future last time, and I was eager to see how much farther into his life I could watch.

Just as I began to peel back the veneer of the dimensions to a much different Moon City, something within this life, in this time, stopped me and dragged me back, like a fishhook in my ethereal eye.

I saw a man hunkered over a desk, peering at some screens. The photo of my son was in someone's hand—my mother's. She was putting it on the table at the diner. The man watching her sped ahead to my arrival and watched us. He brought up a few other pieces of footage. One, actually, of Carl and I outside, that had to have only been an hour ago.

This man was hunting me.

Something about that fact made my desire to see Miles suddenly wane.

Nobody hunted me. I hunted them.

I sought this man out. Knew exactly where he was in the city. The Surefire casino, belonging to the Firecracker Lady. But he wasn't employed by her. Reading his mind and his memories as they flooded into my subconscious, I realized who the man was and that he worked for that crooked intergalactic employment agency, Limbus, Inc., that wished to destroy me.

As it turned out, he had already sent two assassin mechanicals to my house to do just that. Although I could not locate them through their heartbeat, and even if I could find them, I could not read their minds like I read this man's, I wasn't afraid.

I was excited.

I stared at him for a while, in my mind's eyes.

"It's nice to meet you, Dean," I said.

* * *

I had to reserve my strength for the assassin mechanicals. If I killed them with too much force, I wouldn't be able to focus on the growth of my inner spirit, which would cause me to prolong this process further. When I drank from my reserves, I wanted this to be the last time I fed, but if I didn't have the chance to keep my mind in a heightened state for very long, it would limit the access to the ladder of my ascension to godhood. I needed to give myself time to dwell in the mental space that the creator of this universe had once maintained. Despite being more powerful than any kind of machine Limbus could throw at me, I could exert all my energy. I had to be cautious and choose my moves carefully.

When a machete went through my front door, I wondered if I'd have that chance.

I called Carl. He started in on how he'd just sealed up the place and all the reserve bottles were locked up safe and sound. I cut him off mid-story. "I need you to stay where you are."

A second machete went through the door and twisted violently as it was pulled free.

"Why?" Carl asked.

"Do as I say. I'll contact you soon."

"What's going on?"

"I'll call you later."

"But—?"

"Do as I say or no more money. Is that clear?"

"Yes."

"Bye."

I hung up and watched as a large chunk of the door broke apart. A steel-plate face with holes in it centered in the opening for a moment. Then an arm came through, the machete affixed to the elbow joint rather than a forearm and hand. The brutal creation hugged at the door and pulled it outside, off the hinges, and threw it to the side.

I backed up as the metal thing crossed the threshold, swiping its machete hands as it went. Beyond the robot, I could see nothing outside. Dean Fulsome had sent two mechanicals my way, but I could only see this one.

It lunged for me and I sidestepped its attack, grasped its left arm just below the shoulder, and ripped the steel extremity from its socket. It wheeled around with its other weapon and grazed my jaw with the blade. I felt blood course out and wet my neck, but I had not stopped my counterassault—using the machine's momentum, I hurled it over my shoulder. The assassin robot landed on my sofa, which folded around its colossal weight.

The thing was trapped inside the sofa, attempting to free itself. I stepped up just as it took another swipe at me with its remaining arm. Planting my foot on its arm, just past the shoulder, I halted its attacks. I leaned over then and took the corners of its mask, which was not a mask, but part of the machine's face, and pulled it free from all its metal housings amid a small cluster of red and blue sparks. The assassin robot made no sounds of protest, but did wag its head back and forth in panic. The exposed optical circuitry and artificial intelligence core flickered with silver and blue lights, only for a few more seconds before I brought the heel of my boot down on it and crushed it flat as an aluminum can.

The assassin robot's body ceased movement as its functions terminated.

Heart rate hardly increased, I looked up and outside. I had a split second to register what was happening, but my mouth dropped, and I could feel the fresh blood on my skin. A conveyance truck from the lumber yard had pulled up in front of my house during my fight. The chains securing the bundle of imported lumber released and all at once the rumble of hundreds of fifty-foot-long tree trunks came crashing down and rolling toward my house. I got to see the person in the driver's cockpit at the side momentarily. It wasn't a person at all, but a pale-faced synthetic lifeform with black stars for eyes.

The logs crashed into my house and immediately trapped me inside. I coughed through the dirt and dust and held my arm up to my mouth. I went to the window and tried to see out the opening between two logs. I wanted to reach out with my mind, but I had to contain myself. The power urged me to do so, but I didn't want to waste it. Killing the other robot had been easy. I had to ride this out. If this other robot thought I would be trapped here and die, it had made a great mistake. I wasn't like any other mark. I could be in here a long time.

In fact, I could use this to my advantage. I was safe here. I could meditate, I could reach those upper levels of awareness without any interruption. That thing out there had actually done me a great favor.

Quickly, I sat cross-legged on the floor next to the demolished robot and opened my mind to all the universes, drinking in everything. When I did this, I could be paralyzed for a few hours, so it was critical I let my muscles relax and let my senses reach as far as they possibly could. My spirit eyes delved through Moon City to all other star systems and all other versions of their realities. I didn't dwell on the manifestations of my son. I could do that later. Now that people and robots had come after me, there was no time for risking any wasted power. I had to reach that place I'd only scraped before and I had to let my mind reside there for as long as I could handle.

I was making great progress and my body had locked in place as I stretched out farther than I'd ever imagined before. Soon, I'd be able to end a planet with just a moment's thought or, for that matter, begin a new planet, a new star, a new element, a new species.

Something sharp hit my nose. It was immediate, in the here and now, in my house.

Smoke.

Fire.

I realized then what a fool I'd been to have engaged in my meditation without making sure the other robot had been destroyed. It was out there, setting my house on fire with hundreds of dry logs positioned around me like the greatest funeral pyre of all time. And I couldn't break out of my trance yet. I would lose everything I'd tried to achieve.

Sweat poured from my temples as I struggled within myself. The heat hadn't gotten inside, but I could sense it. My eyes were closed but my ears were attuned and I heard the robot whisper something behind the roaring flames.

"Come outside. Please, don't die yet, Moon City Killer."

Chapter 19

My mind continued to ascend and expand over the entire universe. I stopped noting all of the images individually and just experienced, and all the while I was aware of the fiery smell of burning wood around me. I didn't have time to seek other dimensions, and therefore my son, because I was too consumed with this dimension. The process had to be completed before the fire grew out of control and it destroyed all the Deitii's flesh, blood, and bone I needed—for even though I had the reach of God right now, I knew it was limited and that the final feeding still needed to take place.

Sounds of burning support beams crackling overhead made me press harder to find the limits of my newfound power. I could come back from this once I reached it. I had to find the wall where this all stopped. I always had in the past, but now, instead of dreading that moment, I was racing toward it.

Stars and planets whipped past me occasionally, but mostly empty space... blank canvas for a creator to do with as he pleased. I tasted blood and tried to tell myself it was from grinding my teeth, and not that my face was actively melting off from the flames.

No.

I had to control my imagination for it could be the inception of something real. I could literally imagine bursting into flames and it would happen. I had to focus on achieving more mental space in the universe than my present power could contain. I was almost there.

Something hot struck my shoulder.

That wasn't imagination.

I had to get out of this trance with enough power left to escape and deal with the robot. If I quit too soon though, this chance would be squandered.

My breathing came raggedly from a dry throat. Two hot cores burned in my nostrils. The fire was closing in. My mind darted around a galaxy and filled its every crevice with *me*. This was an invasion not only of the materials of time and space, but its emptiness too. That's what God turned out to be, after all, an overlord who pressed his fingerprints into everything and claimed ownership on his creations.

I started to regain a sense of my body. I felt the sweat on my skin and the intense heat surrounding me.

With a scream, I was back. I scrambled to my feet. My home, the house I'd known my entire adult life, was nothing more than a prison of fire and smoke. I disassociated my molecules and ran through the jungle of scarlet and amber claws. Moving forward, I waited until I left the fire far behind. My body reassembled in a rush and I gasped for clean, smoke-free air. My eyes burned and I rubbed at them to regain my sight.

I assumed the robot had taken me for dead and returned to its master. I would attend to that later when—

My eyes settled on a humanoid shape standing on a boulder across the gorge. The pale-faced robot with the star eyes and the purple polo shirt had climbed up there to watch my house burn. It saw me watching it, but it made no move. Somehow, it had known I would make it out alive. The fire had just been a greeting. Right away I gathered that this thing might give me more trouble than the previous assassin.

I walked to the edge of the gorge. I had enough power left in me to leap across and come down on the machine like a giant fist, but as I lifted my eyes, it had left its position on the boulder and I could no longer see it. If this thing had a heartbeat, I would have been able to see it in my mind's eye, but without complete realization of the universe, I could not see *everything*. I would need to get to my reserve and drink the rest today. There could be no further hesitation. I was ready. I was finally ready to be All and Everything.

The fire brigade turned down the dirt road to my house. I walked in the opposite direction and ducked behind a boulder. I couldn't be caught up with the likes of them. And if I couldn't go after the robot directly, I could get it deactivated and out of my hair if I took out its most likely master: Dean Fulsome.

But I could do that without depleting my reserves.

I closed my eyes and dragged up every nightmare from my subconscious, and turned them into living things.

They clawed their way up from the gorge, out of the darkness, into the torchlight. Hundreds of them. My private army sent to kill this Slaughter Man person, this Dean Fulsome, who sat on a sofa with a cat in that same apartment where I'd planted the cyanide gas capsule in the incinerator, his heart beating rapidly. I walked into the darkness and heard the growls of my followers in the distance, all hungry for that very heart. *You should have taken care of the trash. The cyanide might have been an easier way to go, Dean.*

I hurried on. I took out my cell phone to call Carl, but my molecular disassociation must have somehow damaged it. That, or the fire.

I went to toss the phone, but it suddenly rang.

The call was from an unknown number.

"Hello?" I asked.

"Jazon Meyers was mine. You shouldn't have done that. Really."

"Who is this?"

"Are you a god yet?"

I straightened and turned around, looking at every dark corner of every boulder. After I was sure nothing was watching me, I went to hang up.

"I'd like to kill a god. Can you do that for me?" the deep voice whispered. "Can you let me have that? I'll give you a head start."

"I don't need—" I blared. "Who is this? Are you that robot?"

The thing snorted. "I'm the reason gods don't exist anymore."

I tossed the phone on the ground and walked quickly to find the adjacent service road back into town. In the near distance, I heard the life-ending scream of one of my creations and the screams of others around it, bearing witness to its murder.

Chapter 20

Nose gently running, eyes puffy and itchy, Dean sat on the sofa with Butterball on his lap, wondering how everything was playing out with the robots. To put a break in his anxiety, he'd been texting back and forth with Sandra, but the delay was atrocious. Something bothered him about how little she was sharing too. Ever since she went out with her friends.

Nothing happened... the other night. Did it? He texted.

I'm not your ex-wife, she replied. He could imagine the snappiness in her tone.

I just miss you. Don't want you to be unhappy with me.

You're eighty-two trillion miles away. What's there to be unhappy with?

After fifteen minutes, she added, *I didn't even have a drink. Just chatted with the girls about life. I'm still in love with YOU, ya know?*

Dean almost broke his stance on emoticons and sent a heart, but instead replied, *Back at you, beautiful.*

He was so lonely for her, he was about to break another rule and send a selfie, even though he felt it completely demeaning and against the grain of everything that made Dean Fulsome who he was, but this distance... sucked.

Lifting his phone, he got the camera just right, aligning his face in the center of the frame. He wasn't very good with cell phones, but it seemed self-explanatory. Dean put on his best grin, happy Limbus had so generously fixed his crooked teeth when they hired him. Gently, he guided his thumb over the green button to take the photo. His phone vibrated and another button appeared. He pressed it to get rid of it, but answered a visual call instead.

Donaldo stared at him quizzically for a moment on the screen of his phone. "Well, I'm glad you're happy, but Jazon freaking Meyers was stomped to shit!"

Dean bolted upright and Butterball leapt off his lap. "What happened?"

"The AI core in Jazon was completely destroyed. It's unrepairable. Short of him being put into a car crusher made of the finest Fanglion spirit-iron, I have no idea how that even happened. How it's even physically possible."

"Where is Loveman?"

"I don't know. He's gone silent. He's operational, but he's not allowing me to watch his movements."

"What?"

"They have that freedom. Jazon never chose to go silent, but Loveman does it all the time."

"Wonderful." Dean squeezed his forehead where a headache had begun to emerge. "Even if he's tailing the Killer, we have no clue where either of them are."

"Why don't you get some sleep?" Donaldo yawned. "This will sort itself out by the morning. It always does."

"Sleep isn't in my near future."

"Well, stay off the streets. There was a report of a disturbance on the west end of town, something like a riot. They don't have details yet. It might be over the Grettish thing with the Zetú prisoners. They are planning to execute a few of them."

"Let me know if you hear from Loveman," Dean said coldly and hung up.

He sat back against the couch, feeling helpless. The Grettish terror groups only wanted to restore their wealth the Zetú had fairly taken in the United Market Exchange War. The awful thing was that Finny-Min and his community were not a group that reaped any of the financial rewards from the time. The Grettish species were all related through blood, however, and their idea that all species were linked in a similar way made them believe that all species were a large family held accountable as a group, rather than individuals. All this terror group was asking for, in this case, was enough money to rebuild their freighter. But the Zetú government would not negotiate with them.

Dean had read the internal, secret files not released to the galaxy. The terror group was desperate. They'd even suggested contract mercenary missions in exchange for the hostages, but received no response from any government official. Dean understood why. There were many such groups and catering to one would mean they'd need to cater to all of them.

But Finny-Min and his son, Dean... my friends. His mind raced.

Now they were just asking for a lump sum of money again.

His thoughts were broken as his employee Charles Blu emailed him. Dean read it, just for the sake of taking his mind off the present. The email essentially explained how busy Charles was and how he needed to find the time somehow to give his new recruits expense forms translated into Fanglion, but he had no time to coordinate with the translation department. What this meant was that Charles needed help with something he didn't want to do. The staff at the translation department at Limbus could be hard to handle sometimes and intimidating if you didn't know how to deal with them.

Dean told Charles he'd handle it.

He called an extremely high-strung woman named Helenex, who made Dean extremely uncomfortable for about ten minutes before she softened and explained that she could find time around lunch to process the form and send it to Charles. "He suggested you specifically. Said you were the best," Dean told her.

Helenex was extremely flattered.

After they hung up, Dean leaned forward and took a drink of lukewarm water from a porcelain cup. A little redirection never hurt. Now Helenex would be gentler with Charles, and he might actually do his own job next time, rather than involve Dean.

Probably not though.

Why?

Because you're a sucker, he could hear the Firecracker Lady say.

Just then it hit him square between the eyes. Dean sat up straight. A plan formed in his mind. Redirection. He can't fight the Charles incompetence from Moon City, and he couldn't fight the

Grettish terrorist either—but he could gentle them by giving them what they wanted. He didn't have the money to repair their freighter, but he knew someone now who did.

He called back Donaldo and told him to keep a confidential channel open to the Firecracker Lady. "Let her know I'm lining someone up to smuggle the crocoshark venom off the moon for her."

Donaldo jotted it down.

"Still no word from Loveman?"

"Nope. The riot was caused by wild animals though. Thought that was interesting."

"Okay," Dean replied, ignoring him, "get on that secure channel to Firecracker Lady please."

"Yep. Bye."

Dean immediately dialed out to Tasha's department and asked for a direct line to the Terror Group leadership. It took several channels and one disconnection, but since the group waited eagerly for their demands to be met, they were willing to speak to just about anyone.

Their leader was named Rooshish Zthuu. Dean couldn't see the telltale Grettish fedora, but only the burning silver eyes on his phone.

"We know you, Slaughter Man. Friend to Zetú. No friend to ours."

"I *am* a friend, and that's why I'm willing to bargain."

"Speak," replied Zthuu.

"Killing them is not going to get you what you want."

Zthuu's eyes studied him a moment. "We are ignored. Them. You. All. We kill instead. A better end than cowardice."

"I propose a bargain."

"Speak."

"I have work for you on Moon City. The Firecracker Lady has need of smugglers. You would be required to collect crocoshark venom, store it, and ship it off the moon to her buyers. Perhaps she'll even repair your freighter for the job."

Donaldo's text with the secure line address chimed on his phone. Dean was going out on a limb. He didn't know if the Firecracker Lady would completely go for this arrangement, but a little redirection could buy his friends time. Or maybe she could propose another deal for them.

"You work for her?" asked Zthuu.

"No," Dean admitted. "But she told me she had that need. I am getting you a secure line to her. Once you reach her, you may work out the deal. Send me an open channel and I will connect you."

"You do this for the Zetú?"

"Yes. If anything happens to them, she will not trust you to honor your agreement."

Zthuu sniffed, although Dean could not see the Grettish's nose under the shadow of its hat. "This appears to be a Limbus trap."

"This isn't a Limbus communication. You can ask them as much if you don't believe me."

"We will, human. And the Firecracker Lady. Your job is a dangerous one we may not accept."

"I leave that to you, but it *is* a way."

"Send an open channel," said Zthuu and then he abruptly hung up.

Quickly he forwarded the channel to Zthuu's address and sucked in some air through his teeth. Now, he could only hope they negotiated something. The Grettish leader didn't seem too trusting, but he also had his back against the wall. Time would tell.

Dean. Dean. Dean.

He cocked his head. He could have sworn he heard his name.

DeanDeanDeanDeanDean.

Getting up, he stepped over Butterball, who meowed expectantly at him.

DEAN.

DEAN.

DEAN.

DEAN.

A vibration went through the entire building and Dean stumbled back. "What the hell?" he muttered and went to the window.

He looked down below. Monstrous black shapes surrounded the building. They looked more than just wild animals as Donaldo had reported. These things looked like pieces of nightmare and shadow with long teeth and claws, and bleeding eyes that were hungry for...

DEAN.

It was the only word their mouths could form. He could tell in his gut they'd been made just for him, and the person who had made them was the very person he sought to kill.

"He knows where I am now," he whispered.

Calmly, Dean collected his gun off the table. The growls and snarls below grew louder as he went to the kitchen and took a butcher knife out of the drawer.

Chapter 21

The guard for the apartment building had been pulled through the double-pane glass window. Dean couldn't understand how this had even been done, but *it had*. He imagined that the monsters had somehow thrust their hands through the barrier, grabbed him by the shoulders and ripped him through the jagged remnants, but none of that seemed possible—there wasn't a shard of glass remaining, just a mutilated corpse that sunk beneath its bloody uniform, and one of the inky-black manifestations chewing on a left-over piece of flesh behind the left arm. The boomerang shaped game, Returno, that the guard had always been playing when Dean said hello to him, lay in a pool of coagulated, vermillion blood. Across from that large puddle, several dead reg police were also being feasted on.

Dean leveled his butcher's knife.

From around the corner of the street, sliding over the concrete driveway of a single-family dwelling, the shadow creations surged toward Dean. He didn't think any more on it and rushed into them headlong, swinging his butcher's blade at their throats and faces. They popped up before him in an endless succession. The blade went side to side and up and down in a manner that suggested that it knew the direction to go in without Dean's assistance. Boiling black blood hissed and sizzled as it tossed left and right. Open-mouthed horror and pain surrounded him as he killed tens and dozens and double dozens.

He was a robot now. Dean. Fulsome. Slaughter. Man.

He thought about Jazon Meyers.

About Mister Loveman.

He was the same.

Except he had no master.

He only had the misfortune of being a tool to kill.

The berserk rage continued. He felt his entire arm soaked with oil-black blood, from his knuckles to his neck. He remembered enduring this kind of endless murder back in the slaughterhouse in Corona. Back when his marriage was falling apart. Back when punching a hole through a cow's throat was therapeutic, even when he knew damn well it shouldn't, and that he was a horrible person and he had messed up his marriage and it was all his fault and why couldn't he just go away and understand that people like him only brought the rest of the world down and what could he offer that hadn't already been offered before?

Really?

Really?

And he remembered what bullshit it was then. And he remembered what bullshit it was now. But he was killing nonstop again and he had a woman he loved who was just as distant as his ex-wife had been at the time. Except now, he understood what real love was—he understood that it wasn't about dependency, it was about support and inspiration and so many things that he hadn't had earlier in his life. But he couldn't have them now.

He was here.

In Moon City.

Killing.

These.

Things.

The last monster he struck so hard, its head nearly came off its shoulders. It dangled there to the side for a second before the whole body collapsed backward.

More monsters surged around him.

Dean climbed on top of his car.

He was up there for less than a minute when a clawed hand wrapped around his ankle and yanked him down. Air left his lungs as he landed on his back. He couldn't breathe, but he reacted and lifted his butcher knife as a shadow creation leapt for his face. The blade cleaved it in two pieces, and the bloody, black things fell apart around his hands.

He got to his feet, but they grew in number around him. One tugged him down onto one leg. Dean tried to stand, but his head was slammed into the side of the car. Stars and moons cluttered his vision, but he still managed to cut the thing in half.

Then there was a void.

No monsters snapped around him.

Dean stumbled to regain himself.

Powerful hands wrapped around his shoulders.

He turned and swiped with his blade.

The man moved in a blur and caught him around the midsection. Dean felt his body being hurled backward from a force that had the strength of twenty, but the grace of a hundred. He landed several yards away, safely, yet rattled.

This person wasn't a monster like the rest, but something was *other* about him. The warmth of the touch around his waist told Dean it wasn't natural. It was superhuman.

He was to meet the Moon City Killer now. In the flesh.

Dean tried to focus.

His vision focused. The blurring world condensed down to clarity. And when his surroundings were finally clear, he could at last take in the man who stood before him.

His friend, Rick Agate.

Chapter 22

Dressed in black camouflage tactical gear and sporting major artillery, Rick didn't look any different than he had two days ago when he'd supposedly been killed. There wasn't even a scar on his neck from where the knife had gone through. There was something different about Rick's countenance however. His face looked more angular, regal, luminescent almost. He wasn't exactly the same man; it was as though a new intelligence bubbled under the surface of his skin.

"Sorry for roughing you up, buddy." He offered a hand, which Dean reluctantly took and allowed himself to be hauled to his feet with such ease it made him feel a child. "You were hacking up so many of those things, I had to break you out of your fit or you were going to hurt yourself."

Dean didn't buy it. "How did you survive? I saw what happened."

Rick touched his temple thoughtfully. "Looked pretty bad, didn't it?"

"Fatal, yes."

"Turns out that if you drink enough Deitii spinal fluid, your brain doesn't die so easily." A light smile touched his face.

"But—I don't follow you."

"It's not complicated, pal. I've been siphoning off the Moon City Killer's supply. I've been doing it for weeks now, unbeknownst to him. You're the first to know."

"To become powerful," Dean said dryly.

"*More* powerful," Rick added with a crocodile grin.

"So what happens now?"

"You looked famished. See down on that street corner there? Shublish Grill. You're going to wash up in their bathroom and then I'm going to buy you something to eat. They serve LFK burgers throughout third dinner. One of the best places in all of Moon City."

"I'm not hungry."

"Get moving, Dean," said Rick with a sigh. His eyes darkened. "There's a lot of talk about. First, drop the butcher knife." Dean hadn't realized he still gripped the weapon, coated in coagulated, black blood, in his grasp. He let it fall to the ground. He still had his gun in his back pocket, but he had no intention of trying to use it on someone like Rick, even without being suped-up on Deitii juice.

Neither man spoke. When they got to the restaurant, which looked like all other art deco diners in Moon City, Rick took control and got them a table. Then he led Dean to a bathroom in the back corner of the establishment. They walked in and Rick nodded to the basin. "Get that shit off you, buddy."

Dean began to scrub his arms with orange soap and warm water. The basin turned gray as the black blood and gore rinsed off.

"He's much farther along than me—he made those things, you know, to come after you," said Rick with great awe in his voice.

Dean said nothing and continued to wash.

"I told Limbus it was taking me a while to find the Moon City Killer, but I'd really found him right away, probably in twelve hours after I arrived. He'd already grown powerful enough to not worry about what trails he left behind. I watched him make several kills before I got the idea of what he was up to—I saw him move, saw his strength, and I got jealous... I'm not ashamed to admit that. You know?"

"Sure," said Dean as he grabbed a paper towel.

"Getting an edge like that would make me pretty good at my job."

"Far better than your brother." Dean grabbed another paper towel, disappointment and anger surging through him.

Rick chuckled. "You don't know what it's like to be me."

"Nope."

"Shut up, Dean. I got a knife through my damned neck! It was just about healed up when that freaky son of a bitch threw me down a bottomless pit—well, there was a bottom, turns out. It wasn't pleasant, even though my bones healed almost right away too. The hardest part was keeping my heart from beating, playing dead for so long. I'm not as far along as he is and I've only had a few feedings. My fugue state gave me time though to think through some plans, but I had to jump the hell to it once I was pitched over that cliff and was breaking every bone in my body left and right."

"How did he not discover you were stealing his supply?" asked Dean.

Rick's somber face was replaced by a mischievous one. "Your memory is foggy after you drink it. I realized he'd not be able to keep track of how much he had. I watched him. He didn't keep an inventory. He'd drink, go out on a run, and come back to empty jars and not be able to trust his memory enough to grow suspicious. It just worked that way. Hell, I may have even had more than a few bottles myself. I've forgotten too. In the beginning I just thought he'd assume he got ripped off, but then he never seemed to change his movements or secure his supply better. After my own experiences, I figured out why and it couldn't have worked out any better. That's just because it was meant to be. Some people deserve greatness and others don't."

Except for his shirt sleeve stained gray, Dean was clean now. "So you're looking to be God too then?"

"Not even—I don't want to be all-knowing or see and feel everything. You've got me pegged right, buddy. Bottom line, I just want to outdo my brother. I need to be the best at what I do, and I want him to see it and know it and appreciate it, in EVERY dimension."

"How in the hell would you do that?"

Rick opened the bathroom door. "I haven't decided if I'll tell you that part yet."

They walked to their table and sat down. The waitress brought over the menus, but Rick waved her off. "He already knows what he's getting. An LFK, medium." He looked at Dean. "Fries?"

Dean shrugged.

"They have good fries here."

Dean looked at the waitress. "Gimme fries too. And a beer. That local stuff."

"Moon Lager."

"That's the one."

"And for you, sir?" the waitress asked Rick.

"I'm not hungry. Just ice water with an orange slice."

"Oranges haven't arrived yet this week. Freighters are stuck from the Grettish war."

"Well, I'll take it without fruit then. Please hurry on the burger," Rick told her with a polite wink.

"You got it."

When she left, Dean leaned forward. "What's this about? Why are you force feeding me?"

"The LFKs can't be missed." Rick's smile was unnatural, wrong.

"What's it stand for?"

"Lavafuck."

"Sounds lovely."

"Good. As you know, I love introducing my friends to new cuisine. Hope you like spicy."

"I don't actually. I'll have to send it back. I have bad acid reflux. I don't even eat spaghetti sauce anymore. Really messes up my gut."

"That's too bad, but you're eating this burger. It has pureed riot pepper in it—it's like the Carolina reaper pepper back on Earth, except it has some amphetamine components that get the heart jerking pretty good—like a riot in your chest, hence the name. The pepper is too powerful to eat on its own, so it's usually blended into hamburgers or taco meat. I tried it once on Ganymede 35. Really screwed me up."

"What has gotten into you? I thought we were friends."

"Damn, I was wondering how long it would take for you to say that, Slaughter Man."

"Don't call me that," Dean snapped. "I've gone to bat for you. I *got you* this mission."

"I'll tell you more, but you have to cooperate. Eat the burger. Drink your beer. Drink two of them and my water. You'll need it."

"Up yours."

Rick's nostrils flared. "I will kill everyone in here if you don't eat it. Don't make this nasty."

"Bullshit."

His friend remained silent for a moment and stared outside at the bare street. Up on the corner, all the black corpses of the Moon City Killer's monsters lay in heaps. Dean couldn't actually believe he'd killed all of them by himself. It seemed unreal.

"We do what we have to," said the mercenary.

"When it's the right thing to do." Dean could hear the words coming through his teeth. He was tired of being jerked around by the people he cared about the most.

"I *told* you not to come here, Dean," whispered Rick. "Once Tasha got it in her head I needed admin support with the mayor and all that, I said do whatever you could to leave me be or send somebody else who wouldn't get in my way. Remember that above all I told you not to come here. I told you it would be dangerous and you might not make it back home."

"That's how all my offworld jobs are."

"You could have fought harder. Instead, you bent over and showed up, right on the day I could have taken out that bastard and drank his brain down and maybe the rest of his supply. It would have been done. It would have been all I needed. I could have been happy. Limbus would have been happy. You wouldn't be alone here, away from your woman and about to die. Now I have to deal with all this shit I didn't want to, so you're going to eat that burger. It's necessary anyway."

"Necessary? How?"

"You'll see. I've thought this all out."

Dean tamped down his impulse to punch the man in his square smile. "Who are you?"

"I'm the little brother," said Rick, nodding. "I'm the little brother who took all he could take."

"He's your blood."

Rick shook his head and grabbed a salt shaker, spinning it around between his calloused fingers. "You don't have the profession

I have, Dean. My brother won't take this personally. He'll accept that he underestimated me."

"Because you aren't playing fair. You will never be able to say you really beat him."

"I can live with that, especially since every dimension will understand who the greater force is. You see, buddy, it's been a long time since a genuine smile crossed my face, but whenever I think of a universe that holds me up as the greater of the two Agates... I can't help but grin."

"How are you going to do this in every dimension?"

Rick's mouth twisted and he shrugged. "What the hell? You aren't long for this world anyway."

"So you say."

"I've become quite an expert at membrane transport lately. I've read all the studies and trials. There is a way for a single person to hop dimensions."

"It was you," said Dean. "You caused the membranes to slip on me."

The salt shaker spun out of Rick's hands and spilled over the table. He picked it up quickly and pushed it back against the wall next to the pepper and a jar of some green alien spice. "You weren't ever supposed to make it here, Dean... I had that planned for some other schmuck."

"You could have just left me to die."

Rick made an expression of hurt. "Buddy, that's pretty raw of you to say. But anyway, I'm glad it worked out the way it did though. You've done a decent job occupying the Moon City Killer with that robot. Now that he's not suspecting it, on defense and looking for you to kill, I can catch him unawares, put a nice big smile in his neck with my favorite knife and then siphon his brain—it'll be more potent than any Deitii by now—since we've all waited this long. In the beginning I just wanted to kill him and take his stash. Now I *need* the asshole or I'll never be better than my brother. Don't look so surprised! If I'm going into the dimensions to get my brother, I have to be ready."

"Where'd you get the galaxy glass? I know you're planning to get to other dimensions by taking it through the membranes."

Rick's mouth parted in a smile of admiration. "Oh, you're smarter than you look, Dean."

"How'd you get the glass? Those are costly and Friars don't part with them unless they're killed."

The mercenary glanced around. "Where is that burger of yours?"

"How, Rick?" Dean asked again.

Rick cleared his throat. "Courtesy of the Moon City Killer. All the Grettish Friars he slaughtered at the mayor's estate the other day left plenty of their swords behind. I got a few of them stashed back at the transport station."

"I hadn't heard about that."

"No, I guess not. You were too busy overdosing on Constalife."

"You were behind that too?"

"Of course. It all works together, buddy. That and your delicious burger."

The waitress showed up then and put the plate down in front of Dean. The hamburger looked innocent enough except for a bright red cheese melted over its sides.

"Sorry, guys, just a few things I have to say." The waitress read off a notepad. "Any heart problems or nervous system problems, you must disclose before you eat the LFK. Also, has anybody at the table taken a higher dose of Constalife than recommended by the Moon City surgeon general?"

Dean cocked his head at his former friend and narrowed his eyes. Rick held his stare and replied, "No, we are good."

"Please read the warning on the napkin under the plate. Also, I have to ask if either of you has ever acquired the Quantum Flu? Unfortunately, it's another precaution we have to take. It tends to weaken the heart and that also isn't safe."

"We are completely good," Rick answered. "Lifetime Moon City citizens. Never left through a membrane transport."

"Me neither," the waitress said with a flirty wink. "Okay, enjoy! I'll keep the water and beer flowing. Be sure to wash your hands with the towelettes."

Dean stared down at the burger, feeling sick. "You killed that Noggin... I was right there, inside the shack. You had the chance again."

Rick sighed. "The Noggin spotted me when I came back for the extra thermos of Deitii fluid I hid behind your shack. It wasn't personal but I had to do what I had to. Look, I left his damn cat alive. I'm not such a bad guy. So let's get going, eh, compadre? Although it's uncomfortable, I'm going to insist you eat."

Dean grabbed the burger and took a large bite. He immediately felt the heat on the roof of his mouth, but he continued through. The fiery sting actually soaked into his gums and burned the roots of his teeth and his esophagus trembled as the pieces traveled down. A sour churning formed in his stomach right away. His forehead broke out in sweat, which followed a massive army of rolling beads of perspiration down his shoulders and his back. He had to finish the hamburger, but halfway through, he already started gagging.

"Slow down, buddy. You don't have to go so fast."

Dean didn't slow down though. He kept devouring the burger without even drinking his beer or water. If he could just get it all down at once, he'd be able to deal with the fallout rather than prolong the suffering, but this was harsh. It was the worst thing he'd ever chewed up and swallowed. It hardly seemed edible by human standards. His arteries and heart felt like they were going to explode. Rick had planned this for some reason. The overdose of Constalife already had his heart rate up.

He finished eating and downed the beer and his water right away. He started on Rick's glass of water when the man stopped chuckling and began talking. "I know how he watches people. I've been able to do it myself—the beating heart of a living thing is a beacon. The Moon City Killer wants you, Dean—I thought he'd clue in with all that Constalife raging through you, but he's only now sending his little minions your way. I didn't want to make you bait, but it's the only way to get him to come. This way he'll have to come himself. He'll have to make sure you are taken care of. He won't take chances on any more monsters." Rick grabbed his head. "I'm not even as far along as he is and your heartbeat is getting to me."

Dean was about to pass out. He saw Rick throw some money on the table. He felt his body being hoisted up out of the booth seat and being guided back outside. In the distance, he heard the waitress ask if he was okay and Rick say he was fine.

The caverns outside shook with every painful pounding of Dean's chest.

A rope slid around him and tightened. He could do nothing but slump there, against the com pole he'd been placed up on. "We have to get you all set up for your big date," said Rick.

Dean felt like vomiting but he was losing consciousness. His head snapped to the side as Rick struck him across the face. "Keep awake," he cautioned. "And don't have a damned heart attack."

Numbness surged up Dean's left arm and his neck bent with a painful spasm. He realized then he might not be able to fulfill that request.

Chapter 23

I was moving so quickly I couldn't tell which hand unscrewed the jars and which hand slammed them up against my mouth, but I had worked through almost my entire reserve. There could be no further delay with that robot looking for me.

I threw open the last cupboard with a disgusting belch. The entire universe bent around me. I was so ready to accept my destiny and climb up Mount Olympus to live there permanently. Nothing was certain though. I could only wager that the remaining three jars of spinal fluid slurry would be enough. I believed deeply that it would be, just from how close I'd come earlier today, but I would need my food and require enough time to make the transition from flesh to living spirit.

And in the last cupboard I saw the remaining three jars.

All of them empty.

I stared at them in disbelief. This couldn't be happening. These were jars I sent with Carl. I couldn't have ever drunk from them. I reached out and pushed one to the side to see if it was leaking. Stupid to even think that... all three of them wouldn't be leaking. And short of dropping the jars and breaking them, there was no way it all spilled out so *evenly*.

Carl had taken some after he left. Probably stashed them somewhere. That was the only answer. He had taken some for himself, or worse, to sell on the black market. Did he actually believe I was that forgetful?

I listened for his heart beat.

Sure enough, he was only a block away.

I called him, and told him as calmly as I could to meet me at the reserve supply shed. He didn't seem nervous; his heartbeat didn't even increase. Either he was stupid, which I knew he wasn't, or he had a pretty damned good cover-up for this.

Gingerly, I drank down the remaining three.

It wouldn't be enough. I'd cut it too close. I would need to kill at least one other Deitii. I was so angry I hardly noticed when Carl walked in.

I turned to him and his eyes bulged at all the empty jars.

"All of them?" he asked. "Why'd I even bother bringing them—?"

"Shut up," I told him.

He made a face. "Are you feeling okay?"

Sweat dappled my upper lip and I felt cold from the inside out. "You stole from me, boy. I can no longer trust you."

"What the hell are you talking about?"

"I saw the last three jars."

Carl's eyebrow lifted. "What about them? I put everything in the cupboards, just like you told me to. Maybe someone broke in and stole them?"

I lunged forward. He tried to evade me, but being nowhere near as swift and precise as I was, I caught him by the back of the neck.

"Get your hands off me!" he shouted. "You think I stole the sick junk?"

I lifted him off the ground and took him outside. "Disappointing," I whispered. "So very disappointing."

He twisted in my grip, his hands digging at mine to release him. "Please," he said. "You're wrong. I didn't take anything. It had to be somebody else. Believe me!"

I took him up the side of a boulder that cropped out over a small valley of darkness. "I trusted you." The words were hot spit on my quivering lips.

"Please," he begged.

"Over there, do you see?" I asked. "That's where the Midnight Sea is."

"Don't," he cried through his raining tears.

I extended my arm back and became giddy—I wanted to see his body sail over the void and slash in the brine somewhere out there in the blackness—but then something fiery stuck in my eye, and out of reflex, I dropped the kid. I heard his feet hit the dirt and him take off running. I swiveled around just to see the star-eyed robot plunge a dinner fork into my other eye. I growled in rage and met the thing full force. It stabbed me with the fork and what felt like a knife, repeatedly, more than fifty times before I crashed through the side of my supply shed window.

I stood and shook a thousand bits of glass off me, not suffering a single cut. The robot twisted up from the floor, some of its pale, artificial skin hanging with blue-tinged thermal layers. I grabbed the entire cupboard that took up the whole wall and brought it down on the thing. Before it had a chance to make its way back to its feet, I knew I had to act quickly.

I went outside, and rounded the supply shed. There I put my hands against the steel construction and pushed effortlessly. The shed tore from its foundation and flew off the side of outcropping. It crashed down against several large boulders below, spinning and breaking apart in the vast black space.

If the robot hadn't been outright destroyed, it was not coming back up the side of this steep valley any time soon.

I turned and searched for Carl. I wanted to find him and end him, teach him a lesson for complicating my plans. He was heading home, heart pounding hard, yet I couldn't concentrate on its rhythm.

There was only one heartbeat I could focus on.

It belonged to Dean Fulsome.

It sounded like a drum the size of a universe. It made me dizzy and sick to my stomach. It was madness. How had it become so loud? Louder than all the other beings in Moon City? It beat irregular and fast and deep in a way only a failing heart would—except it was living on somehow. I had listened to people with failing hearts. I had listened to people with heart attacks. This wasn't the same. This was like a marching band parade of heart attacks inside one person's chest. It would have killed anybody not overdosed on Constalife. What was this? Was he trying to lure me into a trap?

I had to end it or lose my mind. Why was this happening? I'd been so close. There was no time to pick at this flea any longer. It felt like I was walking into a trap, but I had to make it stop, and I was a slim margin away from godhood. Who could trap me?

The cuts in my eyes sealed shut and my vision returned.

Who indeed?

Dean's heart quaked inside my mind. I went to it, eager to get a respite from the horrible pounding.

Chapter 24

Dean felt on the verge of passing out, but as he hung there, tied to the com pole at the side of the road, one thing, one very small thing, gave him hope.

The head of a nail.

It poked out just enough that he could drag the rope around his wrists across it, back and forth. True, it probably wouldn't cut through for another eight hours, but any hope was good hope at this point. He just wished his chest would stop rattling and his mouth, stomach, eyes, and ears didn't feel like they were engulfed in flames. He kept burping up that burger and it provided more pain than relief.

Rick waited alongside a defunct nightclub across the street. The galaxy glass scimitar looked ridiculously large next to him, but Dean had no doubt the man could wield it without any issues. He wouldn't, of course. Rick needed the Moon City Killer's brain, disgusting as that sounded, and he wouldn't risk eliminating him from all dimensions by using galaxy glass on him. Rick wasn't stupid, however. He knew if he had the best weapon to remove a threat, he had better bring it to the party. He probably already figured out that if this turned out bad, it was better to remove his opposition completely, which would then mean that Rick would go off hunting the Deitii, and one serial killer would have replaced another.

For everybody's sake, Dean hoped they both just killed each other.

He continued to work at the nail, and for some reason, his eyes couldn't leave that sword. Rick's plan was interesting, and it made some interesting ideas twist into Dean's own sweating brain. Redirection... redirection... It was his only hope with the Moon City Killer.

His eyes lifted to Rick as he checked a long survival knife's edge. Dean was pretty sure his old friend would never be redirected. He'd thought of all outcomes and was dead set on his plans.

"Don't do this," Dean shouted. "Rick—"

"I'm still doing what Limbus paid me for, buddy. Now shut it."

A figure walked down the lonesome street. It was the man Dean had watched in the videos. He no longer wore his fedora and his clothing was torn and speckled with dirt and charred in some places. Stab wounds covered his torso and neck but they had scabbed over.

He stopped, just short of Rick's ambush. "Come out, mercenary," he said with an icy tone. "I see now who pilfered my supply of food."

Rick's body relaxed. He looked down and considered the galaxy glass sword.

Do it, thought Dean. *Don't be greedy. Kill the bastard. Wipe him out from every dimension.*

A moment later, Rick rounded the building, just a knife in his hand. He flew at the Moon City Killer, weapon raised overhead. They crashed against one another and grappled together. Rick surprised his opponent by slinging him back against the building. The impact sent cracks through the plaster and bricks busting behind the Moon City Killer's back. With a growl, he went forward and grasped Rick's wrists.

Dean worked at the rope but suddenly the feeling of warm fingers surrounded his own.

"I know a quick way out," said a child's voice.

"Kid, you gotta—"

"My name's Carl. I'm from your apartment building," he said. "Now let me get this"—something hard went past Dean's palm—"off of you."

The rope snapped in half and Dean was free. The kid stood there behind the com pole with a pocket knife. "This way," he instructed.

Rick screamed down the street. A group of conjured monsters had ensnared him and the Moon City Killer walked casually his way.

Carl led Dean to an alley. At the end was a service door near a dumpster. "It's open. We can hide there."

"Good deal," Dean whispered. Over his shoulder, out of the corner of his eye, he saw the Moon City Killer pop Rick Agate's head like a water balloon in his fingers, then plunge a hand through his chest and rip out everything inside. It didn't look like his old friend would be healing from this death.

Soon, the screams ended.

They got to the door. Carl went inside first.

"Thanks for helping me, kid," Dean told him.

Carl turned around just as Dean shut the door behind him and pulled the dumpster toward him. The door opened part way as Carl hollered out to him. Luckily, the dumpster was on wheels and wasn't too full. Dean was able to push it fully against the door.

When he turned back, the Moon City Killer waited at the other end of the alley, the galaxy glass sword in his hand.

"I'm pleased to meet you, Dean Fulsome. I've been busy or we could have done this sooner. I enjoyed the robots you sent me."

"They weren't my idea," Dean said, taking a few steps toward him. "I would have rather killed you myself."

"Now's your chance." The Killer's eyes sparkled.

"You should end this killing."

He snorted. "Why?"

"I watched the video of your conversation with your mother. You said you had a son. Don't you want to see him?"

"He lives in another dimension, not ours. It is impossible."

Dean swallowed and steadied himself. His heart had calmed down a bit but still thundered. "I have an idea if you will listen to it."

"I cannot bear keeping you alive any longer." The Killer moved forward.

"You can be with your son."

He halted a second. "Lies," he said and continued on.

"It's not—if you take that through the membranes with you." Dean pointed to the galaxy glass scimitar pointed straight at him.

The Killer instantly understood, as though slapped across the face. He narrowed his almond-shaped eyes.

"You can go to any dimension you want," Dean concluded. "The transport station is only a couple blocks from here. You could leave now. You're probably the only human resilient enough to withstand the journey."

"You are not so stupid, it would seem. This is something I haven't even considered, but now that I see through the fabric of all things, I know you're right. It truly is a great idea. How did you discover this?"

"I took a seminar on galaxy glass once."

The man chuckled. It sounded like his first ever. He glanced around, looking tired. "My work in Moon City is unfinished. Your Limbus cohort robbed me of my food."

"That may be, but do you really need it now?" Dean asked. "I'd give anything to be back with my..."

"Fiancée," the Killer finished. "Yes, so?"

"I've given you a way to be with your son. Isn't that all you really want anyway?"

"Your sick heart rhythm is righting itself now, Dean Fulsome, but that doesn't mean I should keep you alive."

"Sure," replied Dean. "But you've never killed without reason. If you leave here, you never have to see me again."

The Killer lifted the sword and stood before Dean, considering the edge. For a moment, Dean felt like the sword might be the last thing he saw in this life, but the Moon City Killer nodded and turned back down the alley. Before he disappeared around the corner, he looked over his shoulder.

"You spare this dimension, but give me to another one? I will kill there too, starting with the other version of myself. I cannot decide if you're a coward or a brilliant strategist."

"I usually make enough problems for myself as it is," Dean told him. "The other me will deal with you if he has to."

The Moon City Killer smiled thinly and lifted a hand in farewell.

Dean immediately pulled out his phone and dialed the transport station to inform them there would be an arrival who had no clearance. "Stand down," he ordered. "You'll not want to engage this man. Just leave the controls open for him. Yes, I'm serious... and let me know when he's gone through."

He crumbled to the ground and sat there, heart and head still buzzing.

* * *

The phone conversation with Tasha was over an hour long, but Dean felt strangely comfortable listening to her voice on his phone while he sat against some crates in the dark, quiet building. The strange gyrations of his heart had ceased and the sweat on his body had cooled.

The membrane transport sustained serious damage as it took on the Killer along with the galaxy glass. Such a transfer had only been done a couple times before and the data wasn't shared with anybody outside of Limbus, Inc. Dean had a feeling that the Moon City Killer had gone to where he wanted to go, however. His mission to protect the Deitii had been accomplished... at least in this dimension... but his reward of Golden Transport would not be available.

The station needed countless repairs now according the Tasha, and it could only transport people to Moon City, not away from it. It would take close to three or four months to bring it back online, but it would never be able to make Golden Transports available. Every day he spent here, the time he'd return to Earth would be exponentially greater. So if he left in three months, it would bring him back to Earth three-hundred and sixty plus years later. Even if Sandra agreed to stasis, she would need to take around ten years off throughout the time to not succumb to hibernation damage.

Short of embarking on a suicide mission, like killing the high-commander of a Grettish armada and stealing one of its wormships to journey to another nearby star system where a Golden Transport might be available, Dean slowly came to terms with being a Moon City citizen for the next few months.

Not long to wait.

For him.

He called Sandra. She sounded happy to hear from him, learning the news of the Killer being removed from the dimension. News always traveled fast around Limbus, Inc.'s headquarters. If only Dean could have traveled back to Earth as fast.

He told her he needed to talk about something important, and the joy in her tone quickly diminished.

"I'm sure you've heard about the transport."

"Dean, yes, but we don't have to right now. I'm just glad you're okay—I was so worried, honey. I've had so much to share with you, and I—"

"Look, I have to say this," whispered Dean. "It cannot be. I'm sorry. I can't ask you to go into stasis now. It's asking even more than I originally was asking, and even that was too much."

"Like I said, let's just be calm and talk through some of this. We don't have to make any decisions right now. There's a lot of things we need to talk about. But we can do it together. That's why we are made for each other."

"We're not," Dean said, his whole body trembling. "I don't love you anymore."

"Come on," she told him. "Stop being silly."

"I've learned things out here. I used you as a crutch too long. That's why I left, because deep down inside, I wanted to be away from you."

She was silent for a few breathless moments.

"You can't really mean this."

"I do."

"So this is what you really want?" she asked.

"What I need," he told her, his heart breaking. His eyes warmed with tears but he wouldn't let them fall.

"You don't have to do this."

"Good-bye, Sandra. It was unbelievable for a while."

She hung up on him.

He didn't figure, in that second, it would be the last time he ever heard from her. He was sure she'd call back, pissed off or sad or both, but he promised himself not to let his cards show. Sandra's emotional intelligence surpassed his by light miles, and she knew exactly why he'd chosen to end it. One day she'd forgive him. At least he hoped.

His phone rang again, and he smiled at first, thinking it was her and thinking how great it would be to hear her voice one last time rather than the possibility of never hearing it again.

But it was his employee, Charles Blu.

"So sorry, Dean... I just... Well, I gotta get a mole looked at on my back. I only go to a specialist in the eastern quadrant. Big problem though with my appointment. I don't have time to do my incoming requests for tomorrow. I don't want to stay too late today because I've been having trouble sleeping, you know?"

"Sure," said Dean. "I can handle all the requests. Just forward them to me."

"Thank you, sir. I will call you when I get to the office tomorrow."

"There's no need for you to come back tomorrow."

"Sorry?"

"You're fired, Charles. Clear out your shit after your appointment."

"Dean, really, what's the joke—?"

He hung up. A moment later, Dean burst out laughing, picking himself up from the ground. He moved the dumpster out of the way and checked inside for the kid, Carl, but the resourceful adolescent had made his way out of the building somewhere else.

Returning to the street, Dean spotted a grisly scene up ahead. Sirens wailed in the distance as the reg police continued to respond to all the carnage left behind from the Moon City Killer.

He avoided crossing the street ahead where two monsters ate what was left of Rick Agate's corpse. Dean's stomach was just beginning to settle from that atrocious hamburger he'd been forced to eat, but now it was beginning to gurgle uneasily at the gory sight. Rather unconsciously, he stole one more glance behind as he turned down an adjacent street. The monsters were fighting over what was left of Rick's power-enriched brain. There wasn't much.

Chapter 25

The membranes allowed me to wait within, judging all possibilities. I knew once I left them though the choice would be made and there would be no turning back. So I only chose the one dimension that made the most sense. It was a life with my boy. There were a few I found that had both Miles and his mother alive, but compromises had to be made. I had to choose the one with the perfect version of Miles in it, and in that reality, his mother had overdosed as well.

I couldn't change that. But I had my boy.

His allegiance was so blind, he never noticed the differences between me and the version of the father he'd already grown up with and come to love. Murdering myself, even a different version, was cathartic in a way I'd never ever be able to describe.

But the only thing that mattered was truly this: Miles' love for me, for his father, made me feel more like a god than any Deitii ever had.

And I fundamentally changed him. For the better.

We murdered together. We savored power. We ruled all.

For a great long time.

I eventually met the Slaughter Man again, under very different circumstances.

One day I shall hopefully write again about my experiences with Dean Fulsome.

If we all live long enough to see that day.

Chapter 26

Dean sat on the sofa with the cat. He thought about trying to sleep, but his heart still pounded unnaturally fast. He wouldn't be coming down from the Constalife for probably another full moon day or so. And the hamburger? Well, it was safe to say that another couple trips to the can were in order before he finally purged his system of the riot pepper.

A knock came to the door. He got up, knees cracking, back clenching, and heart *wobbling*. It was a miracle he was still alive for more reasons than he could even begin to count. He went to the peep hole. Two men in suits stood outside. They didn't look like ruffians, but he still put his hand on his firearm in his front right pocket.

"Who is it?" he asked.

"Special agents with the mayor's task force. We want to ask some questions about earlier today, regarding the... suspect you were investigating."

"No thanks," said Dean. "I've got no comment on that."

"Please, Mr. Fulsome. We will not take much of your time."

"I'm not feeling well today, fellas. If you'd like, I'll come down to City Hall later today or early tomorrow and give a report."

"That's gracious of you but the mayor needs to make a statement in two hours about this individual and his whereabouts. He seeks to put citizens at ease. We just need a few statements from you that he will use."

Dean just wanted them gone so he could decompress. "Yeah," he answered, and opened the door.

Immediately, they rushed in and pushed him to the floor. The wind left his lungs just as quickly as his gun left his front pocket. He watched as one of the men looked at it before tossing it into a corner.

Butterball hissed and darted into the hallway.

"Should I get the cat?" asked one of the men. He had a thin mustache that reminded Dean of Zorro.

The other was overweight with a comb-over of limpid chestnut hair and intensely blotchy red skin. "Close the door, asshole."

"Right," said Zorro. He got up, shut the door, and bolted it.

They zip-tied Dean's wrists behind his back. Comb-Over checked the front living space, while Zorro checked the bedroom.

Such an idiot, he thought.

"I take it you're not here for a statement," he muttered.

"No, the statement's been made already," said Comb-Over as he struggled to his feet. "You really should've been watching the feeds on an e-reader. The mayor's bloodline has been challenged by outsiders. He has denied that and publicly blamed Limbus for the killing of Deitii refugees. The citizens are behind him. They know Limbus has only come here to stake a foothold and expand contracts for other galactic governments. You never had an intention of helping the Deitii or this moon. The mayor has vowed to see you and Limbus destroyed. That begins here. We'll see what's in the apartment, what is damaging to the mayor, and then check you into dreamtime—permanently. It will all be more pleasant if you cooperate."

"That's what I do," Dean replied dully.

"Good. So you can start by telling us what all these papers are over there?" asked Comb-Over.

"I'm not totally sure to be honest. They were left by Rick Agate."

"The mercenary? One of the Agate brothers?" The man's brow lifted and his comb-over flexed.

"Yeah, that's the one."

"You're such a bad liar."

"Hey, think what you want to," Dean said. "I haven't had a chance to go through all his research papers. He was here to track the Moon City Killer before he was... killed."

"It was never your intention of taking that monster out," said Comb-Over. "That's why you gave him sanctuary in another dimension."

"So that's what the mayor's been spinning? Fine. Bottom line is the job is done. A dangerous monster has been removed from this moon."

Zorro came back and shrugged his shoulders. "Nothing in the bedroom or the kitchen. Place is clean."

Comb-over man rounded the sofa and stared down at the papers. "We don't have time to sort through all this crap."

"Agreed," said his partner. "So how about the incinerator?"

"Yes, let's just roast it all."

Dean lay there, bound by the wrists, waiting for the slug to the head, but his heart was already thundering, so he couldn't feel more anxious even if he wanted to. He wished he'd listened to Sandra. He wished he'd been the person the Firecracker Lady had chided him over. He wasn't though. He was just a loyal worker bee, an ex-slaughterhouse employee, a sticker, a man who punched a knife through a living thing to start the process of feeding a bunch of people who would never know or care about him. Every pair of sad bovine eyes he'd ever seen flashed before him and he imagined his own eyes looking the same way. He found it ironic that he'd survived a super assassin and a demigod, but wouldn't survive the politics of his job. If he didn't deserve it, the whole affair might have made him sad, but it didn't. Dean was just tired. If anything, he felt the worst about losing his fiancée and how upside down she must feel right now.

The men stuffed around half of the papers into the incinerator.

"Turn it on," said Comb-Over.

Zorro hunkered down at the wall and moved a dial, then pushed a button. The burners lit a second later.

"Sure there isn't anything else here?" Comb-Over asked Dean.

Dean just shook his head.

"We'll come back tomorrow for another once-over," said Comb-Over to Zorro, who nodded with his lips thoughtfully pursed.

"What the hell is that smell?" one of them asked. Dean had closed his eyes briefly so hadn't seen who made the statement. He looked up at saw Comb-Over sniffing the air. "Doesn't smell like burning paper at all. Smells like nuts or something, right?"

"Yeah," said Zorro. "Like... those kind from Earth, the oval ones."

"Almonds."

"Yeah. I feel sick."

"What?"

"Like I'm gonna yack."

"Okay, shut off the damn thing. Something's wrong."

Zorro switched off the incinerator but abruptly vomited on this floor.

"What the hell is the matter with you?" Comb-Over went to help him but suddenly crashed shoulder-first into the wall.

A twinge of nausea settled in Dean's stomach. He knew enough from his confined-spaced classes when he was plant manager at the onion factory that the smell of almonds followed by what these two idiots were going through wasn't just bad, it would be fatal. He didn't know what kind of crap had been on those documents or if something had been in the incinerator itself, but he needed to get out of there fast.

And try not to breathe.

Dean fought to his feet and went to the door. He unlatched the bolt and went to grasp the handle. He jiggled it, but it stuck fast. Rick had tampered with the thing and it was tricky to open even with free hands.

Shit.

Dean suddenly felt dizzy. His mind constructed an implausible plan of sticking a knife in between the door and bolt, and he could wedge it open that way and pull the door free from its catch. It made sense, but not really. In the back of his mind, he realized he just needed a solid grip on the handle.

He went to the kitchen for a knife, blinking through heavy, stinging tears in his eyes. The two thugs in business suits lay in heaps near the incinerator. Dean almost gasped at Zorro's long tongue hanging out of his mouth, reminding him of a dead cow.

Keep your mouth shut, he instructed himself.

But he was already lightheaded from holding his breath.

His hip crashed into the counter as he staggered into the kitchen. He opened the silverware drawer and pulled out a knife. He rounded the counter and went back to the front door.

The knife slipped from his hand.

He looked at it on the floor, forgetting what he might have even wanted to use it for.

He backed up to the door and took the knob. He couldn't jiggle it the right way with his hands tied like this.

The knife!

He could... cut through... somehow.

Dean's eyes fluttered and his body slammed to the floor, his lungs instinctively taking in a deep breath. He tried to remember what gas smelled like almonds and whether it was heavier than air—was it more concentrated near the floor, where he lay?

He held his breath again. His lungs burned.

Something crashed into his side.

The door.

Powerful hands gripped him under his arms and yanked him into the hallway without any care for how his body slammed against the doorjamb on the way out. His rescuer continued to drag him down the hall, a distance away from the room. Dean caught his breath and sucked clean air into his fiery chest. His eyes were goopy and stinging, running with tears.

He heard a door shut and lifted his head. His rescuer had shut the door to the contaminated room and was heading back. Dean's vision was blurred, but the man wore a purple shirt and his face glowed angelic white. He took a knee beside Dean. Before his eyes could clear, Dean noted the shape of Butterball slink in between them, the warm fur brushing his face. The man lifted the cat and held it, stroking it.

Dean's eyes refocused and everything became clear.

"Mr. Loveman."

The star-eyed robot watched him closely. His purple polo shirt was torn, and Dean noticed many slight injuries to his pale, synthetic skin, but otherwise, Mr. Loveman looked unharmed by his encounter with the Moon City Killer.

"I am glad this animal had your DNA attached to it. There are many apartments in the complex, Mr. Fulsome."

"What are you doing here, Loveman?"

"I can't locate my target, Mr. Fulsome," the robot told him. "The membrane transport has no log of his arrival to any planet or body in this known universe. I need your help to locate the Moon City Killer."

The elevator opened and Carl came running down the hall. "Mister!" he cried. "I think two men from the mayor are—" He stopped when he saw the robot.

"They already showed, kid," said Dean. "I'm okay. Get on home."

Carl's head canted at the robot. Mr. Loveman swiveled and handed him the cat.

"You're giving this to me?" he asked.

Loveman looked at Dean. "It's my cat," Dean said, "but yeah, that's a good idea. I need you to watch him a bit."

"What's his name?"

"Butterdi—Butterball."

"You'll give me money for food and litter?" asked Carl, his delight in a new companion apparent.

"Absolutely. But don't come back to my apartment. I'll find you. It isn't safe right now."

"For me too—after my parents found out who my last friend was, they aren't speaking much right now. I'll be staying with my dad at the Commerce Polity. Ask for Carl Riggers."

"Okay, boy."

Butterball twisting in his hold, Carl eyed Mr. Loveman with concern. "He's going to kill you, isn't he, Dean?"

"No," Mr. Loveman told him. "I've put in the request, but my master still needs to sign a release."

There was a long pause between all of them and then Carl finally nodded and walked away. "You'll come by soon?"

"Yes, you have my word, kid." He looked at Loveman. "I need to repay those kind souls who saved me."

Loveman's mouth could not move. It just remained a flat line. The star eyes were black, uncaring. "Where did the Moon City Killer go?"

"We'll talk later, Carl," Dean told the boy.

Carl nodded uncertainly before opening the elevator and getting on with the cat. Once he was gone, Dean scooted back on his hands. "I need this off."

Mr. Loveman noticed the zip-tie around Dean's wrists. He coiled one of his fingers around it, ripped up through the plastic, sending intense pain through Dean's arms. "That'll bruise," he said, wincing.

"You're free," explained the robot. "Now, where can I find the Moon City Killer?"

"He's gone to another plane. A separate dimension. Left through the membrane transport."

"That's impossible unless... he carried galaxy glass."

"He *did*," said Dean, rubbing his wrists.

Loveman leaned away from him. "That is not good news. This doesn't sit well with me. Not at all. It's very disappointing. First he takes Jazon, and now this."

"That's the breaks," said Dean. "I'm sure you'll find someone else to kill."

Mr. Loveman stood and lightly scratched the side of his bone-white face. He spoke then, in his creepy whisper: "Out of your honor to those who have 'saved' you, please notify my master if the Moon City Killer ever returns to this dimension."

Dean nodded. "Sure. Of course. You have my word."

Mr. Loveman took off his flip flops, one at a time, put them under his left arm, and spread his bare, human toes against the cool floor. He sighed with what seemed like an impression of someone feeling something refreshing. He walked toward the elevator with his bare feet against the cool tile floor, leaving like a shadow across ice.

"Thank you," Dean called after him.

The robot said nothing and boarded the elevator.

Before getting to his feet, a call came through.

Tasha.

"Hello," he said, his voice sounding like his throat had a thousand razor blades stuck throughout.

"Thought I might make a deviation from my normal rule and cheer you up, Slaughter Man," she told him. "Come down to the membrane transport station right now."

Dean's heart, still pounding, leapt up in his chest. "Okay... but..."

"I have people on the way to clean the apartment."

He didn't even bother asking how she knew already what had happened.

"Heading to the transport station now," he told her and then hung up.

* * *

Things were frantic at the transport station. The Moon City Killer had left serious damage behind and the repairs had already begun. Nobody could leave through the station, yet it could still receive people. Tasha had told him nothing about who would be coming to see him, but said it would cheer him up. He could use that.

"Standing by," said the tech.

Dean's pulse managed to quicken above its still-elevated rate. The membranes heated to a soft pink glow. He hoped it was her. He needed it to be her. Slowly, the membranes resolved the matter and Dean could see a group of aliens standing there, all with different hair styles. One of them was playing Lady Gaga on his wrist implant.

The Zetú. The deal had gone through after all.

And at the head of the group was Finny-Min and his son. They spotted him right away and ran to him. "Dean!" they cried and wrapped their arms around him. They thanked him profusely and told him they loved him.

Tears threatened to fall from his eyes. "I feel the same way, guys." He looked at them and smiled. "Welcome to your new home."

He got the liaison group to check them in at the apartment, bypassing any attempt at that horrible tavern. They would meet up with him later today after they settled in. He wasn't even sure his apartment was decontaminated yet, but he was on his way to see.

He called Tasha. "Thank you. You're right. That really cheered me up."

"It put you on the fringes again, so I won't speak of your deal with the Grettish group either. Be more careful what you do in the field. I can't cover for you forever. You know what happens to rogues in our group."

"I appreciate everything."

"And, Dean," said Tasha. "I did ask her."

"Who?"

"Sandra. I asked her if she'd like transport here. She declined."

Dean closed his eyes a moment and nodded. "Understood."

"I'll be in touch."

"Thanks again, kid."

Dean pulled the car to the side of the road and killed the engine. He didn't want to do anything at the moment. He couldn't feel anything. Not happy. Not sad. Not lucky. Just numb.

Then his phone rang and it was her.

He looked at it for a few moments. Maybe he shouldn't answer it. That was probably for the best. And then, if he didn't, he'd always wonder what she might have said.

"Hello?" he said lowly.

"I know you don't want to be with me anymore, but there's something I haven't told you. There's a reason I said no."

Dean went still inside. "I'm stuck in Moon City for a while, Sandra. Whatever you have to say is pointless."

"I couldn't go into stasis to wait for you, and I couldn't go into the membrane chamber to meet you there."

"I was told already. You declined."

"I didn't decline *you*. I want to be with you forever. You're everything to me, Dean Fulsome."

He was astonished. "So then why the hell did you turn Tasha's offer down?"

"Because it isn't safe for the baby," she said with some measure. "We're going to be parents. I'm sorry I couldn't tell you sooner. I didn't know what to do. I've been to the doctor and we are both healthy."

The Slaughter Man's mouth dropped open and he glanced around this dream-world he'd suddenly fallen into with silent awe.

"Aren't you going to say anything?" Sandra finally asked.

Fighting through the tremors that coursed through his body, Dean swallowed and replied then with a whisper, "I'm coming back."

She took a deep breath. "It wasn't like you didn't want to in the first place. Now the membrane transport needs repair. You won't make it back here for three hundred some years, Dean."

"I need to call you back."

"Dean, wait—"

"I'll call you back," he repeated and hung up. He dialed out to Donaldo, who picked up on the third ring.

"Hey, my friend, heard the good news about the Killer—"

"Donaldo, I need some help." He cut him off.

"Yes, sure. You know I'm here for anything, of course."

Dean swallowed and closed his eyes. "I need to know where the nearest Grettish armada is located and what kind of transports are available here on Moon City."

"What for, looking to commit suicide?"

"Can you find their location?"

Donaldo paused. "Yeah, I mean, that's no problem. If we can get in touch with anybody who is worth a shit at the Commerce Polity, they can probably tell us the trade route to the nearest armada."

"I think I know a kid who can help us."

"A kid? But wait, hold on, back up a second, aren't you supposed to be training the Zetú? You're not going offworld right now are you? Limbus doesn't usually give second chances, let alone third chances. Tasha won't be able to help you this time. Before I give you anything, you gotta let me know what this is about. I want to keep my job."

"Don't worry about it. You'll be paid for everything. I need to know how fast you can book a mid-range transport once we have the armada's location."

"The Firecracker Lady owns the transport station. So there's that, but if you have the money or the means for her liking, we could book by the end of the day."

"Get on it faster than that," said Dean, before adding, "I'm contacting Christopher Agate to engage his mercenary services."

"The Gem Stone warrior? Are you kidding?"

"No, I'm not," replied Dean. "Oh, and also, I'm going to need to borrow Mr. Loveman."

THE END

Benjamin Kane Ethridge is the Bram Stoker Award® winning author of the novels BLACK & ORANGE, NIGHTMARE BALLAD, BOTTLED ABYSS, as well as countless short stories and articles on writing and being human. Benjamin lives in Southern Florida.

DIVINE SCREAM

A NOVEL

BENJAMIN KANE ETHRIDGE

BRAM STOKER AWARD® WINNING AUTHOR